A NEW-ENGLAN

EARLY AMERICAN WOMEN WRITERS

Hannah Webster Foster, *The Coquette*
Susanna Rowson, *Charlotte Temple*
Tabitha Gilman Tenney, *Female Quixotism*
Rebecca Rush, *Kelroy*
Catharine Maria Sedgwick, *A New-England Tale*

A NEW-ENGLAND TALE;
or, Sketches of New-England Character and Manners

c. 1

Catharine Maria Sedgwick

EDITED AND WITH AN INTRODUCTION BY
Victoria Clements

FOREWORD BY
Cathy N. Davidson

Oxford University Press
New York   Oxford
1995

Oxford University Press

Oxford   New York

Athens   Auckland   Bangkok   Bombay
Calcutta   Cape Town   Dar es Salaam   Delhi
Florence   Hong Kong   Istanbul   Karachi
Kuala Lumpur   Madras   Madrid   Melbourne
Mexico City   Nairobi   Paris   Singapore
Taipei   Tokyo   Toronto

and associated companies in
Berlin Ibadan

Introduction and Notes on the Introduction Copyright © 1995 by Victoria Clements
Foreword Copyright © 1995 by Cathy N. Davidson

First edition *A New-England Tale,* 1822, published
by E. Bliss & E. White, New York

This paperback edition, with new editorial matter, first
published in 1995 by Oxford University Press, Inc.,
200 Madison Avenue, New York, New York 10016

Oxford is a registered trademark of Oxford University Press

Library of Congress Cataloging-in-Publication Data
Sedgwick, Catharine Maria, 1789–1867.
A New-England tale ; or, Sketches of New England character and
manners / Catharine Maria Sedgwick ; edited and with an
introduction by Victoria Clements ; foreword by Cathy N. Davidson.
p.   cm.
Includes bibliographical references (p.).
ISBN 0-19-509327-5
1. New England—Social life and customs—Fiction.   I. Clements,
Victoria, 1956—   .   II. Title.   III. Title: Sketches of New England
character and manners.
PS2798.N43   1995   94-43033   813'.2—dc20

9 8 7 6 5 4 3 2 1
Printed in the United States of America

CONTENTS

PREFACE

Catharine Maria Sedgwick's *A New-England Tale; or, Sketches of New-England Character and Manners* (1822) is the fifth title to appear in the Early American Women Writers series. Both a critical and a popular success in its day, it has not been reprinted since the mid-nineteenth century. Its republication marks an important addition to American literary history. Motivated by aesthetic nationalism, Sedgwick recreated early American dialects, settings, historical events, social issues, and ideological debates in her novels in order to "add something to the scanty stock of native American literature." In this, she resembled her contemporaries Washington Irving and James Fenimore Cooper. Indeed, when Cooper toured Europe, many readers who turned out to meet him thought he was the author of *Redwood* (1824), a popular novel by Catharine Maria Sedgwick.

Sedgwick, however, should be remembered for another contribution to American literature as well. Although wary of organized women's movements, she makes women characters central to her novels and, perhaps equally important, shows the ways in which urgent social issues such as abolitionism, religious freedom, or prison reform are also "women's issues." For example, in *Hope Leslie* (1827), her most popular book, Sedgwick reverses some of the racial prejudices of the more standard captivity narrative not only by giving a relatively sympathetic rendering of Native American religious and social customs, but also by sanctioning a marriage between a white woman and an Indian and suggesting ways in which one character, Faith Leslie, might be better off in her Indian life than she was in her restrictive, misogynistic Puritan community. The book is thus simultaneously a commentary on the treatment of Native Americans and of middle-class white women in the young United States.

Sedgwick's social concerns are often illuminated through a well-known plot device. A female protagonist rises from poverty to success through a series of trials occasioned by her being abandoned or orphaned (or both). In virtually all of her novels, marriage is the reward for women, but before the final marriage that ties up the plot, Sedgwick's heroines engage in a series of adventures in which they prove themselves to be feisty, independent, strong-willed, and morally fierce.

Jane Elton, the heroine of *A New-England Tale*, combats poverty and the repressive sadism of an aunt and various other relatives who use Calvinist principles to justify domestic tyranny. As Victoria Clements argues in her introduction to this volume, Jane's turn away from Calvinism reflects Sedgwick's own quiet rebellion against her Calvinist forebears as well as against some aspects of her socially prominent community. Reversing the tendency of the eighteenth-century novel that promises it will be founded on "truth," *A New-England Tale* begins with the disclaimer: "It can scarcely be necessary to assure the reader, that no personal allusions, however remote, were intended to be made to any individual." No one was fooled by this disavowal. The unnamed village in the novel had too much of the feel of Sedgwick's own Stockbridge, Massachusetts, and there were some who took offense that their lives and their religion were taken to task so publicly.

A New-England Tale was popular on both sides of the Atlantic. Jane Elton's trials and her liberation made for fascinating reading in 1822 and continue to provide a unique perspective on the Calvinist strain in American culture. One of Sedgwick's most intriguing devices is the introduction of a peripheral character called "Crazy Bet," a woman who serves as Jane's ambiguous guide in throwing off the shackles of Calvinist (and conventionally feminine) propriety. If Calvinism, like nineteenth-century codes of femininity, is about repression and restriction, Bet is an emblem of unfettered emotion and unrestricted movement. Like the Fools in Shakespeare's plays, Crazy Bet can speak her mind because, by usual social definitions, she has lost it. In one scene, Bet screams wildly at the memory of two grand, entwined old beech trees, one of which perished from a broken heart after the other was chopped down. The scene allows for a respectful, pantheistic celebration of nature in which the two women (one an orphan, one unquietly mad) enact Transcendentalism in a personalized, intimate, passionate, and sentimental register.

In a variety of tales—everything from folk stories to Nancy Drew mystery novels—a young, motherless girl throws off the oppression embodied by a repressive or sometimes even evil female figure (typically a stepmother or an aunt) in order to find her own way, often with the help of a female guide who exists outside normal conventions. Bet and Jane represent precisely this allegorical formula that expands a young woman's gender horizons. Bet, the "wild woman," becomes Jane's guide away from the callous family and toward a life filled with love and nature. Leading Jane over a dangerous pass, into a dark wood and at nightfall, Bet warns her young friend: "Go carefully over this lower ledge, there is a narrow foot-hold there; let not your foot slip on the wet leaves, or the soft moss. I am in the spirit, and I must mount to the summit." There is more tenderness here than Jane ever encountered in her aunt's home— and more adventure.

Following Crazy Bet, Jane Elton mounts figuratively to the summit— in psychological, religious, moral, emotional, and even economic terms. In the process, she comes to view American life and religion through a unique and often oppositional perspective. There are blind spots, certainly, in Sedgwick's depiction of middle-class Protestant mores, but both the fantasy of Jane's ascendant life and the complexity of Sedgwick's religious and social critique make *A New-England Tale* compelling reading today.

INTRODUCTION

When Catharine Maria Sedgwick published *A New-England Tale; or, Sketches of New-England Character and Manners* (1822), many in her native Stockbridge, Massachusetts, were angered by her novelized indictment of New England Calvinism. Writing shortly after the book's publication to her close friend Susan Higginson Channing, sister-in-law of the distinguished Unitarian minister William Ellery Channing, Sedgwick noted, "Some of my friends here have, as I learn, been a little troubled [by the book], but, after the crime of confessed Unitarianism, nothing can surprise them." Despite the light tone of the letter, Sedgwick was so anxious about public reaction to the novel that she published it anonymously, also telling Susan Channing, "I could not endure the idea that I had written myself out of the affections of my own people." Her concerns were not unfounded. As Sedgwick's brother Harry put it, "the only difficulty with the book is the unfavorable representation of the New England character. . . . The orthodox do all they can to put it down . . . and the New Englanders feel miffed."

Yet *A New-England Tale* sold. In the same letter Harry reports that the book "was going off very rapidly . . . and would soon be entirely exhausted." A second printing followed just four months after the first, minus the subtitle *Sketches of New-England Character and Manners* and with a new preface intended to mollify the "miffed." Although exact sales figures are unavailable, it appears that the book sold extremely well— the second edition was also "exhausted" in another two months. But the commercial success of *A New-England Tale* did little to reduce the censure Sedgwick obviously received at the hands of "the most bigoted," or to assuage her resultant discomfort.[1]

That the novel's setting was a barely disguised Stockbridge no doubt contributed to the outrage of its detractors. The town's inhabitants and clergy are portrayed in a distinctly unflattering light. In the tale's first paragraph we meet "prying neighbors;" shortly thereafter we are introduced to the clergyman, "one of those, who are more zealous for sound doctrine, than benevolent practice." We are urged to "look around the circle of our acquaintance, and observe how few there are among those whom we believe to be Christians, who govern their daily conduct by Christian principles, and regulate their temporal duties by the strict Christian rule."[2] Since Sedgwick's "circle of acquaintance" was based in Stockbridge, its citizens smarted under such disloyalty from one of their own.

The novel's primary representative of dogmatic Calvinism is the heroine's aunt, Mrs. Wilson, a tyrannical zealot who professes the church doctrine but who fails to live by its spirit. The heroine, Jane Elton, orphaned and left penniless at the age of twelve, is forced to live with Mrs. Wilson and is subject to hard labor and endless trials of her fundamental, non-Calvinist Christianity while under her aunt's roof. Not the least of these trials are her various interactions with her cousins, Elvira and David, both of whom rebel against their mother's iron hand with acts of deceit and moral lassitude, frequently involving the unwilling Jane in their nefarious schemes. Jane is sustained through her tribulations by the comfort of her friends, chief among whom is the hero, Robert Lloyd, a Quaker who purchases Jane's parents' home when it is auctioned. The complex plot includes many interwoven sub-plots, but the novel's emphasis is undeniably on the repressive, hypocritical Calvinist attitudes of Mrs. Wilson and her church brethren, which are consistently shown to be the source of great unhappiness to those who must submit to them.

But while Sedgwick's purpose in writing the tale was to expose the "thraldom of orthodox [Calvinist] despotism"[3] and to defend the more tolerant Christianity she had chosen, the term "Unitarian" never appears

---

1. Mary E. Dewey, ed., *Life and Letters of Catharine Maria Sedgwick* (New York: Harper & Bros., 1871) 151–157.

2. *A New-England Tale,* 9, 11, 13.

3. Catharine Sedgwick to Susan Higginson Channing, 25 Sept. 1821. This letter is included in the voluminous Catharine Maria Sedgwick Papers 1798–1867 held by the Massachusetts Historical Society and is quoted here by permission.

in the text, suggesting she was profoundly aware of the ramifications of her decision to reject the theology that had held New England firmly in its grasp for more than two hundred years. The sixth of seven surviving children of Theodore Sedgwick and Pamela Dwight, Catharine grew up with a thorough understanding of the significance of her position as daughter of a politically prominent and socially connected Massachusetts family. Theodore's career had taken him through the state and the Federal legislatures, culminating in his tenure as Speaker of the U.S. House of Representatives. He had been active in the Revolutionary War and was a noted Federalist campaigner for the Constitution. The Dwight family was numbered among the Colonial aristocracy known as the "River Gods" of the Connecticut River Valley, where Pamela's father had been a successful lawyer and land speculator.

As was appropriate to her aristocratic status, Sedgwick attended various schools for girls in New England. Although she frequently lamented her lack of the rigorous formal education that was common for boys, she nevertheless participated in the intellectually stimulating atmosphere of the Sedgwick home in Stockbridge, where she was encouraged to read widely and often. All four of the Sedgwick brothers were active in Massachusetts law, and the eldest in Massachusetts politics. Youngest sibling Charles's wife Elizabeth ran a well-respected school for young ladies; among its many noted pupils was Emerson's daughter Ellen. The brothers' marriages connected the Sedgwick family to Jonathan Edwards and to early-American historian George Richards Minot. Both of Catharine's sisters married distinguished lawyers.[4] The Sedgwick family name was one that justified righteous New England pride.

As Mary Kelley points out, Sedgwick's Federalist origins and the prominent cultural position occupied by her family engendered in her an elitist sense of moral responsibility to "the majority."[5] She believed "we should feel more pleasure in the affection of our inferiors than in the praise of our superiors, and nothing could indemnify me for the loss of the kind feeling of my humble country neighbors."[6] In 1821, at the age of thirty-one, Sedgwick knew full well that her adherence to the then

---

4. Catharine herself never married, worth noting in a century in which nine out of ten women did. Her conflicting attitudes toward marriage are perhaps best expressed in her autobiography and journals and in her last novel, *Married or Single?*, published in 1857.

5. Introduction, *The Power of Her Sympathy: The Autobiography and Journals of* Catharine Maria Sedgwick, ed. Mary Kelley (Boston: Massachusetts Historical Society and Northeastern UP, 1993) 31.

6. Dewey 157–158.

Calvinist-based Congregationalist church, bastion of New England respectability and righteousness, lent the institution credibility and helped promote its sociopolitical aims at a time when Calvinism and the sects it inspired were clearly losing cultural ground. She found the religious controversy that pitted Calvinism and Unitarianism against one another "a subject of continual pain and anxiety," worrying that her adoption of the "new faith" would result in the loss of her "many dear friends, who never will change their opinions, who would be shocked and deeply wounded by what they would consider [her] apostasy." Even though Sedgwick's father reportedly had made a deathbed conversion to Unitarianism in the presence of William Ellery Channing in 1813, and even though Sedgwick's brother Henry joined the Unitarian Society in New York in 1819, soon followed by brother Robert, Catharine's defection from Congregationalism was comparatively slow in coming.

In April 1821, however, she wrote her sister Frances that she had left Calvinist John Mitchell Mason's church in New York (where she spent her winters), of which she had long been a member. She noted that "some of the articles of the creed of that Church . . . appear to me both unscriptural and very unprofitable, and, I think, very demoralizing." Her decision to leave the congregation was not an easy one. The idea was so "painful" that she remained a member until she felt it her "imperative duty to leave." Finally, she told her sister, "I thought myself bound not to lend [my] sanction to what seems to me a gross violation of the religion of the Redeemer, and an insult to a large body of Christians entitled to respect and affection. . . . I know I have risked much and lost much, for I have many friends whose confidence and affection constitute a large portion of my happiness, who have not liberality to think there is any religion beyond the pale of orthodoxy."[7] By September, she had joined the Unitarians.

Sedgwick's rejection of Calvinist orthodoxy and her acceptance of Unitarianism gave credence in her circle of influence (a circle that was substantially enlarged with the publication of A *New-England Tale*[8]) to a rapidly expanding movement toward a more humanized—to some, dangerously liberal—Christianity. That such a paradigm shift in religious

7. Dewey 117–19.

8. The novel's first appearance earned it an entirely laudatory thirty-four-page review (containing excerpts) in the New York–based *Literary & Scientific Repository*, ed. Col. Charles K. Gardner, vol. IV, no. 8 (May 1822) 336–70. It also earned a favorable mention in the widely circulated *North American Review*, ironically in a review of Cooper's *The Spy*, vol. XV, n.s. vol. VI, no. 1 (July 1822) 279.

thinking would have far-reaching effects on the political and cultural makeup of the United States, a nation that had for all intents and purposes begun its life as a theocracy, there could be little doubt. With the publication of A New-*England Tale,* Sedgwick took her place among the ranks of those who would actively promote this shift, forging for herself a dynamic role in both the moral and literary development of the emerging American character and setting out on what would be a long, distinguished career as a writer.

A New-England Tale marks an important transition in the development of the American sentimental novel, a transition prompted in part by growing interest in what role women would play in the new republic. The prominent novels of the late eighteenth and early nineteenth centuries were primarily interested in the threat of seduction for a young, inherently defenseless woman—indeed, the first two novels in the Early American Women Writers series, Susanna Rowson's *Charlotte Temple* and Hannah Foster's *The Coquette,* rely on the theme of seduction. But Jane Elton is no Charlotte, no Eliza Wharton. Seduction is never an issue for Jane. As women came increasingly to be regarded in the nineteenth century as guardians of the nation's morality, the possibility of seduction for the heroine of the sentimental novel became unacceptable to middle-class readers and writers.

Jane's concern lies, as it will for countless heroines in the ensuing fifty years, with how she will provide for herself in a culture that offers her a choice between what is often the lesser of two evils: marriage, or a single life characterized by limited avenues through which to earn money. Both options are potentially disastrous. A single woman with no independent wealth was vulnerable to social stigma and, more important, to abject poverty and its effects. A married woman gave up all rights to custody of her children and to ownership or control of property under the laws of coverture in the early part of the century. She had no right to make her own will, and if her husband died without one, the law apportioned her only one third of her husband's estate. A woman was vulnerable in the best of marriages to ruined health or even death through too frequent childbirth,[9] and a bad marriage could subject her as well to the excesses

---

9. Sedgwick's own mother gave birth to ten children in little more than fifteen years, which may have accounted in part for her crippling depression. Despite the fact that Sedgwick's sister Eliza's marriage was apparently a happy one, Sedgwick writes in her autobiography that she thinks Eliza "had a hard life of it—indifferent health and the pain and drudgery of bearing twelve children." *Power of Her Sympathy* 87.

of an abusive husband, for law and custom gave him ownership of his wife's physical person. A successful union with a kind and generous man was perhaps the best a young woman with no inherited means could hope for in 1822.

This challenge to the young, white, middle-class woman to successfully negotiate the hazards of the road before her is the focus of the group of novels identified by Nina Baym in her 1978 landmark study as "woman's fiction," the subgenre that displaces the novel of seduction in the development of the American sentimental novel. As Baym notes, "These novels, deploying different settings and a wide variety of incidents, all tell about a young woman who has lost the emotional and financial support of her legal guardians—indeed who is often subject to their abuse and neglect—but who nevertheless goes on to win her own way in the world."[10] All are written by white, middle-class women and consider women to be their audience.[11] Nearly all begin with the heroine's loss of her mother, or of both parents, and end with her marriage. The period between these events is marked by the heroine's encounters with various obstacles, significant among them being her effort to gain or retain her Christian faith. Jane Elton maintains her Christian spirit through numerous challenges to it, including a romance with the county's most eligible cad, and she is rewarded in the end with a beautiful home and a considerate and wealthy husband. *A New-England Tale is* arguably the first of the vast group of popular novels written via this formula.

These novels enjoyed unprecedented popularity from the early 1820s through the 1870s.[12] Their success, however, failed to earn them a place in the American literary canon. Indeed, their very popularity often served to justify their exclusion from the canon, according to critics who dismissed popular novels in favor of "literature." Only in the last fifteen years have feminist scholars rediscovered these texts and asserted their interest in them as a legitimate subject for literary study.[13] Although these

10. Nina Baym, *Woman's Fiction: A Guide to Novels by and about Women in America, 1820–1870,* 2d ed. (Urbana: U Illinois P, 1993) ix.

11. Black writers deconstructed the genre in works such as Harriet Jacobs' *Incidents in the Life of a Slave Girl* and Frances Harper's *Iola Leroy, or Shadows Uplifted.*

12. For details see Mary Kelley, *Private Woman, Public Stage: Literary Domesticity in Nineteenth-Century America,* (New York: Oxford UP, 1984) chap. 1.

13. See particularly Baym; Cathy N. Davidson, *Revolution and the World: The Rise of the Novel in America* (1986); Judith Fetterley, ed., Introduction, *Provisions: A Reader from 19th-Century American Women* (Bloomington: Indiana UP, 1985); Susan Harris, *19th-Century American Women's Novels: Interpretive Strategies* (New York: Cambridge UP, 1990); Shirley Samuels, ed., *The Culture of Sentiment: Race, Gender, and Sentimentality in Nineteenth-Century America* (New York: Oxford UP,

novels often include the active promotion of a "cult of true womanhood" whose ideals are seemingly antithetical to current feminist values, they also reveal the conflicted attitudes with which nineteenth-century women addressed their subordinate legal and political status and the social convention of "separate spheres." Woman's fiction is characterized by a serious regard for social reform, economic issues, and issues of community, concerns that differ significantly from the focus on the individual typical of canonized early- and mid-nineteenth-century men's fiction, which reinforces the work of literary theorists who have identified a tendency in women's discourse to privilege community over the individual.[14] Also, as Jane Tompkins has pointed out, the "psycho-political situation [of the heroines of woman's fiction] is just as relevant today as it was in 1850. [The heroine] is a vulnerable, powerless, and innocent person victimized by those in authority over her. Since we have all at one time or another been in her position, we cannot help sharing her emotional point of view."[15]

For contemporary readers reared on a steady diet of buckskin, rifles, bizarre murders, and whale flaying, it is refreshing to study nineteenth-century fiction that takes as its subject the lives and thoughts of women. Through *A New-England Tale* and its successors, we can inquire into how apples were dried, how clothing was manufactured at home, how women sought to educate themselves, and how women traversed the obstacle course of the marriage market, subjects virtually ignored by Cooper, Poe, and Melville. Additionally, what has been demonstrated by Tompkins, Cathy N. Davidson, Susan Harris, and others is that popular fiction by women in the nineteenth century is marked by the same sort of textual ambiguities and stylistic complexity that have been the focus of most recent critical discussion of canonized nineteenth-century men's texts. The ways in which issues of representation are addressed by the woman writer, the incompatibility of ideology and fictive genres, the gap

---

1992); Jane Tompkins, *Sensational Designs: The Cultural Work of American Fiction, 1790–1860* (New York: Oxford UP, 1985); Rutgers UP American Women Writers Series; Joyce Warren, ed., *The (Other) American Traditions: Nineteenth-Century Women Writers* (New Brunswick, N.J.: Rutgers UP, 1993). This is by no means a comprehensive list, but names major contributions to this field of study.

14. See Nina Auerbach, *Communities of Women: An Idea in Fiction* (Cambridge: Harvard UP, 1978); Fetterley, Introduction, *Provisions*; Marilyn Mobley, *Folk Roots and Mythic Wings in Sarah Orne Jewett and Toni Morrison* (Baton Rouge: Louisiana State UP, 1991); Sandra Zagarell, "Narrative of Community: The Identification of a Genre," *Signs 13* (1988).

15. Jane Tompkins, ed., Afterword, in *The Wide, Wide World* by Susan Warner, 1850 (New York: Feminist Press, 1987) 585.

between the sign and the referent, conversations with other texts, and the tension between the subject and the object can all be identified in *A New-England Tale* and the hundreds of women's novels that follow it, laying to rest the connoisseurist critical tradition that consigned these texts to oblivion in the early part of the twentieth century.

In the preface to *A New-England Tale*, Sedgwick asserts that her "original design" was

> even more limited and less ambitious than what has been accomplished. It was simply to produce a very short and simple moral tale . . . and if in the course of its production it has acquired anything of a peculiar or local cast, this should be chiefly attributed to the habits of the writer's education, and that kind of accident which seems to control the efforts of those who have not been the subjects of strict intellectual discipline, and have not sufficiently premeditated their own designs.

In a letter to Susan Channing, Sedgwick claims she "began that little story for a tract," a pamphlet comprised of stories of Christian exemplars and related scriptural references, millions of which were circulated in the nineteenth century. She goes on to explain that she "had no plans, and the story took a turn that seemed to render it quite unsuitable for a tract."[16] The language of both preface and letter calls attention to the way the genre of the novel has transformed Sedgwick's discourse: the "accident [the shift in genre] . . . seems to control [her] efforts;" that the tale "took a turn" suggests volition, as if the work had a purpose of its own that countered Sedgwick's "original design." In permitting the "accident," the shift from tract to novel, Sedgwick made in her first literary effort a courageous leap into a groundless genre that would require her text to give voice to a wide array of social, religious, and philosophical attitudes, some of which might differ from her own—for in its demand for verisimilitude, or the depiction of the "real world," the novel is compelled to give voice to the various ideologies that constitute that world.

The political, social, and religious ideologies that compete for the reader's attention in *A New-England Tale* reflect the cultural upheaval that occupied early nineteenth-century America. Democratic egalitarianism struggles with Federalist elitism. Patriarchal gender codes are both validated and questioned. Dogmatic New England Calvinism, ideologi-

16. Dewey 153–54.

cally dependent on an authoritarian God of Wrath, is shown in opposition to the liberal Christianity that relies on an all-powerful God of Mercy. Both of these socio-religious positions are interrogated by a recurring assertion of the power of the individual, of the Self. A vigorous dialogue between diametrically opposed ideological positions might be said to characterize *A New-England Tale*, just as such a dialogue characterized the early nineteenth-century United States. As Cathy N. Davidson demonstrates in *Revolution and the Word: The Rise of the Novel in America* (1986), the popularity in the developing nation of a genre that thrived on cultural conflict was no accident. Particularly for women, excluded from public debate and decision on matters religious, social, and political, the novel provided an engagement with both sides of controversial issues that directly concerned them.

These early nineteenth-century ideological debates were significantly inspired by German philosopher Immanuel Kant's *Critique of Pure Reason* (1781). Prior to Kant's influence, it was generally accepted that objects (or nature, a fixed external world) provided the subject (or the mind) with order, structuring human experience and knowledge. Kant contended that the reverse was in fact the case, that the mind gave order to the external world, or, in other words, that the subject created the object. Following Kant's claim that "Mind is the law-giver to nature," any interpretation of the external world could be brought into question. If the mind (the subject, or the Self) created the world (the object), who was to say whose mind was right? The widespread social, economic, and religious reforms that characterized the mid-nineteenth century can be accounted for in part by the swift growth of this tension between subject and object. In the United States, the increased validation of the subject, along with concomitant social and political changes, led to the interrogation of certain "objective," essentialist "truths" (such as the innate superiority of whites and men), consciously or unconsciously employed by members of enfranchised groups to assure their positions. This, in turn, resulted in an increase in the authority of formerly marginalized groups, such as women, children, African-Americans, and workers. The struggle for supremacy between the subject and the object thus had momentous implications for the emerging cultural politics of the United States.

Sedgwick's novel exhibits an uneasy tension between these two fundamentally opposed philosophical positions, between a world ordered by the subject, or the Self, and a world ordered by the object, in which truth lies outside the Self. The text's efforts are ostensibly directed toward supplanting one object-centered ideology with another: The rigid Calvinist ideology practiced by Mrs. Wilson and her cohorts, in which the all-powerful Object is the God of Wrath, is displaced by the ideology espoused by Jane and her friends, whose all-powerful Object is a God of Mercy. But just as significant as this ideological contest is the novel's elevation of authorship through its persistent reminders of the autonomous subject that orders this fictive world. Such a validation of the authorial subject, ultimately a validation of Self, serves to question the supremacy of the Object and the corollary powerlessness of the individual subject. Moreover, as fiction—something invented, something created from nothing—the novel owes its very existence to an authorial subject, necessarily calling attention to the power of that subject. For the white, middle-class woman author, schooled in a habit of spiritual, intellectual, and literary dependence on God and men, the prospect of wielding such power must have been both daunting and exhilarating.

The authorial subject's narrative voice in *A New-England Tale* is the intrusive collective "we" typical of the era, suggesting on one level, as Susan Harris has noted, the assumption of a "diffused personality that speaks for the authority of a changing New England culture."[17] At times wickedly ironic, its principal target is the hypocritical practitioners of Calvinism the book seeks to undermine. But this voice also functions to emphasize the omniscience of the authorial subject—it knows things the characters do not. When David Wilson threatens to kill himself, Jane acquiesces to his demands, but the narrative voice has "reason to believe thc pistol was neither primed nor loaded."[18] Although Robert Lloyd, identified as "a self-examiner," asserts he "should be perfectly happy" if Erskine, Jane's knavish suitor, "were but worthy" of her, the text knows "he would not, even in that case, have been perfectly happy. He did not . . . clearly define all his feelings on this trying occasion."[19]

The authorial subject also governs the tale's numerous narratives within the narrative, which attest to that subject's ability to transcend the constraints of a fundamental ordering principle of objective reality, chronological time. The story of David Wilson's mistress, the unfortunate Mary Oakley; the story of John Mountain's lawsuit; and the events of Erskine's duel are all told in loudly announced flashbacks, persistently calling attention to the capability of the novelist. In the pages detailing the final

17. Harris 52.
18. *A New-England Tale*, 96.
19. Ibid., 108.

meeting between Jane and Erskine and Erskine's subsequent departure from the village, the action shifts from the present to the past and back again several times, rendering time entirely fluid. While Mary Oakley sleeps, the narrator will "take the liberty to avail ourselves of our knowledge of her history, and offer our readers a slight sketch of it"[20]; the subsequent narrative begins with Mary's birth and eventually dramatizes recent events leading to her appearance in John's hut. John's lawsuit has taken place several weeks before John tells Jane, "'if you have patience to hear an old man's story, I will tell you mine.'"

What immediately follows, though, is John's poetic description of his life with his wife Sarah—not a chronology-bound "story" of actual events occurring in time and space, but subjective discourse, which John foregrounds as being such when he says, "'This has not much to do with my lawsuit.'" The text here calls attention to itself as text, a manifestation of subject, rather than to its supposed ability to deliver so-called objective reality, what actually happened. When the details of the lawsuit finally are revealed, chief among them is the fact that one corrupt lawyer "poured out such a power of words, that he seemed to take away people's senses. . . . [His] fine oration put reason quite out of the question."[21] In John's narrative within the narrative, we are offered a warning against the bewitching power of discourse, revealing the narrator's ambiguity regarding her own textual power. Nevertheless, when the events of the novel are neatly wrapped up and the kindly John and Sarah are assured happiness ever after, the pious Jane (with whom the reader identifies) is prompted to exclaim, "Oh, it is as beautiful a conclusion of their lives, as if it had been conjured up by a poet."[22] Jane, whom we might by this point in the novel legitimately expect to attribute this turn in her friends' fortunes to Providence, reminds us instead of the command of the author.

As I have suggested, the repeated assertion of the power of the authorial subject in *A New-England Tale* and the texts that would follow it was problematic for the nineteenth-century woman writer and reader.[23] In the early nineteenth century United States, as Barbara Welter notes, "The attributes of True Womanhood, by which a woman judged herself and was judged by her husband, her neighbors and society could be

---

20. Ibid., 89.

21. Ibid., 117–119.

22. Ibid., 152.

23. For further discussion of this, see Mary Kelley's *Private Woman, Public Stage*, which takes as its subject the conflict over gender roles experienced by writers of woman's fiction.

divided into four cardinal virtues—piety, purity, submissiveness and domesticity."[24] Female submissiveness was inscribed in the practical, statute-governed, day-to-day workings of the country, for, despite the privileged status awarded her vital, God-given responsibility for the national morality, woman's intellectual and physical inferiority was almost universally accepted by men and women alike. Medical science colluded with cultural and political convention to affirm this social order. Gender roles were based on supposed objective, observable, biological phenomena—woman's reproductive function rendered her weak and nervous, hence economically and psychologically dependent on men.[25] Submissiveness and piety were inextricably intertwined, for piety required submission, indeed, complete self-effacement, if not to men, then to God.

The assertion of an author-izing Self demanded, on some level, a radical departure from the role of True Woman for the female writer of fiction, one that could conceivably result in ostracism and alienation. The necessary complicity of the female reader was equally fraught. All the more frightening was the possibility that the assertion of Self could have dire consequences for the well-being of the immortal soul, whose self-effacement was divinely ordained. It is understandable, then, that the tentative narratorial exploration of a female Self prompted by authorship in *A New-England Tale is* almost outweighed by the many ways in which that Self is negated. For example, the novel's conspicuous over-reliance on quotations (many of which are taken from the Bible and almost all of which are taken from texts by men) reveals a lack of confidence in the authority of its own voice. The plot's general confirmation of patriarchal gender codes (Jane is "rescued" from Erskine through the intervention of the hero, whom she finally marries) and the novel's almost hyperbolic insistence on Jane's dependence on the Almighty offer a marked contrast to the autonomy of the female narrator. The exploration of the author-izing Self is mediated by an anxious reliance on external, object-ive authorities, just as the reliance on those authorities is problematized by the author-izing Self.

This simultaneous destabilizing of both culturally sanctioned and cul-

24. Barbara Welter, "The Cult of True Womanhood: 1820–1860," *American Quarterly* XVIII (Summer 1966) 152.

25. See Barbara Ehrenreich and Deirdre English, *For Her Own Good: 150 Years of the Experts' Advice to Women* (New York: Anchor Books, 1989) and Carroll Smith-Rosenberg, *Disorderly Conduct: Visions of Gender in Victorian America* (New York: Oxford UP, 1985) for discussion of the relationship between medicine and women in the nineteenth century.

turally vilified ideological positions provides much of the textual energy that drives *A New-England Tale*. For instance, despite its conflicted interest in human autonomy, the novel for the most part tacitly accepts the legal, social, and political subordination of women. Sedgwick herself never sanctioned the women's rights movement, even allowing the heroine of *Married or Single?* (1857) to claim the term "women's rights" had been rendered "odious" by its supporters.[26] *A New-England Tale* accepts without question the "natural" division of men and women into separate social spheres, the woman's sphere characterized by the virtues named above, as evidenced in the suggestion that Jane's influence may "cure" Erskine of his "faults" of drinking, gambling, and sophistry.[27] Jane's chief advisor, family servant Mary Hull, avows that with Jane's "tutoring, . . . who knows what [Erskine] may become, when he sees how good and how beautiful it is to have the whole heart and life ordered and governed by the christian rule."[28] And when only the boys perform at the exhibition with which Jane's school term concludes, the narrator approvingly notes, "The young ladies were with obvious and singular propriety excluded from any part in [it]."[29]

A New-England Tale does contain, however, momentary flickers of discontent with women's lesser social and legal position. The novel disregards "propriety" enough to allow the writer of the exhibition's prize composition, who turns out to be a girl, to read that composition aloud before a "promiscuous" audience (one composed of both men and women). The implication is that writing gives a woman both license and opportunity to cross codified gender barriers and speak her thoughts directly to women and men alike. Dissatisfaction with patriarchal gender codes also appears in the narrator's description of Jane's mother, who, we are told, "had that passiveness which, we believe, is exclusively a feminine virtue." The narrator's prompt, albeit parenthetical, addendum, "(if virtue it may be called)," and the ruin to which passivity leads Jane's mother undeniably question both the wisdom and the rectitude of such passivity for women.[30] Furthermore, when Jane's cousin Elvira elopes with her French dancing teacher, the narrator is careful to point out the discrepancy in their wedding vows, noting the justice required "from the

26. Sedgwick, *Married or Single?* (New York: Harper & Bros., 1857) 153.
27. *A New-England Tale*, 122.
28. Ibid., 109–110.
29. Ibid., 51.
30. Ibid., 10.

bridegroom the usual promise to love and cherish; and from the bride, to love, cherish, and obey."[31] Again, the novel strikes an uncomfortable balance: the implied criticism of prevailing gender codes questions the novel's general adherence to those codes, while its adherence to the gender codes problematizes its criticism of them.

This same sort of disorienting balancing act manifests in the novel's contradictory presentation of class and its repeated insistence that the post-Revolutionary American culture is characterized by economic, educational, and political equality. The narrator's assessment of the "prosperous condition of all classes in our happy country . . . where they [have] neither the miseries of poverty, nor the temptations of riches" is based significantly on her claim that the United States takes "care to give the poor man learning" and that there are therefore "no dark corners of ignorance" to be found in "this blessed region."[32] Nevertheless, despite the text's obvious efforts to celebrate an egalitarian American culture, Sedgwick's inheritance of a legacy of Federalist elitism is readily apparent in *A New-England Tale*. Sedgwick notes in her autobiography that her father was firmly committed to a republic organized around "a strong aristocratic element," and that he maintained "a thorough distrust of 'the people,' . . . dread[ing] every upward step they made, regarding elevation as a depression, in proportion to their ascension[,] of the intelligence and virtue of the country."[33] As if in response to this inherited suspicion of the average citizen, the characters that populate *A New-England Tale* fall into two distinct groups—"the people" and the "aristocratic element."

The independently wealthy Lloyd, for instance, admires "the ingenuity and contentment" of the peddler he meets on the mountain, noting the peddler's "enjoyment of the . . . 'glorious privilege,' of every New-England man, of 'being independent.'" But his "pleasure [is] somewhat abated by an appearance of a want of neatness and order" in the peddler's cabin. Lloyd also sees that "neither the complexion of the floor nor of the children seemed to have been benefited" by the stream that runs through the dwelling.[34] Despite the peddler's "independence," his inabil-

---

31. Ibid., 142.

32. *A New-England Tale*, 12, 28, 152, 48. This laudatory and inaccurate description of the American educational system, which ignores the system's exclusion of blacks and Native Americans and its inherent discrimination against girls and the poor, seems particularly odd coming from Sedgwick, who vehemently acknowledged the second-rate quality of her own education in comparison to that of her male peers.

33. Sedgwick, *Power of Her Sympathy* 64.

34. *A New-England Tale*, 32.

ity to keep his home clean and his children healthy mark him as Lloyd's social inferior. Mary Hull, introduced as a "faithful domestic," prompts the narrator's dissertation on the character of American servants:

> We know it is common to rail at our domestics. Their independence is certainly often inconvenient to their employers; but, as it is the result of the prosperous condition of all classes in our happy country, it is not right nor wise to complain of it. We believe there are many instances of intelligent and affectionate service . . . that are rarely equalled . . . where ignorance and servility mark the lower classes.[35]

The narrator acknowledges that her complaint with regard to "our" domestics is neither right nor wise, but she does not fail to make it. And if Mary Hull is not "servile," she certainly knows her place—she knows, for example, that Lloyd is "a gentleman far above her condition in life."[36] Likewise, when the novel's happy ending promises marriage for both her and Jane, Mary notes the similarity in their romances, but quickly qualifies her remark, saying, "not that I mean to compare myself to you, or James [her intended] to Mr. Lloyd, but it is the *nature of the feeling*—it is the same in the high and the low, the rich and the poor."[37]

This assumption of the universal nature of feeling is a key element of the sentimental ideology, which characterizes a substantial portion of the woman's fiction that follows *A New-England Tale* and which plays a significant role in the hypothetical egalitarianism promulgated by Jacksonian Democrats in the first half of the nineteenth century. Sentimentalism values profound but controlled feeling and shared emotions as the foundation for a salutary social order. Proponents of the sentimental ideology, both male and female,[38] accept and promote the belief that the moral well-being of the growing United States will only result from the successful dissemination of a Christian "ethic of social love [that differs from] self-love and link[s] love to wisdom, responsibility, rationality, and self-command."[39]

We cannot help but notice that the characters in *A New-England Tale* who manifest this Christian ethic of social love are, with the notable

35. Ibid., 12.
36. Ibid., 36.
37. Ibid., 160.
38. Sentimentalism is, however, correctly associated with white, middle-class women, who were its chief purveyors, mostly through the writing of tracts, novels, short stories, advice manuals, etc.
39. Baym 25.

exception of Jane and Lloyd, members of the "lower classes." Mary Hull and her suitor James; John Mountain and his wife Sarah; Mrs. Hervey, the mistress of the boarding house where Jane eventually resides; and various others who assist Jane in her travails all practice selfless generosity and trust in the provisions of the Almighty for their well-being. The characters shown to be lacking in feeling and moral virtue are members of the landed class: Erskine and his friends, Mrs. Wilson and her children, Jane's father and his sisters, the church elders. Certainly, the stereotyping of the "noble worker" or "faithful domestic" might be regarded as one more instance of the text's essentially patronizing presentation of the lower class, but the manner in which the novel validates the lower class through the uniformly positive actions of its members nevertheless serves to destabilize the narrator's elitist class commentary, which, in turn, undercuts the text's validation of the working class. As it does in its exploration of the Self and its examination of gender roles, Sedgwick's novel establishes a restless balance between presumably antithetical positions in its presentation of class.

In its curiously conflicted appraisal of American culture in 1822, *A New-England Tale* presages the role that will be played by woman's fiction in the general interrogation of religious, political, and social authority that will characterize the first half of the century and generate the liberal reform activity of the ensuing thirty years. Later examples of the genre will speak out against poverty, slavery, alcoholism, and unfair labor practices. Strangely, though, a distinctly ambivalent presentation of the struggle for women's social and political rights continues to characterize woman's fiction all the way through to its gradual disappearance in the final decades of the century. Perhaps, as Judith Fetterley points out, "pressures on women to be selfless . . . impaired their ability to speak out in their own behalf." Mary Kelley further notes that "woman's immersion in her own peculiar history made ultimate self- and social knowledge elusive and the foreboding nature of the life to be understood forestalled personal resolution. To criticize or perhaps condemn the life was to criticize or condemn the self."[40] Apparently, for both practical and psychological reasons, the writers of woman's fiction required boundaries in their exploration of women's capacity for authority, boundaries that excluded the investigation of their own socio-political oppression.

---

40. Fetterley 13 and Kelley, quoted in Fetterley 13.

During the late 1840s and '50s, of course, the women's rights movement in America would nevertheless flourish, provoking dramatic improvements in women's legal rights and in educational and professional opportunities for women. In 1847, for example, Elizabeth Blackwell entered Geneva Medical School, the first American woman to do so. By 1850, most white women were literate, and women dominated the teaching profession. By 1860, fourteen of the thirty-three existing states had adopted legislation granting property rights to married women. But the women's rights movement would demand of its participants an almost superhuman courage and commitment, for it would be loudly and viciously attacked from all sides. Eventually it would be sidetracked by the Civil War, reorganizing with any real force only after the turn of the century in the campaign for women's suffrage. The flow of woman's fiction, however, continued unabated, from the publication of *A New-England Tale* through the 1870s. Despite its equivocal stance on women's rights, the genre consistently introduced and reinforced the power of the author-izing female Self into the experience of countless writers and readers, laying a subtle foundation for the advances in women's equality that would gradually transform the national culture.

Sedgwick's novel was a pioneer, a scout into the seemingly treacherous territory of nineteenth-century woman's autonomy. A result of the fortunate confluence of genre, gender, and historical moment, *A New-England Tale* clearly demonstrates that one of the means by which that territory was explored was the popular novel.

NOTE ON THE TEXT

The text is printed from the University Microfilms, Inc. microfilm of the first edition held by the University of Michigan Library, which appears in UMI's American Culture Series. The first edition was published anonymously in New York by E. Bliss and E. White in March of 1822.

In this edition, early nineteenth-century punctuation and spelling have been retained. The modern reader will note minor irregularities in the use of quotation marks in dialogue and the heavy use of commas and semi-colons. Spelling, although substantially regularized by 1822 (Webster's *American Dictionary of the English Language* appeared in 1812), is antiquated to the modern eye and retains an English flavor: for example, "vigour" (vigor), "pretence" (pretense), "labour" (labor), "favourite" (favorite), "divers" (diverse), "humour" (humor), "fidgetted" (fidgeted), "gayety" (gaiety), "ach" (ache), "woful" (woeful), etc.

The modern reader will also be aware of well over one hundred unattributed quotations and allusions, many of which are biblical. Rather than interrupt the reading experience with myriad, perhaps gratuitous footnotes, we have elected to leave the detective work to the reader.

A second edition of *A New-England Tale,* with a new preface, also published by Bliss and White and also anonymously, appeared in July 1822. Changes between this and the first edition are minimal, limited mostly to orthography, correction of typographical errors (and the addition of new ones), changes in capitalization (Quaker, for example, is printed for the most part with a lower-case *q* in the second edition), and the occasional rephrasing. Jane's assertion that William Penn was the only colonial leader to "treat the natives [American Indians] with justice" is appended with a footnote acquitting Winthrop, Winslow, Bradford, Mayhew, and Williams. The peddler's reference to "sauce" is footnoted to explain it as a New England term for vegetables. The second edition was also published in 1822 in London by John Miller.

In 1849, G.P. Putnam in New York began a uniform edition of Sedgwick's work, but only three novels were published—*Clarence* (1849), *Redwood* (1849), and *A New England Tale* (1852). In this third edition, the hyphen in the title was dropped, and the novel was attributed to Sedgwick and accompanied by three "miscellanies" entitled "A Berkshire Tradition," "The White Scarf," and "Fanny McDermot." These volumes were reprinted in 1854 by J.C. Derby in Boston and Phillips, Sampson & Co. in New York.

The 1852 edition differs substantially from the 1822 edition, but no essential elements of plot, setting, or character are altered. Spelling is modernized (although still appearing somewhat antiquated to the modern reader) and Americanized (the "u" is often dropped from words such as "labor" and "color"), commas and semi-colons are removed, capitalization is altered. More important, the prose is quite visibly edited. Word choice is frequently altered, sentence structures are re-worked, sentences and phrases are deleted, new sentences and phrases are added. Robert Lloyd's family history is completely omitted, suggesting a general tightening of narrative style.

SELECTED BIBLIOGRAPHY

Primary

Sedgwick wrote more than twenty novels, didactic tales, children's books, and collections of short pieces, as well as numerous magazine pieces. The following are those currently most available.

"Cacoethes Scribendi." In *Provisions: A Reader from 19th-Century American Women*. Ed. Judith Fetterley. Bloomington: Indiana UP, 1985. 49–59.

Hope Leslie; or, Early Times in the Massachusetts. 1827. Ed. Mary Kelley. American Women Writers Ser. New Brunswick, NJ: Rutgers UP, 1987.

"Old Maids." In *Old Maids: Short Stories by Nineteenth Century U.S. Women Writers*. Ed. Susan Koppelman. Boston: Pandora, 1984. 8–26.

The *Power of Her Sympathy: The Autobiography and Journals of Catharine Maria Sedgwick*. Ed. Mary Kelley. Boston: Massachusetts Historical Society & Northeastern UP, 1993.

Redwood: A Tale. 1824. New York: Garrett Press, 1969. (Now available through Irvington Press, Manchester, NH.)

Biographical

Brooks, Gladys. *Three Wise Virgins*. New York: E. P. Dutton & Co., 1957.

Dewey, Mary E., ed. *Life and Letters of Catharine Maria Sedgwick*. New York: Harper & Bros., 1871.

Foster, Edward Halsey. *Catharine Maria Sedgwick*. Twayne's United States Authors Series 233. New York: Twayne, 1974.

Kelley, Mary. *Private Woman, Public Stage: Literary Domesticity in Nineteenth-Century America*. New York: Oxford UP, 1984.

Critical

Bardes, and Suzanne Gossett. *Declarations of Independence: Women and Political Power in 19th-Century American Fiction.* New Brunswick, N.J.: Rutgers UP, 1990.

Baym, Nina. *Woman's Fiction: A Guide to Novels by and about Women in America, 1820–1870.* 2d ed. Urbana: U Illinois P, 1993.

Fetterley, Judith, ed. Introduction to "Cacoethes Scribendi." *Provisions: A Reader from 19th-Century American Women.* Bloomington: Indiana UP, 1985. 41–49.

Fick, Thomas H. "Catharine Sedgwick's 'Cacoethes Scribendi': Romance in Real Life." *Studies in Short Fiction 27* (1990): 567–76.

Harris, Susan. *19th-Century American Women's Novels: Interpretive Strategies.* New York: Cambridge UP, 1990.

Nelson, Dana. "Sympathy as Strategy in Sedgwick's Hope Leslie." *The Culture of Sentiment: Race, Gender, and Sentimentality in Nineteenth-Century America.* Ed. Shirley Samuels. New York: Oxford UP, 1992. 191–202.

Singley, Carol J. "Catharine Maria Sedgwick's *Hope Leslie:* Radical Frontier Romance." *The (Other) American Traditions: Nineteenth-Century Women Writers.* Joyce Warren, ed. New Brunswick, NJ: Rutgers, 1993. 39–53.

ACKNOWLEDGMENTS

Ann Romines introduced me to Sedgwick and her contemporaries, and Chris Sten encouraged my initial exploration of *A New-England Tale*. Were it not for their breadth of vision, I might never have discovered my love and respect for woman's fiction. I am indebted to Cathy N. Davidson and to Linda Robbins of Oxford University Press for fostering that same respect in the Early American Women Writers Series and for guiding me through the publishing process. Rich King at the Gelman Library at George Washington University went the extra mile in tracking down elusive texts, and research librarians at the Library of Congress provided invaluable assistance. I am especially grateful for the guidance and generosity of Rich De Prospo, whose insights into this novel are woven throughout my own. Thanks are also due to Dick and Joan Clements, Linda Clements, Dean Hebert, and a host of colleagues and friends, whose support and encouragement have contributed to the production of this book in more ways than can be explained here.

A NEW-ENGLAND TALE

A NEW-ENGLAND TALE;

or,
Sketches of
New-England Character and Manners

But how the subject theme may gang,
Let time and chance determine;
Perhaps it may turn out a sang,
Perhaps turn out a sermon.

BURNS

NEW-YORK:
PUBLISHED BY E. BLISS & E. WHITE, 128 BROADWAY.
1822.
J. Seymour, Printer.

TO
MARIA EDGEWORTH,
AS A
SLIGHT EXPRESSION
OF THE
WRITER'S SENSE OF HER EMINENT SERVICES
IN THE
GREAT CAUSE
OF
HUMAN VIRTUE AND IMPROVEMENT,
THIS HUMBLE TALE
IS RESPECTFULLY DEDICATED.

PREFACE

The writer of this tale has made an humble effort to add something to the scanty stock of native American literature. Any attempt to conciliate favour by apologies would be unavailing and absurd. In this free country, no person is under any obligation to write; and the public (unfortunately) is under no obligation to read. It is certainly desirable to possess some sketches of the character and manners of our own country, and if this has been done with any degree of success, it would be wrong to doubt that it will find a reception sufficiently favourable.

The original design of the author was, if possible, even more limited and less ambitious than what has been accomplished. It was simply to produce a very short and simple moral tale of the most humble description; and if in the course of its production it has acquired any thing of a peculiar or local cast, this should be chiefly attributed to the habits of the writer's education, and that kind of accident which seems to control the efforts of those who have not been the subjects of strict intellectual discipline, and have not sufficiently premeditated their own designs.

It can scarcely be necessary to assure the reader, that no personal allusions, however remote, were intended to be made to any individual, unless it be an exception to this remark, that the writer has attempted a sketch of a real character under the fictitious appellation of "Crazy Bet."

March 30, 1822.

A NEW-ENGLAND TALE

CHAPTER I

Oh, ye! who sunk in beds of down,
Feel not a want but what yourselves create,
Think for a moment on his wretched fate,
Whom friends and fortune quite disown.

Burns.

Mr. Elton was formerly a flourishing trader, or, in country phrase, a merchant, in the village of ———. In the early part of his life he had been successful in business; and having a due portion of that mean pride which is gratified by pecuniary superiority, he was careful to appear quite as rich as he was. When he was at the top of fortune's wheel, some of his prying neighbours shrewdly suspected, that the show of his wealth was quite out of proportion to the reality; and their side glances and prophetic whispers betrayed their contempt of the offensive airs of the purse-proud man.

The people in the village of ——— were simple in their habits, and economical in their modes of life; and Mr. Elton's occasional indulgence in a showy piece of furniture, or an expensive article of dress for himself or for his wife, attracted notice, and, we fear, sometimes provoked envy, even from those who were wiser and much better than he was. So inconsistent are men—and women too—that they often envy a display of which they really despise, and loudly condemn the motive.

Mrs. Elton neither deserved nor shared the dislike her husband received in full measure. On the contrary, she had the good-will of her neighbours. She never seemed elated by prosperity; and, though she occasionally appeared in an expensive Leghorn hat, a merino shawl, or a fine lace, the gentleness and humility of her manners, and the uniform benevolence of her conduct, averted the censure that would otherwise have fallen on her. She had married Mr. Elton when very young, without much consideration, and after a short acquaintance. She had to learn, in the bitter way of experience, that there was no sympathy between them; their hands were indissolubly joined, but their hearts were not related; he was 'of the earth, earthy'—she 'of the heavens, heavenly.' She had that passiveness which, we believe, is exclusively a feminine virtue, (if virtue it may be called,) and she acquiesced silently and patiently in her unhappy fate, though there was a certain abstractedness in her manner, a secret feeling of indifference and separation from the world, of which she, perhaps, never investigated, certainly never exposed the cause.

Mr. Elton's success in business had been rather owing to accidental circumstances, than to his skill or prudence; but his vanity appropriated to himself all the merit of it. He adventured rashly in one speculation after another, and, failing in them all, his losses were more rapid than his acquisitions had been. Few persons have virtue enough to retrench their expenses, as their income diminishes; and no virtue, of difficult growth, could be expected from a character where no good seed had ever taken root.

The *morale*, like the *physique*, needs use and exercise to give it strength. Mrs. Elton's had never been thus invigorated. She could not oppose a strong current. She had not energy to avert an evil, though she would have borne any that could have been laid on her, patiently. She knew her husband's affairs were embarrassed; she saw him constantly incurring debts, which she knew they had no means of paying; she perceived he was gradually sinking into a vice, which, while it lulls the sense of misery, annihilates the capacity of escaping from it—and yet she silently, and without an effort, acquiesced in his faults. They lived on, as they had lived, keeping an expensive table, and three or four servants, and dressing as usual.

This conduct, in Mrs. Elton, was the result of habitual passiveness; in Mr. Elton, it was prompted by a vain hope of concealing from his neighbours a truth, that, in spite of his bustling, ostentatious ways, they had known for many months. This is a common delusion. We all know that, from the habits of our people in a country town, it is utterly impossible for the most watchful and skilful manœuver, to keep his pecuniary affairs secret from the keen and quick observation of his neighbours. The expedients practised for concealment are much like that of a little child, who shuts his own eyes, and fancies he has closed those of the spectators; or, in their effect upon existing circumstances, may be compared to the customary action of a frightened woman, who turns her back in a carriage when the horses are leaping over a precipice.

It may seem strange, perhaps incredible, that Mrs. Elton, possessing the virtues we have attributed to her, and being a religious woman, should be accessary to such deception, and (for we will call "things by their right names") dishonesty. But the wonder will cease if we look around upon the circle of our acquaintance, and observe how few there are among those whom we believe to be Christians, who govern their daily conduct by Christian principles, and regulate their temporal duties by the strict Christian rule. Truly, narrow is the way of perfect integrity, and few there are that walk therein.

There are too many who forget that our religion is not like that of the ancients, something set apart from the ordinary concerns of life; the consecrated, not the "daily bread;" a service for the temple and the grove, having its separate class of duties and pleasures; but is "the leaven that leaveneth the whole lump," a spirit to be infused into the common affairs of life. We fear Mrs. Elton was not quite guiltless of this fault. She believed all the Bible teaches. She had long been a member of the church in the town where she lived. She daily read the scriptures, and daily offered sincere prayers. Certainly, the waters of the fountain from whence she drank had a salutary influence, though they failed to heal all her diseases. She was kind, gentle, and uncomplaining, and sustained, with admirable patience, the growing infirmities and irritating faults of her husband. To her child, she performed her duties wisely, and with an anxious zeal; the result, in part, of uncommon maternal tenderness, and, in part, of a painful consciousness of the faults of her own character; and, perhaps, of a secret feeling she had left much undone that she ought to do.

Mr. Elton, after his pecuniary embarrassments were beyond the hope of extrication, maintained by stratagem the appearance of prosperity for some months, when a violent fever ended his struggle with the tide of fortune that had set against him, and consigned him to that place where there is 'no more work nor device.' His wife was left quite destitute with her child, then an interesting little girl, a little more than twelve years old. A more energetic mind than Mrs. Elton's might have been discouraged at the troubles which were now set before her in all their extent, and with tenfold aggravation; and she, irresolute, spiritless, and despondent, sunk under them. She had, from nature, a slender constitution; her health declined, and, after lingering for some months, she died with resignation, but not without a heart-rending pang at the thought of leaving her child, poor, helpless, and friendless.

Little Jane had nursed her mother with fidelity and tenderness, and performed services for her, that her years seemed hardly adequate to, with

an efficiency and exactness that surprised all who were prepared to find
her a delicately bred and indulged child. She seemed to have inherited
nothing from her father but his active mind; from her mother she had
derived a pure and gentle spirit, but this would have been quite insufficient
to produce the result of such a character as hers, without the aid of her
mother's vigilant, and, for the most part, judicious training. In the
formation of her child's character, she had been essentially aided by a
faithful domestic, who had lived with her for many years, and nursed Jane
in her infancy.

We know it is common to rail at our domestics. Their independence is
certainly often inconvient to their employers; but, as it is the result of the
prosperous condition of all classes in our happy country, it is not right
nor wise to complain of it. We believe there are many instances of intel-
ligent and affectionate service, that are rarely equalled, where ignorance
and servility mark the lower classes. Mary Hull was endowed with a mind
of uncommon strength, and an affectionate heart. These were her jewels.
She had been *brought up* by a pious mother, and early and zealously
embraced the faith of the Methodists. She had the virtues of her station
in an eminent degree: practical good sense, industrious, efficient habits,
and *handy ways*. She never presumed formally to offer her advice to Mrs.
Elton; her instincts seemed to define the line of propriety to her; but she
had a way of suggesting hints, of which Mrs. Elton learnt the value by
experience. This good woman had been called to a distant place, to attend
her dying mother, just before the death of Mrs. Elton; and thus Jane was
deprived of an able assistant, and most tender friend, and left to pass
through the dismal scene of death, without any other than occasional
assistance from her compassionate neighbours.

On the day of Mrs. Elton's interment, a concourse of people assembled
to listen to the funeral sermon, and to follow to the grave one who had
been the object of the envy of some, and of the respect and love of many.
Three sisters of Mr. Elton were assembled with their families. Mrs. Elton
had come from a distant part of the country, and had no relatives in ——.

Jane's relations wore the decent gravity that became the occasion; but
they were of a hard race, and neither the wreck their brother had made,
nor the deep grief of the solitary little creature, awakened their pity. They
even seemed to shun manifesting towards her the kindness of common
sympathy, lest it should be construed into an intention of taking charge
of the orphan.

Jane, lost in the depths of her sufferings, seemed insensible to all external things. Her countenance was of a death-like paleness, and her features immoveable; and when, during the sermon, an address was made to her personally by the clergyman, she was utterly unable to rise, one of her aunts, shocked at the omission of what she considered an essential decorum, took her by the arm, and almost lifted her from her seat. She stood like a statue, her senses seeming to take no cognizance of any thing. Not a tear escaped, nor a sigh burst from her breaking heart. The sorrow of childhood is usually noisy; and this mute and motionless grief, in a creature so young, and one that had been so happy, touched every heart.

When the services were over, the clergyman supported the trembling frame of the poor child to the place of interment. The coffin was slowly let down into the house appointed for all. Every one who has followed a dear friend to the grave, remembers with shuddering the hollow sound of the first clods that are thrown on the coffin. As they fell heavily, poor Jane shrieked, "oh, mother!" and springing forward, bent over the grave, which, to her, seemed to contain all the world. The sexton, used as he was to pursue his trade amidst the wailings of mourners, saw something peculiar in the misery of the lone child. He dropped the spade, and hastily brushing away the tears that blinded him with the sleeve of his coat, "Why does not some one," he said, "take away the child? This is no place for such a heart-broken thing." There was a general bustle in the crowd, and two young ladies, more considerate, or perhaps more tender-hearted, than the rest, kindly passed their arms around her, and led her to her home.

The clergyman of ——— was one of those, who are more zealous for sound doctrine, than benevolent practice; he had chosen on that occasion for his text, "The wages of sin is death," and had preached a long sermon in the vain endeavour of elucidating the doctrine of original sin. Clergymen who lose such opportunities of instructing their people in the operations of providence, and the claims of humanity, ought not to wonder if they grow languid, and selfish, and careless of their most obvious duties. Had this gentleman improved this occasion of illustrating the duty of sympathy, by dwelling on the tenderness of our blessed Lord, when he wept with the bereaved sisters at the grave of Lazarus: had he distilled the essence of those texts, and diffused their gracious influence into his sermon—"Bear ye one another's burthens;" "Weep with those who weep;" "Inasmuch as ye have done it unto one of these, ye have done it unto me;"—had his preaching usually been in conformity to the teaching of our Saviour, could the scene have followed, which it is our business to relate?

We fear there are many who think there is merit in believing certain doctrines; who, mistaking the true import of that text, "by grace are ye saved," quiet themselves with having once in their lives passed through what they deemed conviction and conversion, and from thence believe their salvation is secure. They are like the barren fig-tree; and unless they are brought to true repentance, to showing their "faith by their works," we fear they will experience its just fate.

The house, furniture, and other property of Mr. Elton had lain under an attachment for some time previous to Mrs. Elton's death, but the sale had been delayed in consideration of her approaching dissolution. It was now appointed for the next week; and it therefore became necessary that some arrangement should be immediately made for the destitute orphan.

The day after the funeral, Jane was sitting in her mother's room, which, in her eyes, was consecrated by her sickness and death; the three aunts met at Mr. Elton's house; she heard the ladies approaching through the adjoining apartment, and hastily taking up her Bible, which she had been trying to read, she drew her little bench behind the curtain of her mother's bed. There is an instinct in childhood, that discerns affection wherever it exists, and shrinks from the coldness of calculating selfishness. In all their adversity, neither Jane, nor her mother, had ever been cheered by a glimmering of kindness from these relatives. Mrs. Elton had founded no expectations on them for her child, but with her usual irresolution she had shrunk from preparing Jane's mind for the shocks that awaited her.

The three sisters were led in by a young woman who had offered to stay with Jane till some arrangement was made for her. In reply to their asking where she was, the girl pointed to the bed.

"There," she said, "taking on *despotly.*—A body would think," added she, "that she had lost her uncles and aunts as well as her father and mother. And she might as well," (she continued, in a tone low enough not to be heard,) for any good they will do her."

The eldest sister began the conference by saying, "That she trusted it was not expected she should take Jane upon her hands—that she was not so well off as either of her sisters—that to be sure she had no children; but then Mr. Daggett and herself *calculated* to do a great deal for the Foreign Missionary Society; that no longer ago than that morning, Mr. D. and she had agreed to pay the expense of one of the young Cherokees at the School at ———; that there was a great work going on in the world, and as long as they had the heart given them to help it, they could not feel it their duty to withdraw any aid for a mere worldly purpose!"

Mrs. Convers (the second sister) said that she had not any religion, and she did not mean to pretend to any; that she had ways enough to spend her money without sending it to Owyhee or the Foreign School; that she and her husband had worked hard, and saved all for their children; and now they meant they should make as good a figure as any body's children in the country. It took a great deal of money, she said, to pay the dancing-master, and the drawing-master, and the music-master; it was quite impossible for her sisters to think how much it took to dress a family of girls genteelly. It was not now, as it used to be when they were girls: now-a-days, girls must have merino shawls, and their winter hats, and summer hats, and prunella shoes, and silk stockings;—it was quite impossible to be decent without them. Besides, she added, as she did not live in the same place with Jane, it was not natural she should feel for her. It was her decided opinion, that Jane had better be put out at once, at some place where she could do light work till she was a little used to it; and she would advise too, to her changing her name, the child was so young she could not care about a name, and she should be much mortified to have it known, in the town of ———, that her daughters had a cousin that was a *hired girl*.

There was something in this harsh counsel which touched Mrs. Wilson's (the younger sister's) pride, though it failed to awaken a sentiment of humanity. She said she desired to be thankful that she had been kept from any such sinful courses as sending her children to a dancing-school; nobody could say she had not done her duty by them; the minister's family was not kept more strict than hers.

"No," said Mrs. Convers, "and by all accounts is not more disorderly."

"Well, that is not our fault, Mrs. Convers, if we plant and water, we cannot give the increase."

Mrs. Wilson should have remembered that God does give the increase to those that rightly plant, and faithfully water. But Mrs. W.'s tongue was familiar with many texts, that had never entered her understanding, or influenced her heart.

Mrs. Wilson continued—"Sister Convers, I feel it to be my duty to warn you—you, the daughter and granddaughter of worthy divines who abhorred all such sinful practices, that you should own that you send your children to dancing-school, astonishes and grieves my spirit. Do you know that Mr. C—, in reporting the awakening in his parish, mentions that not one of the girls that attended dancing-school were among the converts, whereas two, who had engaged to attend it, but had received a remarkable warning in a dream, were among the first and brightest?"

"I would as soon," she continued, "follow one of my children to the grave, as to see her in that broad road to destruction, which leads through a ball-room."

"It is easy enough," replied Mrs. Convers, (adjusting her smart mourning cap at the glass) "to run down sins we have no fancy for."

Mrs. Wilson's ready answer was prevented by the entrance of Jane's humble friend, who asked, if the ladies had determined what was to be done with the little girl.

Mrs. Wilson in her vehemence had quite forgotten the object of their meeting, but now brought back to it, and instigated by a feeling of superiority to Mrs. Convers, and a little nettled by the excuses of Mrs. Daggett, which she thought were meant as a boast of superior piety, she said, that she had no dancing-masters to pay, and had not "*that* morning agreed" to adopt a Cherokee—she could afford to take Jane for a little while. The child, she said, must not think of depending upon her for life, for though she was a widow, and could do what she was a mind to her with her own, she could not justify herself in taking the children's meat"— and she would have added—"throw it to the dogs,"—but she was inter- rupted by a person who, unregarded by the ladies, had taken her seat among them.

This was a middle aged woman, whose mind had been unsettled in her youth by misfortunes. Having no mischievous propensities, she was allowed to indulge her vagrant inclinations, in wandering from house to house, and town to town, her stimulated imagination furnishing continual amusement to the curious by her sagacious observations, and unfailing mirth to the young and vulgar, by the fanciful medley in which she arrayed her person. There were some who noticed in her a quickness of feeling that indicated original sensibility, which, perhaps, had been the cause of her sufferings. The dogs of a surly master would sometimes bark at her, because her dress resembled the obnoxious livery of the beggar—a class they had been taught to chase with pharisaical antipathy. But except when her timid nature was alarmed by the sortie of dogs, which she always called the devil's servants, crazy Bet found a welcome wherever she went.

It is common for persons in her unfortunate circumstances to seek every scene of excitement. The sober, sedate manners of the New-England people, and the unvaried tenor of their lives, afford but few of these. Wherever there was an awakening, or a camp-meeting; crazy Bet was sure to be found; she was often seen by moonlight wandering in the church-yard, plucking the nettles from the graves, and wreathing the monuments with ground-pine. She would watch for whole nights by the side of a grave in her native village, where twenty years before were deposited the remains of her lover, who was drowned on the day before they were to have been married. She would range the woods, and climb to the very mountain's-top, to get sweet flowers, to scatter over the mound of earth that marked his grave. She would plant rose bushes and lilies there, and when they bloomed, pluck them up, because she said their purity and brightness mocked the decay below.

She has been seen, when the sun came rejoicing over the eastern mountain's brow, and shot its first clear brilliant ray on the grave, to clap her hands, and heard to shout, "I see an angel in the sun, and he saith 'Blessed and holy is he that hath part in the first resurrection: on such, the second death hath no power; but they shall be priests of God and of Christ, and shall reign with him a thousand years.'"

Poor Bet was sure to follow in every funeral procession, and sometimes she would thrust herself amidst the mourners, and say, "the dead could not rest in their graves, if they were not followed there by one true mourner." She has been seen to spring forward when the men were carelessly placing the coffin in the grave with the head to the east, and exclaim, "are ye heathens, that ye serve the dead thus? Know ye not the 'Lord cometh in the east.'" She always lingered behind after the crowd had dispersed, and busily moved and removed the sods; and many a time has she fallen asleep, with her head resting on the new-made grave, for, she said, there was no sleep so quiet as 'where the wicked did not trouble.'

The quick eye of crazy Bet detected, through their thin guise, the pride and hypocrisy and selfishness of the sisters. She interrupted Mrs. Wilson as she was concluding her most inappropriate quotation, 'Throw it to the dogs;' said she, 'It is more like taking the prey from the wolf.' She then rose, singing in an under voice,

> "Oh! be the law of love fulfilled
> In every act and thought,
> Each angry passion far removed,
> Each selfish view forgot."

She approached the bed, and withdrawing the curtain, exposed the little sufferer to view. She had lain the open Bible on the pillow, where she had often rested beside her mother, and laying her cheek on it had fallen asleep. It was open at the 5th chapter of John, which she had so often read to her mother, that she had turned instinctively to it. The page was blistered with her tears.

Careless of the future, which to her seemed to admit no light, her exhausted nature had found relief in sleep, at the very moment her aunts were so unfeelingly deciding her fate. Her pale cheek still wet with her tears, and the deep sadness of a face of uncommon sweetness, would have warmed with compassion any breast that had not been steeled by self-ishness.

"Shame, shame, upon you!" said the maniac, "has pride turned your hearts to stone, that ye cannot shelter this poor little ewe-lamb in your fold? Ah! ye may spread your branches, like the green bay tree, but the tempest will come, and those who look for you shall not find you; but this little frost-bitten bud shall bloom in the paradise of God for ever and ever."

Untying a piece of crape which she had wound around her throat, (for she was never without some badge of mourning,) she stooped and gently wiped the tears from Jane's cheek, saying, in a low tone, "Bottles full of odours, which are the tears of saints;" then rising, she carefully closed the curtains, and busied herself for some minutes in pinning them together. She then softly, and on tiptoe, returned to her seat; and taking some ivy from her broken straw bonnet, began twisting it with the crape. "This," said she, "is a weed for Elder Carrol's hat; he lost his wife yesterday, and I have been to the very top of Tauconnick to get him a weed, that shall last fresh as long as his grief. See," added she, and she held it up laughing, "it has begun to wilt already; it is a true token."

She then rose from her seat, and with a quick step, between running and walking, left the room; but returning as suddenly, she said slowly and emphatically, "Offend not this little one; for her angel does stand before my Father. It were better that a mill-stone were hanged about your neck." Then curtseying to the ground, she left them.

Bet's solemn and slow manner of pronouncing this warning, was so different from her usually hurried utterance, that it struck a momentary chill to the hearts of the sisters. Mrs. Daggett was the first to break the silence.

"What does she mean?" said she. "Has Jane experienced religion?"

"Experienced religion!—no," replied Mrs. Wilson. "How should she? She has not been to a meeting since her mother was first taken sick; and no longer ago than the day after her mother's death, when I talked to her of her corrupt state by nature, and the opposition of her heart, (for I felt it to be my duty, at this peculiar season, to open to her the great truths of religion, and I was faithful to her soul, and did not scruple to declare the whole counsel,) she looked at me as if she was in a dumb stupor. I told her the judgments of an offended God were made manifest towards her in a remarkable manner; and then I put it to her conscience, whether if she was sure her mother had gone where the worm dieth not and the fire is not quenched, she should be reconciled to the character of God, and be willing herself to promote his glory, by suffering that just condemnation. She did not reply one word, or give the least symptom of a gracious understanding. But when Mrs. Hervey entered, just as I was concluding, and passed her arm around Jane, and said to her, 'My child, God does not willingly grieve or afflict you,' the child sobbed out, 'Oh no! Mrs. Hervey, so my mother told me, and I am sure of it.'

"No, no," she added, after a moment's hesitation; "this does not look as if Jane had a hope. But, sister Daggett, I wonder you should mind any thing crazy Bet says. She is possessed with as many devils as were sent out of Mary Magdalen."

"I don't mind her, Mrs. Wilson; but I know some very good people who say, that many a thing she has foretold has come to pass; and especially in seasons of affliction, they say, she is very busy with the devil."

"I don't know how that may be," replied Mrs. Wilson, "but as I mean to do my duty by this child, I don't feel myself touched by Bet's crazy ranting."

Mrs. Daggett, nettled by her sister's hint, rose and said, "that, as she was going in the afternoon to attend a meeting in a distant part of the town, (for," said she, "no one can say that distance or weather ever keeps me from my duties,) she had no more time to waste."

Mrs. Convers' husband drove to the door in a smart gig, and she took leave of her sisters, observing, she was glad the child was going to be so well provided for. As she drove away, crazy Bet, who was standing by the gate, apparently intently reading the destiny of a young girl, in the palm of her hand, fixed her eyes for a moment on Mrs. Convers, and whispered to the girl, "all the good seed that fell on that ground was choked by thorns long ago."

Mrs. Wilson told Jane's attendant, Sally, to inform her, she might come to her house the next day, and stay there for the present.

CHAPTER II

Or haply prest with cares and woes,
Too soon thou hast began
To wander forth.   Burns.

Jane received the intelligence of her destination without the slightest emotion. The world was "all before her," and she cared not whither led her "mournful way."

Happily for her, her humble friend mentioned in the beginning of her history, Mary Hull, returned on that day, after having performed the last act of filial duty. Jane poured all her sorrows into Mary's bosom, and felt already a degree of relief that she had not believed her condition admitted.

Such is the elastic nature of childhood; its moral, like its physical constitution, is subject to the most sudden changes.

Mary having assuaged the wounds of her youthful friend with the balm of tender sympathy and just consolation, undertook the painful, but necessary, task of exposing to Jane, the evils before her, that she might fortify her against them; that, as she said, being "fore-warned, she might be fore-armed."

She did not soften the trials of dependance upon a sordid and harsh nature. She told her what demands she would have on her integrity, her patience, and her humility.

"But, my child," said she, "do not be down-hearted. There has One 'taken you up who will not leave you, nor forsake you.' 'The fires may be about you, but they will not kindle on you.' Make the Bible your counsellor; you will always find some good word there, that will be a bright light to you in the darkest night: and do not forget the daily sacrifice of prayer; for, as the priests under the old covenant were nourished by a part of that which they offered, so, when the sacrifice of praise is sent upward by the broken and contrite heart, there is a strength cometh back upon our own souls: blessed be his name, it is what the world cannot give."

Mary's advice fell upon a good and honest heart, and we shall see that it brought forth much fruit.

The evening was spent in packing Jane's wardrobe, which had been well stocked by her profuse and indulgent parents. Mary had been told, too, that the creditors of Mr. Elton would not touch the wearing apparel of his wife. This was, therefore, carefully packed and prepared for removal; and Mary, who with her stock of heavenly wisdom had some worldly prudence, hinted to Jane, that she had better keep her things out of the sight of her craving cousins.

Jane took up her mother's Bible, and asked Mary, with a trembling voice, if she thought she might be permitted to take that.

"Certainly," replied Mary, "no one will dispute your right to it; it is not like worldly goods, we will not touch the spoils, though we were tempted by more than the 'goodly Babylonish garment, the two hundred shekels of silver, and the wedge of gold' that made Achan to sin."

In obedience to the strictest dictates of honesty, Mary forbore from permitting her zeal for Jane's interests to violate the letter of the law. She was so scrupulous, that she would not use a family trunk, but took a large cedar chest of her own to pack the clothes in.

While they were busily occupied with these preparations, Jane received a note from her aunt, saying, that she advised her to secure some small articles which would never be missed: some of "the spoons, table-linen, her mother's ivory workbox," &c. &c. The note concluded—"As I have undertaken the charge of you for the present, it is but right you should take my advice. There is no doubt my brother's creditors have cheated him a hundred fold the amount of these things, for, poor man! with all his faults, he was so generous, any body could take him in; besides, though these things might help to pay the expense I must be at in keeping you, they will be a mere nothing divided among so many creditors—the dust on the balance."

"Poor woman!" said Mary, to whom Jane had handed the note, "I am afraid she will load the balance with so much of this vile dust, that when she is weighed her scale will be "found wanting." No, Jane, let us keep clean hands, and then we shall have light hearts."

The next morning arrived, and Mary arose before the dawn, in order to remove Jane early, and save her the pain of witnessing the preparations for the vendue. Jane understood her kind friend's design, and silently acquiesced in it, for she had too much good sense to expose herself to any unnecessary suffering. But when every thing was in readiness, and the moment of departure arrived, she shrunk back from Mary's offered arm, and sinking into a chair, yielded involuntarily to the torrent of her feelings. She looked around upon the room and its furniture as if they were her friends.

It has been said by one, who well understands the mysteries of feeling, that objects which are silent every where else, have a voice in the home of our childhood. Jane looked for the last time at the bed, where she had often sported about her mother, and rejoiced in her tender caresses—at the curtains, stamped with illustrations of the Jewish history, which had often employed and wearied her ingenuity in comprehending their similitudes—at the footstool on which she had sat beside her mother; and the old family clock,

> "Whose stroke 'twas heaven to hear,
> When soft it spoke a promised pleasure near."

Her eye turned to the glass, which now sent back her wo-begone image, and she thought of the time, but a little while past, when elated with gratified vanity, or joyful anticipation, she had there surveyed her form arrayed in finery—now, the rainbow tints had faded into the dark cloud.

She rose, and walked to the open window, about which she had trained a beautiful honey-suckle. The sun had just risen, and the dew-drops on its leaves sparkled in his rays.

"Oh, Mary!" said she, "even my honey-suckle seems to weep for me."

A robin had built its nest on the vine; and often as she sat watching her sleeping mother, she had been cheered with its sprightly note, and maternal care of its young. She looked to the next—the birds had flown;—

"They too," she exclaimed, "have deserted this house of sorrow."

"No, Jane;" replied Mary, "they have been provided with another home, and He who careth for them, will care much more for you."

Mary might have quoted (but she was not addicted to any profane works,) the beautiful language of a native poet—

> "He who from zone to zone
>   Guides through the boundless sky their certain flight,
> In the long way that you must trace alone
>   Will guide your steps aright."

"We shall not," she said, "be at your aunt's in time for breakfast; here, tie on your hat, you will need all your strength and courage, and you must not waste any on flowers and birds."

Jane obeyed the wise admonition of her friend; and with faltering steps, and without allowing herself time to look again at any thing, hastily passed through the little court yard in front of their house.

The morning was clear and bright; and stimulated by the pure air, and nerved by the counsels Mary suggested as they walked along, Jane entered her new home with a composed, timid manner.

Perhaps her timidity appealing to Mrs. Wilson's love of authority, produced a softer feeling than she had before shown to Jane; or perhaps, (for scarcely any nature is quite hardened,) the forlornness of the child awakened a transient sentiment of compassion,—she gave her her hand, and told her she was welcome. The children stared at her, as if they had never seen her before, but Jane's down-cast eye, a little clouded by the gathering tears, saved her from feeling the gaze of their vulgar curiosity.

Jane, in entering the family of Mrs. Wilson, was introduced to as new a scene as if she had been transported to a foreign country.

Mrs. Wilson's character might have been originally cast in the same mould with Mr. Elton's, but circumstances had given it a different modification. She had married early in life a man, who, not having energy enough for the exercise of authority, was weak and vain, tenacious of the semblance, and easily cozened by the shadow, when his wife retained the substance. Mrs. Wilson, without having the pride of her nature at all subdued, became artful and trickish; she was sordid and ostentatious, a careful fellow-worker with her husband in the acquisition of their property, she secured to herself all the praise in the expending it. Whenever a contribution was levied for an Education or Tract Society, for Foreign Missions, the Cherokees, or Osages,—Mrs. Wilson accompained her donation, which on the whole was quite handsome, with a remark, that what she did give, she gave with a willing heart; that, women could not command much money, but it was the duty of wives to submit themselves to their husbands. After Mrs. Wilson became sole mistress of her estate, the simple and credulous, who remembered her professions, wondered her gifts were not enlarged with her liberty. But Mrs. Wilson would say, that the widow was the prey of the wicked, and that her duty to her children prevented her indulging her generous feelings towards those pious objects which lay nearest her heart.

Mrs. Wilson had fancied herself one of the subjects of an awakening at an early period of her life; had passed through the ordeal of a church-examination with great credit, having depicted in glowing colours the opposition of her natural heart to the decrees, and her subsequent joy in the doctrine of election. She thus assumed the form of godliness, without feeling its power. Are there not many such: some who, in those times of excitement, during which many pass from indifference to holiness, and many are converted from sin to righteousness, delude themselves and others with vain forms of words, and professions of faith?

Mrs. Wilson was often heard to denounce those who insisted on the necessity of good works, as Pharisees;—she was thankful, she said, that she should not presume to appear before her Judge with any of the 'filthy rags of her own righteousness;'—it would be easy getting to heaven if the work in any way depended on ourselves;—any body could 'deal justly, love mercy, and walk humbly.' How easy it is, we leave to those to determine, who have sought to adjust their lives by this divine rule.

Mrs. Wilson rejected the name of the Pharisee, but the proud, oppressive, bitter spirit of the Jewish bigot was manifest in the complacency with which she regarded her own faith, and the illiberality she cherished towards every person, of every denomination, who did not believe what she believed, and act according to her rule of right. As might be expected, her family was regulated according to 'the letter,' but the 'spirit that giveth life' was not there. Religion was the ostensible object of every domestic arrangement; but you might look in vain for the peace and good will which a voice from heaven proclaimed to be the objects of the mission of our Lord.

Mrs. Wilson's children produced such fruits as might be expected from her culture. The timid among them had recourse to constant evasion, and to the meanest artifices to hide the violation of laws which they hated; and the bolder were engaged in a continual conflict with the mother, in which rebellion often trampled on authority.

Jane had been gently led in the bands of love. She had been taught even more by the example than the precepts of her mother.

She had seen her mother bear with meekness the asperity and unreasonableness of her father's temper, and often turn away his wrath with a soft answer.

The law of imitation is deeply impressed on our nature. Jane had insensibly fallen into her mother's ways, and had, thus early, acquired a habit of self-command. Mrs. Elton, though, alas, negligent of some of her duties, watched over the expanding character of her child, with

Christian fidelity. "There she had garnered up her heart." She knew that amiable dispositions were not to be trusted, and she sought to fortify her child's mind with Christian principles. She sowed the seed, and looked with undoubting faith for the promised blessing.

"I must soon sleep," she would say to Mary, "but the seed is already springing up. I am sure it will not lack the dews of Heaven; and you, Mary, may live to see, though I shall not, 'first the blade, then the ear, and after that the full corn in the ear.'"

Mary had seconded Mrs. Elton's efforts. She looked upon herself as a humble instrument; but she was a most efficient one. She had a rare and remarkable knack at applying rules, so that her life might be called a commentary on the precepts of the Gospel. Mary's practical religion had, sometimes, conveyed a reproach (the only reproach a Christian may indulge in) to Mrs. Wilson, who revenged herself by remarking, that "Mary was indulging in that soul-destroying doctrine of the Methodists— *perfection*;" and then she would add, (jogging her foot, a motion that, with her, always indicated a mental parallel, the result of which was, 'I am holier than thou,') there is no error so fatal, as resting in the duties of the second table." Mrs. Wilson had not learned, that the duties of the second table cannot be done, if the others are left undone; the branches must be sustained by the trunk; for he, from whose wisdom there is no appeal, has said, "If ye love me, ye will keep my commandments."

Happily for our little friend, Mary was not to be removed far from her; an agreeable situation was, unexpectedly, offered to her grateful acceptance.

CHAPTER III

Now Spring returns, but not to me returns
The vernal year my better days have known;
Dim in my breast life's dying taper burns,
And all the joys of life with health are flown.
Bruce.

A few weeks before the death of Mrs. Elton, a Mr. Lloyd, a Quaker, who was travelling with his wife and infant child, for the benefit of Mrs. Lloyd's health, had stopped at the inn in ———. Mrs. Lloyd was rapidly declining with a consumption. On this day she had, as is not unfrequent in the fluctuation of this disease, felt unusually well. Her cough was lulled by the motion of the carriage, and she had requested her husband to permit her to ride further than his prudence would have dictated.

The heat and unusual exertion, proved too much for her. In the evening she was seized with a hemorrhage, which reduced her so much as to render it unsafe to move her. She faded away quietly, and fell into the arms of death as gently as a leaf falleth from its stem, resigning her spirit in faith to him who gave it.

An extraordinary attachment subsisted between Mr. and Mrs. Lloyd, which had its foundation in the similarity of their characters, education, views, and pursuits; and had been nourished by the circumstances that had drawn and kept them together.

The father of Mr. Lloyd was an Englishman; he, with his wife, and only son Robert, then eight years old, had emigrated to Philadelphia. Mrs. Elwyn, the sister of Mrs. Lloyd, a widow, with an only daughter, accompanied them. The severities of a long and tempestuous voyage, operating on a very timid spirit and delicate constitution, completely undermined Mrs. Elwyn's health, and she survived the voyage but a few days.

Before her death she gave her daughter to her sister, saying to her, "Let her be thine own, dear Anne. She is but one year younger than thy Robert; and, if it please God so to incline their hearts, let them be united, that, as we have not been divided in life, our children may not be. Keep her from the world and its vanities, and train her for Heaven, dear sister."

Mrs. Lloyd loved her sister so devotedly, that she would, at any time, have yielded her wishes to Mrs. Elwyn's; but that was unnecessary, for in this plan they perfectly coincided.

The children were educated together, and were so much alike in their characters, that one seemed the soft reflection of the other. The habits of the family were secluded and simple; formed on the model of the excellent leader of their sect, William Penn, who, Mr. Lloyd used to say, it was his aim to follow, in all that he followed Christ. Benevolence was his business, and he went to it as regularly as a merchant goes to his compting-house. He finally fell a victim to his zeal, in the service of his fellow-creatures; or rather, to use one of his last expressions which had in it the sweet savour of piety and resignation, "He was taken from his Father's work to his Father's rest."

During one of those seasons when Philadelphia suffered most from the ravages of the yellow fever, Mr. Lloyd sent the young people to lodgings on the banks of the Schuylkill, while he and his wife remained in the city to administer relief to the poor sufferers, who were chained by poverty to the scene of this dreadful plague. Constant fatigue and watchfulness impaired the strength of this excellent pair. They both took the fever and died. They were mourned by their children, as such parents should be, with deep, but not complaining grief.

Robert was but sixteen at the time of his father's death. At the age of twenty-one he married Rebecca Elwyn. As Robert led his bride out of the meeting, where, with the consent and hearty approbation of their Society, they had been united, the elders said, they were as goodly a pair as their eyes ever rested on; and their younger friends observed, they were sure their love was as "fervent, mutual, and dear," as William Penn himself could have desired. Three years glided on in uninterrupted felicity. Excepting when they were called to feel for others' woes, their happiness was not darkened by a single shadow; nor did it degenerate into selfish indulgence, but, constantly enlarging its circle, embraced within its compass all that could be benefitted by their active efforts and heavenly example. They lived after the plain way of their sect; not indulging in costly dress or furniture, but regulating all their expenses by a just and careful economy, they seldom were obliged to stint themselves in the indulgence of their benevolent propensities.

Three years after their marriage Mrs. Lloyd gave birth to a girl. This event filled up the measure of their joy. A few weeks after its birth, as Mr. Lloyd took the infant from its mother's bosom and pressed it fondly to his own, he said, "Rebecca, the promise is to us and our children; the Lord grant that we may train His gift in His nurture and admonition."

"Thou mayest, dear Robert; God grant it," Rebecca mournfully replied; "but the way is closed up to me. Do not shudder thus, but prepare thy mind for the 'will of the Lord.' I could have wished to have lived, for thy sake, and my little one; but I will not rebel, for I know all is right."

Mr. Lloyd hoped his wife was needlessly alarmed; but he found from her physician, that immediately after the birth of the child, some alarming symptoms had appeared, which indicated a hectic. Mrs. Lloyd had begged they might be concealed from her husband from the generous purpose of saving him, as long as possible, useless anxiety. The disease, however, had taken certain hold, and that morning, after a conversation with her physician, during which her courage had surprised him, she had resolved to begin the difficult task of fortifying her husband for the approaching calamity.

Spring came on, and its sweet influences penetrated to the sick room of Rebecca. Her health seemed amended, and her spirits refreshed; and when Mr. Lloyd proposed that they should travel, she cheerfully consented. But she cautioned her husband not to be flattered by an apparent amendment, for, said she, "though my wayward disease may be coaxed into a little clemency, it will not spare me."

As she prophesied, her sufferings were mitigated, but it was but too manifest that no permanent amendment was to be expected. The disease made very slow progress; one would have thought it shrunk from marring so young and so fair a work. Her spirit, too, enjoyed the freedom and beauty of the country. As they passed up the fertile shores of the Connecticut, Rebecca's benevolent heart glowed with gratitude to the Father of all, at the spectacle of so many of her fellow-creature's enjoying the rich treasures of Providence; cast into a state of society the happiest for their moral improvement, where they had neither the miseries of poverty, nor the temptations of riches. She would raise her eyes to the clear Heaven, would look on the "misty mountain's top," and then on the rich meadows through which they were passing, and which were now teeming with the summer's fulness, and would say, "Dear Robert, is there any heart so cold, that it does not melt in this vision of the power and the bounty of the Lord of heaven and earth? Do not sorrow for me, when I am going to a more perfect communion with Him, for I shall see him as he is."

From the Connecticut they passed by the romantic road that leads through the plains of West Springfield, Westfield, &c. There is no part our country, abundant as it is in the charms of nature, more lavishly adorned with romantic scenery. The carriage slowly traced its way on the side of a mountain, from which the imprisoned road had with difficulty been won;—a noisy stream dashed impetuously along at their left, and as they ascended the mountain, they still heard it before them leaping from rock to rock, now almost losing itself in the deep pathway it had made, and then rushing with increased violence over its stony bed.

"This young stream," said Mr. Lloyd, "reminds one of the turbulence of headstrong childhood; I can hardly believe it to be the same we admired, so leisurely winding its peaceful way into the bosom of the Connecticut."

"Thou likest the sobriety of maturity," replied Rebecca, "but I confess that there is something delightful to my imagination in the elastic bound of this infant stream; it reminds me of the joy of untamed spirits, and undiminished strength."

The travellers' attention was withdrawn from the wild scene before them to the appearance of the heavens, by their coachman, who observed, that "never in his days had he seen clouds make so fast; it was not," he said, "five minutes since the first speck rose above the hill before them, and now there was not enough blue sky for a man to swear by:—but," added he, looking with a lengthening visage to what he thought an interminable hill before them, "the lightning will be saved the trouble of coming down to us, for if my poor beasts ever get us to the top, we may reach up and take it."

Having reached the summit of the next acclivity, they perceived by the road's side, a log hut; over the door was a slab, with a rude and mysterious painting, (which had been meant for a foaming can and a plate of gingerbread,) explained underneath by "cake and beer for sale." This did not look very inviting, but it promised a better shelter from the rain, for the invalid, than the carriage could afford. Mr. Lloyd opened the door, and lifted his wife over a rivulet, which actually ran between the sill of the house and the floor-planks that had not originally been long enough for the dimensions of the apartment.

The mistress of the mansion, a fat middle-aged woman, who sat with a baby in her arms at a round table, at which there were four other children eating from a pewter dish in the middle of the table, rose, and having ejected the eldest boy from a chair by a very unceremonious slap, offered it to Mrs. Lloyd and resumed her seat; quietly finishing her meal. Her husband, a ruddy, good-natured, hardy looking mountaineer, had had the misfortune, by some accident in his childhood, to lose the use of both his legs, which were now ingeniously folded into the same chair on which he sat. He turned to the coachman, who, having secured his horses, had just entered, and smiling at his consternation, said, "Why, friend, you look scare't, pretty pokerish weather, to be sure, but then we don't mind it up here;" then turning to the child next him, who, in gazing at the strangers, had dropped half the food she was conveying to her mouth, he said,—"*Desdemony*, don't scatter the 'tatoes so."—"But last week," he continued, resuming his address to the coachman, "there was the most *tedious* spell of weather I have seen sen the week before last thanksgiving, when my wife and I went down into the lower part of Becket, to hear Deacon Hollister's funeral *sarmont*—Don't you remember, Tempy, that musical fellow that was there?—'I don't see,' says he, 'the use of the minister preaching up so much about hell-fire,' says he, 'it is a very good doctrine,' says he, 'to preach down on Connecticut River, but,' says he, 'I should not think it would frighten any body in such a cold place as Becket.'"

A bright flash, that seemed to fire the heavens, succeeded by a tremendous clap of thunder, which made the hovel tremble, terrified all the groupe, excepting the fearless speaker—

"A pretty smart flash to be sure; but, as I was saying, it is nothing to that storm we had last week.—*Velorus*, pull that hat out of the window, so the gentleman can see.—There, sir," said he, "just look at that big maple tree, that was blown down, if it had come one yard nearer my house, it would have crushed it to atoms. Ah, this is a nice place as you will find any where," he continued, (for he saw Mr. Lloyd was listening attentively to him,) "to bring up boys; it makes them hardy and spirited, to live here with the wind roaring about them, and the thunder rattling right over their heads: why they don't mind it any more than my woman's spinning-wheel, which, to be sure, makes a dumb noise sometimes."

Our travellers were not a little amused with the humour of this man, who had a natural philosophy that a stoic might have envied. "Friend," said Mr. Lloyd, "you have a singular fancy about names; what may be the name of that chubby little girl who is playing with my wife's fan?"

"Yes, sire, I am a little notional about names; that girl, sir, I call *Octavy*, and that lazy little dog that stands by her, is *Rodolphus*."

"And this baby," said Mr. Lloyd, kindly giving the astonished little fellow his watch-chain to play with, "this must be Vespasian or Agricola."

"No, sir, no; I met with a disappointment about that boy's name—what you may call a slip between the cup and the lip—when he was born, the women asked me what I meant to call him? I told them, I did not mean to be in any hurry; for you must know, sir, the way I get my names, I buy a book of one of those pedlers that are going over the mountain with tin-ware and brooms, and books and pamphlets, and one notion and another; that is, I don't buy out and out, but we make a swap; they take some of my wooden dishes, and let me have the *vally* in books; for you must know I am a great reader, and mean all my children shall have larning too, though it is pretty tough scratching for it. Well, Sir, as I was saying about this boy, I found a name just to hit my fancy, for I can pretty generally suit myself; the name was Sophronius; but just about that time, as the deuce would have it, my wife's father died, and the gin'ral had been a very gin'rous man to us, and so to compliment the old gentleman, I concluded to call him Solomon Wheeler."

Mr. Lloyd smiled, and throwing a dollar into the baby's lap, said, "There is something, my little fellow, to make up for your loss." The sight and the gift of a silver dollar produced a considerable sensation among the mountaineers. The children gathered round the baby to examine the splendid favour. The mother said, "The child was not old enough to make its manners to the gentleman, but he was as much beholden to him as if he could." The father only seemed insensible, and contented himself with remarking, with his usual happy nonchalance, that he "guessed it was easier getting money down country, than it was up on the hills."

"Very true, my friend," replied Mr. Lloyd, "and I should like to know how you support your family here. You do not appear to have any farm."

"No, Sir," replied the man, laughing, "it would puzzle me, with my legs, to take care of a farm; but then I always say, that as long as a man has his wits, he has something to work with. This is a pretty cold sappy soil up here, but we make out to raise all our sauce, and enough besides to fat a couple of pigs on; then, Sir, as you see, my woman and I keep a stock of cake and beer, and tansy bitters—a nice trade for a cold stomach; there is considerable travel on the road, and people get considerable dry by the time they get up here, and we find it a good business; and then I turn wooden bowls and dishes, and go out peddling once or twice a year; and there is not an old wife, or a young one either for the matter of that, but I can coax them to buy a dish or two; I take my pay in provisions or clothing; all the cash I get, is by the beer and cake: and now, Sir, though I say it, that may be should not say it, there is not a more independent man in the town of Becket than I am, though there is them that's more forehanded; but I pay my minister's tax, and my school tax, as reg'lar as any of them."

Mr. Lloyd admired the ingenuity and contentment of this man, his enjoyment of the privilege, the "glorious privilege," of every New-England man, of "being independent." But his pleasure was somewhat abated by an appearance of a want of neatness and order, which would have contributed so much to the comfort of the family, and which, being a Quaker, he deemed essential to it. He looked at the little stream of water we have mentioned, and which the rain had already swollen so much that it seemed to threaten an inundation of the house; and observing that neither the complexion of the floor nor of the children seemed to have been benefited by its proximity, he remarked to the man, that he "should think a person of his ingenuity would have contrived some mode of turning the stream."

"Why, yes, Sir," said the man, "I suppose I might, for I have got a book that treats upon hydrostatics and them things; but I'm calculating to build in the fall, and so I think we may as well musquash along till then."

"To build! Do explain to me how that is to be done?"

"Why, Sir," said he, taking a box from the shelf behind him, which had a hole in the centre of the top, through which the money was passed in, but afforded no facility for withdrawing it, "my woman and I agreed to save all the cash we could get for two years, and I should not be afraid to venture, there is thirty dollars there, Sir. The neighbours in these parts are very kind to a poor man; one will draw the timber, and another will saw the boards, and they will all come to raising, and bring their own spirits into the bargain. Oh, Sir, it must be a poor shack that can't make a turn to get a house over his head."

Mr. Lloyd took ten dollars from his pocketbook, and slipping it into the gap, said, "There is a small sum, my friend, and I wish it may be so expended as to give to thy new dwelling such conveniences as will enable thy wife to keep it neat. It will help on the trade too; for depend upon it, there is nothing makes a house look so inviting to a traveller as a cleanly air."

Our mountaineer's indifference was vanquished by so valuable a donation. "You are the most gin'rous man, Sir," said he, "that ever journeyed this way; and if I don't remember your advice, you may say there is no such thing as gratitude upon earth."

By this time the rain had subsided, the clouds were rolling over, the merry notes of the birds sallying from their shelters, welcomed the returning rays of the sun, and the deep unclouded azure in the west promised a delightful afternoon.

The travellers took a kind leave of the grateful cottagers, and as they drove away—"Tempy," said the husband, "if the days of miracles weren't quite entirely gone by, I should think we had 'entertained angels unawares.'"

"I think you might better say," replied the good woman, "that the angels have entertained us; any how, that sick lady will be an angel before long; she looks as good, and as beautiful, as one now."

It was on the evening of this day, that Mr. and Mrs. Lloyd arrived at the inn in the village of ———, which, as we have before stated, was the scene where her excellent and innocent life closed. She expressed a desire, that she might not be removed; she wished not to have the peace of her mind interrupted by any unnecessary agitation. Whenever she felt herself a little better, she would pass a part of the day in riding. Never did any one, in the full flush of health, enjoy more than she, from communion with her Heavenly Father, through the visible creation. She read with understanding the revelations of his goodness, in the varied expressions of nature's beautiful face.

"Do you know," said she to her husband, "that I prefer the narrow vales of the Housatonick, to the broader lands of the Connecticut? It certainly matters little where our dust is laid, if it be consecrated by Him who is the 'resurrection and the life;' but I derive a pleasure which I could not have conceived of, from the expectation of having my body repose in this still valley, under the shadow of that beautiful hill."

"I, too, prefer this scenery," said Mr. Lloyd, seeking to turn the conversation, for he could not yet but contemplate with dread, what his courageous wife spoke of with a tone of cheerfulness. "I prefer it, because it has a more domestic aspect. There is, too, a more perfect and intimate union of the sublime and beautiful. These mountains that surround us, and are so near to us on every side, seem to me like natural barriers, by which the Father has secured for His children the gardens He has planted for them by the river's side."

"Yes," said Rebecca, "and methinks they enclose a sanctuary, a temple, from which the brightness of His presence is never withdrawn. Look," said she, as the carriage passed over a hill that rose above the valley, and was a crown of beauty to it; "look, how gracefully and modestly that beautiful stream winds along under the broad shadows of those trees and clustering vines, as if it sought to hide the beauty that sparkles so brightly whenever a beam of light touches it. Oh! my Rebecca," said she, turning fondly to her child, "I could wish thy path led along these still waters, far from the stormy waves of the rude world—far from its 'vanities and vexation of spirit.'"

"If that is thy wish, my love," said her husband, looking earnestly at her, "it shall be a law to me."

Mrs. Lloyd's tranquillity had been swept away for a moment, by the rush of thought that was produced by casting her mind forward to the destiny of her child; but it was only for a moment. Her's was the trust of a mind long and thoroughly disciplined by Christian principles. Her face resumed its wonted repose, as she said, "Dear Robert, I have no wish but to leave all to thy discretion, under the guidance of the Lord."

It cannot be deemed strange that Mr. Lloyd should have felt a particular interest in scenes for which his wife had expressed such a partiality. He looked upon them with much the same feeling that the sight of a person awakens who has been loved by a departed friend. They seemed to have a sympathy for him; and he lingered at ———— without forming any plan for the future, till he was roused from his inactivity by hearing the sale of Mr. Elton's property spoken of. He had passed the place with Rebecca, and they had together admired its secluded and picturesque situation. The house stood at a little distance from the road, more than half hid by two patriarchal elms. Behind the house, the grounds descended gradually to the Housatonick, whose nourishing dews kept them arrayed in beautiful verdure. On the opposite side of the river, and from its very margin, rose a precipitous mountain, with its rich garniture of beach, maple, and linden; tree surmounting tree, and the images of all sent back by the clear mirror below; for the current there was so gentle, that, in the days of fable, a poet might have fancied the Genius of the stream had paused to woo the Nymphs of the wood.

Mr. Lloyd had no family ties to Philadelphia. He preferred a country life; not supinely to dream away existence, but he hoped there to cultivate and employ a "talent for doing good;" that talent which a noble adventurer declared he most valued, and which, though there is a field for its exercise, wherever any members of the human family are, he compassed sea and land to find new worlds in which to expend it.

Mr. Lloyd purchased the place and furniture, precisely as it had been left on the morning of the sale by Jane and her friend Mary.

CHAPTER IV

She, half an angel in her own account,
Doubts not hereafter with the saints to mount,
Tho' not a grace appears on strictest search,
But that she fasts, and item, goes to church.

Cowper.

The excellent character of Mary Hull had been spoken of to Mr. Lloyd by his landlady, and he was convinced that she was precisely the person to whom he should be satisfied to commit the superintendence of his family. Accordingly, on the evening of the sale, he sent a messenger to Mrs. Wilson's with the following note:—

"Robert Lloyd, having purchased the place of the late Mr. Elton, would be glad to engage Mary Hull to take charge of his family. Wages, and all other matters, shall be arranged to her satisfaction. He takes the liberty to send by the messenger, for Jane Elton, a work-box, dressing-glass, and a few other small articles, for which he has no use, and which, he hopes, she will do him the favour to retain, on account of the value they must have in her eyes."

Mrs. Wilson had no notion that any right could be prior to hers in her house. She took the note from the servant, and, notwithstanding he ventured to say he believed it was not meant for her, she read it first with no very satisfied air, and then turning to one of the children, she told her to call Mary Hull to her. The servant placed the things on the table, and left the room.

"So," said she to Jane, who was looking at her for some explanation of the sudden apparition of the work-box, &c.—"So, Miss, you have seen fit to disobey the first order I took the trouble to give you. I should like to know how you dared to leave these things after my positive orders."

"I did not understand your note, Ma'am, to contain positive orders; and Mary and I did not think it was quite right to take the things."

"Right! pretty judges of right to be sure. She a hired a girl, and a Methodist into the bargain. I don't know how she dares to judge over my head; and you, Miss, I tell you once for all, I allow no child in my house to know right from wrong; children have no reason, and they ought to be very thankful, when they fall into the hands of those that are capable of judging for them. Here," said she to Mary, who now entered in obedience to her summons; "here is a proposal of a place for you, from that Quaker that buried his wife last week. I suppose you call yourself your own mistress, and you can do as you like about it; but as you are yet a young woman, Mary Hull, and this man is a Quaker widower, and nobody knows who, I should think it a great risk for you to live with him; for, if nothing worse comes of it, you may be sure there is not a person in this town that won't think you are trying to get him for a husband.

Mary was highly gratified with the thought of returning to the place where she had passed a large and happy portion of her life, and she did not hesitate to say, that "she should not stand so much in her own light as to refuse so excellent a place; that from all she had heard said of Mr. Lloyd, he was a gentleman far above her condition in life; and therefore she thought no person would be silly enough to suppose she took the place from so foolish a design as Mrs. Wilson suggested; and she should take care that her conduct should give no occasion for reproach."

"Well," said Mrs. Wilson, chagrined that her counsel was not compulsory, "it does amaze me to see how some people strain at a gnat, and swallow a camel."

Mary did not condescend to notice this remark, but proceeded quietly to remove the articles Mr. Lloyd had sent, which she succeeded in doing, without any further remark from Mrs. Wilson, who prudently restrained the exercise of her authority while there was one present independent enough to oppose its current.

"Oh, Mary," said Jane, when they were alone, how glad I am you are going to live with such a good man; how happy you must be!" "And I too, Mary;" and she hastily brushed away a tear, "I am; at least I should be very happy when I have such a kind friend as you are so near to me."

"Yes, yes, dear Jane, try to be happy, this foolish aunt of yours will try you like the fire, but I look to see you come out of it as gold from the furnace: keep up a good heart, my child, it is a long lane that never turns."

The friends separated, but not till Mary had with her usual caution carefully packed away Jane's new treasures, saying, as she did it, "that it was best to put temptation out of sight."

Mary's plain and neat appearance, and her ingenuous sensible countenance, commended her at once to Mr. Lloyd's favour, and she entered immediately upon the duties of her new and responsible situation.

We must now introduce those who are willing to go further with us in the history of Jane Elton, to the family of Mrs. Wilson, where they will see she had a school for the discipline of christian character.

"Jane," said Mrs. Wilson to her on the morning after Mary's departure, "you know, child, the trouble and expense of taking you upon my hands is very great, but it did not seem suitable that being my brother's daughter you should be put out at present: you must remember, child, that I am at liberty to turn you away at any time, whereas, as you will always be in debt to me, you can never be at liberty to go when you choose. It is a great trial to me to take you, but the consciousness of doing my duty and more than my duty to you, supports me under it. Now as to what I expect from you:—in the first place, my word must be your law; you must not hesitate to do any thing that I require of you; never think of asking a reason for what I command—it is very troublesome and unreasonable to do so. Visiting, you must give up entirely; I allow my children to waste none of their time in company: meetings I shall wish you to attend when you have not work to do at home; for I do not wish you to neglect the means of grace, though I am sensible that your heart must be changed before they can do you any good. You must help Martha do the ironing, and assist Elvira with the clear starching and other matters; Nancy will want your aid about the beds; Sally is but young, and requires more care than I can give her, for my time is at present chiefly spent in instructing the young converts; and therefore I shall look to you to take the charge of Sally, and I expect you to take charge of mending and making for David when he comes home; the other boys will want now and then a stitch or two; and, in short, Miss, (and she increased the asperity of her tone, for she thought Jane's growing gravity indicated incipient rebellion,) you will be ready to do every thing that is wanted of you."

Jane was summoning resolution to reply, when both her and her aunt's attention was called to a rustling at the window, and crazy Bet thrust her head in—

"Go on," said she, "and fill up the measure of your iniquities, load her with burthens heavy and grievous to be borne, and do not touch them with one of your fingers.—There, Jane," said she, throwing her a bunch of carnations, "I have just come from the quarterly meeting, and I stopped as I came past your house, and picked these, for I thought their bright colours would be a temptation to the Quaker. And I thought too," said she, laughing, "there should be something to send up a sweet smelling savour from the altar where there are no deeds of mercy laid."

"Out of my yard instantly, you dirty beggar!" said Mrs. Wilson.

Bet turned, but not quickening her step, and went away, singing, "Glory, glory, hallalujah."

"Aunt," said Jane, "do not mind the poor creature. She does not mean to offend you. I believe she feels for me; for she has been sheltered many a time from the cold and the storms in our house."

"Don't give yourself the least uneasiness, Miss. I am not to be disturbed by a crazy woman; but I do not see what occasion there is for her feeling for you. You have not yet answered me."

"I have no answer to make, Ma'am," replied Jane, meekly, "but that I shall do my best to content you. I am very young, and not much used to work, and I may have been too kindly dealt with; but that is all over now."

"Do you mean, Miss, to say, that I shan't treat you kindly?"

"No, aunt, but I meant—excuse me, if I meant any thing wrong."

"I did expect, Miss, to hear some thankfulness expressed."

"I do, Ma'am, feel grateful, that I have a shelter over my head; what more I have to be grateful for, time must determine."

There was a dignity in Jane's manner, that, with the spirit of the reply, taught Mrs. Wilson, that she had, in her niece, a very different subject to deal with from her own wilful and trickish children. "Well, Miss Jane, I shall expect no haughty airs in my house, and you will please now to go and tell the girls to be ready to go with me to the afternoon conference, and prepare youself to go also. One more thing I have to say to you, you must never look to me for any clothing; that cunning Mary has packed away enough to last you fifty years. With all her methodism, I will trust her to feather your nest, and her own too."

Alas! thought Jane, as she went to execute her aunt's commission, what good does it do my poor aunt to go to conference? Perhaps this question would not have occurred to many girls of thirteen, but Jane had been accustomed to scan the motives of her conduct, and to watch for the fruit. The aid extended to our helpless orphan by her pharisaical aunt, reminds us of the "right of asylum" afforded, by the ancients to the offenders who were allowed to take shelter in the temples of their gods, and allowed to perish there.

She found the girls very much indisposed to the afternoon meeting. Martha said, she "would not go to hear Deacon Barton's everlasting prayers; she had heard so many of them, she knew them all by heart."

Elvira had just got possession, by stealth, of a new novel; that species of reading being absolutely prohibited in Mrs. Wilson's house, she had crept up to the garret, and was promising herself a long afternoon of stolen pleasure. "Oh, Jane," said she, "why can't you go down and tell Mother you can't find me. Just tell her, you guess I have gone down to Miss Baneker's, to inquire whether the tracts have come; that's a good thought; that will quiet her;" and she was resuming her book, when seeing Jane did not move, she added, "I'll do as much for you any time."

"I shall never wish you to do as much for me, Elvira."

"I do not think it is so very much, just to go downstairs; besides, Jane," she added, imperiously, "Mother says, you must do whatever we ask you to."

Elvira was so habituated to deceit, that it never occurred to her, that the falsehood was the difficult part of the errand to Jane; and when Jane said, "Cousin Elvira, I will do whatever is reasonable for you, and no more; any thing that is true, I will tell your Mother for you;" she laughed in derision.

"Pooh, Jane, you have brought your deaconish nonsense to a poor market. It was easy enough to get along with the truth with your mother, because she would let you have your own way on all occasions; but I can tell you, disguises are the only wear in our camp!"

"I shall not use them, Elvira. I should dread their being stripped off."

"Oh, not at all. Mother seldom takes the trouble to inquire into it; and if she does, now and then, by accident, detect it, the storm soon blows over. She has caught me in many a white lie, and black one too, and she has not been half so angry as when I have torn my frock, or lost a glove. Why, child, if you are going to fight your battles with Mother with plain truth, you will find yourself without shield or buckler."

"Ah, Elvira!" replied Jane, smiling,

> "That's no battle, ev'ry body knows,
> Where one side only gives the blows."

"That's true enough, Jane. Well, if you will not help me off from the conference, I must go.—Sweet Vivaldi," said she, kissing her book, and carefully hiding it in a dark corner of the garret, "must I part with thee?"

"One would think," said Jane, "you was parting with your lover."

"I am, my dear. I always fancy, when I read a novel, that I am the heroine, and the hero is one of my favourites; and then I realize it all, and it appears so natural."

Elvira was not, at heart, an ill-natured girl; but having a weak understanding, and rather a fearful unresisting temper, she had been driven by her Mother's mode of treatment into the practice of deceit; and she being the weaker party, used in her warfare, as many arts as a savage practises towards a civilized enemy. A small stock of original invention may be worked up into a vast deal of cunning. Elvira had been sent one quarter to a distant boarding-school, where her name had attracted a young lady, whose head had been turned by love-stories. They had formed a league of eternal friendship, which might have a six months' duration; and Elvira had returned to her home, at the age of sixteen, with a farrago of romance superadded to her home-bred duplicity.

Martha was two years older than her sister, and more like her mother: violent and self-willed, she openly resisted her Mother's authority, whenever it opposed her wishes. From such companions, Jane soon found she had nothing to expect of improvement or pleasure; but, though it may seem quite incredible to some, she was not unhappy. The very labour her aunt imposed on her was converted into a blessing, for it occupied her mind, and saved her from brooding on the happy past, or the unhappy present. She now found exercise for the domestic talents Mary had so skilfully cultivated. Even the unrelenting Mrs. Wilson was once heard to say, with some apparent pleasure, that "Jane was gifted at all sorts of work." Her dexterous hand was often put in requisition by her idle and slatternly cousins, and their favour was sometimes won by her kind offices. But more than all, and above all, as a source of contentment and cheerfulness—better far than ever was boasted of perennial springs, or "Amreeta cups of immortality"—was Jane's unfailing habit of regulating her daily life by the sacred rules of our blessed Lord. She would steal from her bed at the dawn of day, when the songs of the birds were interpreting the stillness of nature, and beauty and fragrance breathing incense to the Maker, and join her devotions to the choral praise. At this hour she studied the world of truth and life, and a holy beam of light fell from it on her path through the day. Her pleasures at this social period of her life were almost all solitary, except when she was indulged in a visit to Mary, whose eye was continually watching over her with maternal kindness. The gayety of her childhood had been so sadly checked by the change of her fortunes, that her countenance had taken rather a serious and reserved cast. Mr. Lloyd's benevolent feelings were awakened by her appearance; and Mary, whose chief delight was in expatiating on the character of her favourite, took care to confirm his favourable impressions by setting in the broadest light her former felicity, her present trials, and her patience in tribulation.

Mary had orders to leave the furniture in a little room that had formerly been assigned to Jane, precisely as she left it, and to tell Jane that it was still called, and should be considered, her room.

"And that beautiful honeysuckle, Jane," said Mr. Lloyd to her, "which thy tasteful hand has so carefully trained about the window, is still thine."

These, and many other instances of delicate attention from Mr. Lloyd, saved her from the feeling of forlornness that she might otherwise have suffered.

CHAPTER V

"I am for other, than for dancing measures."
As You Like It.

A few months after Jane entered her aunt's family, an unusual commotion had been produced in the village of —— by an event of rare occurrence. This was no less than the arrival of a dancing-master, and the issuing of proposals for a dancing-school.

This was regarded by some very zealous persons as a ruse de guerre of the old Adversary, which, if not successfully opposed, would end in the establishment of his kingdom.

The plan of the disciple of Vestris, was to establish a chain of dancing-schools from one extremity of the county to the other; and this was looked upon as a mine which would be sprung to the certain destruction of every thing that was 'virtuous and of good report.' Some clergymen denounced the impending sin from their pulpits. One said that he had searched the Bible from Genesis to Revelation, and he could not find a text that expressly treated of that enormity, but that was manifestly because it was a sin too heinous to be spoken of in holy writ; he said that dancing was one of the most offensive of all the rites of those savage nations that were under the immediate and *visible* government of the prince of this world; and, finally, he referred them to the church documents, those precious records of the piety, and wisdom, and purity of their ancestors; and they would there find a rule which prohibited any church-member from frequenting, or being present at, a ball, or dance, or frolic, or any such assembly of Satan; and they would moreover find that such transgressions had been repeatedly punished by expulsion from the church, and exclusion from all christian ordinances. Some of this gentleman's brethren contented themselves by using their influence in private advice and remonstrance; and a few said they could not see the sin nor the danger of the young people's indulging, with moderation, in the healthful exercise and innocent recreation adapted to their season of life; that what the moral and pious Locke had strenuously advocated, and the excellent Watts approved, it did not become them to frown upon; but they should use their efforts in restraining the young people within the bounds of moderation.

The result was that our dancing-master obtained a few schools, and one in the village which enjoyed the privilege of such a light as Mrs. Wilson. She, filled with alarm, 'lifted up her voice and spared not.' Some of her warmest admirers thought her clamour had more of valour in it than discretion.

Notwithstanding the violence of the opposition, and perhaps aided by it, the dancing-school was at length fairly established, and some of the elderly matrons of the village, who considered dances as the orgies of Satan, were heard to confess that when properly regulated, they might furnish an amusement not altogether unsuited to youth, and that they did not, in point of propriety, suffer by a comparison with the romps, forfeits, and cushion-dances of *their* younger days.

At Mrs. Wilson's instance, two new weekly meetings were appointed, on the same evenings with the dancing-school; the one to be a conference in the presence of the young people, and the other a catechetical lecture for them. These her daughters were compelled to attend, in spite of the bold and turbulent opposition of Martha, and the well-concerted artifices of Elvira.

Elvira expressed her surprise at Jane's patience under the new dispensation. "To be sure, Jane," she said, "you have not the trial that I have, about the dancing-school, for a poor girl can't expect such accomplishments.—I do so long to dance! It was in the mazy dance Edward Montreville first fell in love with Selina;—but then these odious—these hateful meetings! Oh, I have certainly a *natural* antipathy to them; you do not always have to attend them; mother is ready enough to let you off, when there is any hard job to be done in the family;—well, much as I hate work, I had rather work than go to meeting. Tell me honestly, Jane, would not you like to learn to dance, if you was not obliged to wear deep mourning, and could afford to pay for it?"

Jane, all used as she was to the coarseness of her cousins, would sometimes feel the colour come unbidden to her cheeks, and she felt them glow as she replied, "I learned to dance, Elvira, during the year I spent at Mrs. B.'s boarding school."

"La, is it possible? I never heard you say a word about it."

"No," said Jane; "many things have happened to me that you never heard me say a word about."

"Oh! I dare say, Miss Jane. Every body knows your cold, reserved disposition. My sensibility would destroy me, if I did not permit it to flow out into a sympathizing bosom."

"But now, Jane," said she, shutting the door, and lowering her voice, "I have hit upon a capital plan to cheat mother. There is to be a little ball to-night, after the the school; and I have promised Edward Erskine to go with him to it. For once, Jane, be generous, and lend me a helping-hand. In the first place, to get rid of the meeting, I am going to put a flannel round my throat, to tell my mother it is very sore, and I have a head-ach; and then I shall go to bed; but as soon as she is well out of the house, I shall get up and dress me, and wind that pretty wreath of yours, which I'm sure you will lend me, around my head, and meet Erskine just at the pear-tree, at the end of the garden. Then, as to the return, you know you told mother you could not go to meeting, because you was going to stay with old Phillis, and I just heard the Doctor say, he did not believe she would live the night through. This is clear luck, what mother would call providential. At any rate, you know, if she should not be any worse, you can sit up till 12 o'clock, and I will just tap at Phillis's bed-room window, and you won't refuse, Jane, to slip the bolt of the outside door for me."

Jane told her she could not take part in her projects; but, Elvira trusting to the impulse of her cousin's good-nature, adhered to her plan.

Mrs. Wilson was not, on this occasion, so keen-eyed as usual. She had, that very day, received proposals of marriage from a broken merchant, and though she had no idea of jeopardizing her estates and liberty, she was a good deal fluttered with what she would fain have believed to be a compliment to her personal charms. Every thing succeeded to Elvira's most sanguine expectations. Her mother went to the conference. Elvira, arrayed in all the finery her own wardrobe supplied, and crowned with Jane's wreath, went off to her expecting gallant, leaving Jane by the bedside of Phillis; and there the sweet girl kindly watched alone, till after the return of the family from the conference, till after the bell had summoned the household to the evening prayer, and till after the last lingering sound of fastening doors, windows, &c. died away.

The poor old invalid was really in the last extremity; her breathing grew shorter and more interrupted; her eyes assumed a fearful stare and glassiness. Jane's fortitude forsook her, and she ventured to call her aunt, who had but just entered the room, when the poor creature expired.

In the last struggle she grasped Jane's hand, and as her fingers released their hold, and the arm fell beside her, Jane raised it up, and gently laying it across her body, and retaining the hand for a moment in her own, she said, "Poor Phillis! how much hard work you have done with this hand, and how many kindnesses for me. Your troubles are all over, now."

"You take upon you to say a great deal, Jane," replied her aunt. "Phillis did not give me satisfying evidence of a saving faith."

"But," said Jane, as if she did not quite comprehend the import of her aunt's remark, "Phillis was very faithful over her little."

"That's nothing to the purpose, Jane," answered Mrs. Wilson.

Jane made no reply, unless the tear she dropped on her old friend might be deemed one, and Mrs. Wilson added,

"Now, child, you must get the things together, to lay her out." Then saying, that Phillis's sickness had been a bill of cost to her, and quite overlooking her long life of patient and profitable service, she gave the most sordid directions as to the selection of provisions for the last wants of the poor menial. Jane went out of the room to execute her orders.

She had scarcely gone, when Mrs. Wilson heard the window carefully raised, and some one said, "Here I am, Jane; go softly and slip the bolt of the west door, and don't for the world wake the old lady." By any brighter light than the dim night lamp that was burning on the hearth, Elvira could not have mistaken her dark harsh visaged mother for her fair cousin. A single glance revealed the truth to Mrs. Wilson. The moonbeams were playing on the wreath of flowers, and Edward Erskine, who was known as the ringleader of the ball-faction, stood beside Elvira. She smothered her rage for a few moments, and creeping softly to the passage, opened the door, and admitted the rebel, who followed her to Phillis's room, saying, "Oh, Jane, you are a dear good soul for once. I have had an ecstatic time. Never try to persuade me not to trick the old woman." By this time they had arrived at Phillis's room, where Jane had just entered with a candle in her hand.

Mrs. Wilson turned to her child, who stood confounded with the sudden detection, "I have caught you," said she, almost bursting with rage; "caught you both!" Then seizing the wreath of flowers, which she seemed to look upon as the hoisted flag of successful rebellion, she threw it on the floor; and crushing it with her foot, she grasped the terrified girl, and pushed her so violently that she fell on the cold body of the lifeless woman: "and you, viper!" continued the furious creature, turning to Jane, "is this my reward for warming you in my bosom? You, with your smooth hypocritical face, teaching my child to deceive and abuse me. But you shall have your reward. You shall see whether I am to be browbeaten by a dependant child, in my own house."

Jane had often seen her aunt angry, but she had never witnessed such passion as this, and she was for a moment confounded; but like a delicate plant that bends to the ground before a sudden gust of wind, and then is firm and erect as ever, she turned to Mrs. Wilson, and said, "Ma'am, I have never deceived or aided others to deceive you."

"I verily believe you lie!" replied her aunt, in a tone of undiminished fury.

Jane looked to her cousin, who had recoiled from the cold body of Phillis, and sat in sullen silence on a trunk at the foot of the bed,—"Elvira," said she, "you will do me the justice to tell your mother I had no part in your deception." But Elvira, well pleased to have any portion of the storm averted from her own head, had not generosity enough to interpose the truth. She therefore compromised with her conscience, and merely said,— "Jane knew I was going."

"I was sure of it,—I was sure of it; I always knew she was an artful jade; 'still waters run deep;' but she shall be exposed, the mask shall be stripped from the hypocrite."

"Aunt," said Jane, in a voice so sweet, so composed, that it sounded like the breath of music following the howlings of an enraged animal, "Aunt, we are in the chamber of death; and in a little time you, and I, and all of us, shall be as this poor creature; as you will then wish your soul to be lightened of all injustice—spare the innocent now; you know I never deceived you; Elvira knows it; I am willing to bear any thing it pleases God to lay upon me, but I cannot have my good name taken, it is all that remains to me."

This appeal checked Mrs. Wilson for a moment, she would have replied, but she was interrupted by two coloured women, whom she had sent for, to perform the last offices for Phillis. She restrained her passion, gave them the necessary directions, and withdrew to her own room: where, we doubt not, she was followed by the rebukes of her conscience; for however neglected and stifled, its 'still small voice' will be heard in darkness and solitude.

It may seem strange, that Mrs. Wilson should have manifested such anxiety to throw the blame of this affair on Jane; but however a parent may seek by every flattering unction vanity can devise, to evade the truth, the misconduct of a child will convey a reproach, and reflect dishonour on the author of its existence.

Jane and Elvira crept to their beds without exchanging a single word. Elvira felt some shame at her own meanness; but levity and selfishness always prevailed in her mind, and she soon lost all consciousness of realities, and visions of dances and music and moonlight floated in her brain; sometimes 'a change came o'er the spirit of her dream,' and she shrunk from a violent grasp, and she felt the icy touch of death; and wherever she turned, a ray from her cousin's mild blue eye fell upon her, and she could not escape from its silent, beautiful reproach. The mother and the daughter might both have envied the repose of the solitary abused orphan, who possessed 'a peace they could not trouble.' She soon lost all memory of her aunt's rage and her cousin's injustice, and sunk into quiet slumbers. In her dream she saw her mother tenderly smiling on her; and heard again and again the last words of the old woman: "the Lord bless you, Miss Jane! the Lord will bless you, for your kindness to old Phillis."

If Mrs. Wilson had not been blinded by self-love, she might have learnt an invaluable lesson from the melancholy results of her own malgovernment. But she preferred incurring every evil, to the relinquishment of one of the prerogatives of power. Her children, denied the appropriate pleasures of youth, were driven to sins of a much deeper die, than those which Mrs. Wilson sought to avoid could have had even in her eyes; for surely the very worst effects that ever were attributed to dancing, or to romance-reading, cannot equal the secret dislike of a parent's authority, the risings of the heart against a parent's tyranny, and the falsehood and meanness that weakness always will employ in the evasion of power; and than which nothing will more certainly taint every thing that is pure in the character.

The cool reflection of the morning pointed out to Mrs. Wilson, as the most discreet, the very line of conduct justice would have dictated. She knew she could not accuse Jane, without exposing Elvira, and besides she did not care to have it known that her sagacity had been outwitted by these children. Therefore, though she appeared at breakfast more sulky and unreasonable than usual, she took no notice of the transactions of the preceding night, and they remained secret to all but the actors in them; except that we have reason to believe, from Mr. Lloyd's increased attention to Jane, shortly after, that they had been faithfully transmitted to him by Mary Hull, the balm of whose sympathy it cannot be deemed wonderful our little solitary should seek.

CHAPTER VI

These are fine feathers, but what bird were they plucked from.

Esop.

There is nothing in New-England so eagerly sought for, or so highly prized by all classes of people, as the advantages of education. A farmer and his wife will deny themselves all other benefits that might result from the gains that have accrued to them from a summer of self-denial and toil, to give their children the *privilege* of a grammar-school during the winter. The public, or as they are called the *town-schools*, are open to the child of the poorest labourer. As knowledge is one of the best helps and most certain securities to virtue, we doubtless owe a great portion of the morality of this blessed region, where there are no dark corners of ignorance, to these wise institutions of our pious ancestors.

In the fall subsequent to the events we have recorded, a school had been opened in the village of ———, of a higher and more expensive order, than is common in a country town. Every mouth was filled with praises of the new teacher, and with promises and expectations of the knowledge to be derived from this newly opened fountain; all was bustle and preparation among the young companions of Martha and Elvira for the school; for Martha, though beyond the usual school-going age, was to complete her education at the new seminary.

The dancing school had passed without a sigh of regret from Jane; but now she felt severely her privation. Her watchful friend, Mary Hull, remarked the melancholy look that was unheeded at her aunt's; and she inquired of Jane, "Why she was so downcast?"

"Ah, Mary!" she replied, "it is a long time since I have felt the merry spirit which the wise man says, is 'medicine to the heart.'"

"That's true, Jane; but then there's nobody, that is, there's nobody that has so little reason for it as you have, that has a more cheerful look."

"I have great reason to be cheerful, Mary, in token of gratitude for my kind friends here; and," added she, taking Mr. Lloyd's infant, who playfully extended her arms to her, "you and I are too young, Rebecca, to be very sad." The child felt the tear that dewed the cheek to which she was pressed, and looking into Jane's face, with instinctive sympathy, burst into tears. Mr. Lloyd entered at this moment, and Jane hastily replacing the child in Mary Hull's lap, and tying on her hat, bade them farewell.

Mr. Lloyd asked for some explanation. Mary believed nothing particular had happened. "But," she said, "the poor girl's spirit wearies with the life she leads, and its no wonder; it is a great change from a home and mother, to such a workhouse and such a task-woman."

Mr. Lloyd had often regretted, that it was so little in his power to benefit Jane. The school occurred to him, and as nothing was more improbable than that Mrs. Wilson would, herself, incur the expense of Jane's attendance, he consulted with Mary as to the best mode of doing it himself, without provoking Mrs. Wilson's opposition, or offending her pride. A few days after, when the agent for the school presented the subscription list to Mrs. Wilson for her signature, she saw there, to her utter astonishment, Jane Elton's name. The agent handed her an explanatory note from Mr. Lloyd, in which he said, "that as it had been customary to send one person from the house he now occupied to the 'subscription school,' he had taken the liberty to continue the custom. He hoped the measure would meet with Mrs. Wilson's approbation, without which it could not go into effect."

Mrs. Wilson, at first, said, it was impossible; she could not spare Jane; but afterwards, she consented to take it into consideration. The moment the man had shut the door, she turned to Jane, and misunderstanding the flush of pleasure that brightened her usually pale face, she exclaimed, "And so, Miss, this is one of your plans to slip your neck out of the yoke of duty."

Jane said, she had nothing to do with the plan, but she trusted her aunt would not oblige her to lose such a golden opportunity of advantage. Mrs. Wilson made various objections, and Jane skilfully obviated them all. At last she said, "There would be a piece of linen to make up for David, and that put it quite out of the question, for," said she, "I shall not take the girls from their studies; and even you, Miss Jane, will probably have the grace to think my time more precious than yours."

"Well, aunt," said Jane, with a smile so sweet that even Mrs. Wilson could not entirely resist its influence, "if I will get the linen made by witch or fairy, may I go?"

"Why, yes," replied her aunt; "as you cannot get it made without witches or fairies, I may safely say you may."

Jane's reliance was on kindness more potent than any modern magic; and that very evening, with the light-bounding step of hope, she went to her friend Mary's, where, after having made her acknowledgments to Mr. Lloyd with the grace of earnestness and sincerity, she revealed to Mary the only obstacle that now opposed her wishes. Mary at once, as Jane expected, offered to make the linen for her; and Jane, affectionately thanking her, said, she was sure her aunt would be satisfied, for she had often heard her say, "Mary Hull was the best needle woman in the county."

Mrs. Wilson had seen Jane so uniformly flexible and submissive to her wilful administration, and in matters she deemed of vastly more consequence than six months schooling, that she was all astonishment to behold her now so persevering in her resolution to accomplish her purpose. But Jane's and Mrs. Wilson's estimate of the importance of any given object was very different. The same fortitude that enabled Jane to bear, silently and patiently, the "oppressor's wrong," nerved her courage in the attainment of a good end.

Mrs. Wilson had no longer any pretence to oppose Jane's wishes; and the following day she took her place, with her cousins, at Mr. Evertson's school. Her education had been very much advanced for her years; so that, though four years younger than Martha Wilson, she was, after a very careful examination by the teacher, classed with her. This was a severe mortification to Martha's pride; she seemed to feel her cousin's equality an insult to herself, and when she reported the circumstance to her mother, she said, she believed it was all owing to Jane's soft answers and pretty face; or "may be the Quaker, who takes such a mighty fancy to Jane, has bribed Mr. Evertson."

"Very likely, very likely," answered her mother. "It seems as if every body took that child's part against us."

Jane, once more placed on even ground with her companions, was like a spring relieved from a pressure. She entered on her new pursuits with a vigour that baffled the mean attempts of the family at home to impede or hinder her course. She was not a genius, but she had that eager assiduity that "patient attention," to which the greatest of philosophers attributed the success which has been the envy and admiration of the world. There was a perpetual sunshine in her face, that delighted her patron. He had thought nothing could be more interesting than Jane's pensive dejected expression; but he now felt, that it was beautiful as well as natural for the young plant to expand its leaves to the bright rays of the sun, and to rejoice in his beams. Mary Hull was heard to say, quite as often as the beauty of the expression would justify, the Lord be thanked, our dear young lady once more wears the "cheerfulness of countenance that betokens a heart in prosperity."

Double duties were laid on Jane at home, but she won her way through them. The strict rule of her aunt's house did not allow her to "watch with the constellations," but she "made acquaintance with the gray dawn," and learnt by "employing them well," (the mode recommended by Elizabeth Smith,) the value of minutes as well as hours. The bad envied her progress, the stupid were amazed at it, and the generous delighted with it. She went, rejoicing on her way, far before her cousins, who, stung by her manifest superiority, made unwonted exertions; and Martha might have fairly competed with her for the prizes that were to be given, had she not often been confused and obstructed by the perversities of her temper.

The winter and the spring winged their rapid flight. The end of the term, which was to close with an exhibition, approached. The note of busy preparation was heard in every dwelling in the village of ———. We doubt if the expectation of the tournament at Ashby de la Zouche excited a greater sensation among knights-templars, Norman lords, and wandering chevaliers, than the anticipation of the exhibition produced upon the young people of ———. Labour and skill were employed and exhausted in preparations for the event. One day was allotted for the examination of the scholars, and the distribution of prizes; and another for the *exhibition*, during which the young men and boys were to display those powers that were developing for the pulpit, and the bar, and the political harangue. The young ladies were with obvious and singular propriety excluded from any part in the exhibition, except that on the first drawing *aside*, (for they did not know enough of the scenic art to draw *up* the curtain,) the prize composition was to be read by the writer of it.

The old and the young seemed alike interested in promoting the glories of the day. The part of a king, from one of Miss More's Sacred Dramas, was to be enacted, and there was a general assembly of the girls of the village to fit his royal trappings. A purple shawl was converted by a little girl of ready invention into a royal robe of Tyrian dye. The crown blazed with jewelry, which to too curious scrutiny appeared to be not diamonds, but paste; not gold, but gold-leaf, and gold beads; of which fashionable New-England necklace, as tradition goes, there were not less than sixty strings, lent for the occasion by the kind 'auld wives' of the village. An antiquated belle who had once flourished in the capital, completed the decoration of the crown by four nodding ostrich plumes, whose 'bend did certainly awe the world' of ————. There might have been some want of congruity in the regalia, but this was not marked by the critics of ————, as not one of the republican audience had ever seen a *real crown*.

A meeting was called of the trustees of the school, and the meeting-house (for thus in the land of the Puritans the churches are still named,) was assigned as the place of exhibition. In order not to invade the seriousness of the sanctuary, the pieces to be spoken were all to be of a moral or religious character. Instrumental music, notwithstanding the celebrations of Independence in the same holy place were pleaded as a precedent, was rigorously forbidden. The arrangements were made according to these decrees, from which there was no appeal, and neither, as usually happens with inevitable evils, was there much dissatisfaction. One of the boys remarked, that he wondered the deacons (three of the trustees were deacons,) did not stop the birds from singing, and the sun from shining, and all such gay sounds and sights. Oh that those, who throw a pall over the innocent pleasures of life, and give, in the eye of the young, to religion a dark and gloomy aspect, would learn some lessons of theology from the joyous light of the sun, and the merry carol of the birds!

A floor was laid over the tops of the pews, which was covered by a carpet lent by the kind Mr. Lloyd. A chair, a present from Queen Anne to the first missionary to the Housatonick Indians, and which, like some other royal gifts, had cost more than it came to, in its journey from the coast to the mountainous interior, furnished a very respectable throne, less mutable than some that have been filled by real kings, for it remained a fixture in the middle of the stage, while kings were deposed and kingdoms overthrown. Curtains, of divers colours and figures, were drawn in a cunningly devised manner, from one end of the church to the other.

The day of *examination* came, and our deserving young heroine was crowned with honours, which she merited so well, and bore so meekly, that she had the sympathy of the whole school—except that (for the truth must be told,) of her envious cousins. When the prizes for arithmetic, grammar, geography, history, and philosophy, were one after another, in obedience to the award of the examiners, delivered to Jane, by her gratified master, Martha Wilson burst into tears of spite and mortification, and Elvira whispered to the young lady next her, "She may have her triumph now, but I will have one worth a hundred prizes to-morrow, for, I am sure that my composition will be preferred to hers."

To add the zest of curiosity and surpise to the exhibition, it had been determined that the writer of the successful piece should not be known till the withdrawing of the curtain disclosed the secret. The long expected day arrived. One would have thought, from the waggons and chaises that poured in from the neighbouring towns, that a cattle show, or a hanging, or some such 'merry-making matter,' was going on in the village of ———. The church was filled at an early hour, and pews, aisles, and galleries crowded as we have seen a less holy place at the first appearance of a foreign actor. The teacher and the clergyman were in the pulpit; the scholars ranged on benches at the opposite extremities of the stage; the crowd was hushed into reverent stillness while the clergyman commenced the exercises of the day by an appropriate prayer. The curtains were hardly closed, before they were again withdrawn, and the eager eyes of the assembly fell on Elvira. A shadow of disappointment might have been seen flitting across Mr. Lloyd's face at this moment, while Mary Hull, who sat in a corner of the gallery, half rose from her seat, sat down again, tied and untied her bonnet, and, in short, manifested indubitable signs of a vexed spirit; signs, that in more charitable eyes than Mrs. Wilson's certainly would have gone against the obnoxious doctrine of 'perfection.' Elvira was seated on the throne, ambitiously arrayed in a bright scarlet Canton crape frock, a white sarsenet scarf, fantastically thrown over her shoulders. Her hair, in imitation of some favourite heroine, flowed in ringlets over her neck, excepting a single braid, with which, as she fancied, '*à la grecque*,' she had encompassed her brow, and, to add to this confusion of the classical and the pastoral orders, instead of the crescent of Diana in the model, she had bound her braid with blue glass beads.

"Who is that? who is that?" was whispered from one to another.

"The rich widow Wilson's daughter," the strangers were answered.

Mrs. Wilson, whose maternal pride (for maternal tenderness she had not) was swollen by the consciousness of triumph over Jane, nodded and whispered to all within her hearing, "My daughter, sir"—"my daughter, ma'am; you see, by the bill, the prize composition is to be spoken by the writer of it."

Elvira rose and advanced. She had requested that she might speak instead of reading her piece, and she spouted it with all the airs and graces of a sentimentalist of the beau monde. When she dropped her courtesy, and returned to her companions, her usually high colour was heightened by the pride of success and the pleasure of display. Some were heard to say, "She is a beauty;" while others shook their heads, and observed, "The young lady must have great talents to write such a piece, but she looked too bold to please them."

Before the busy hum of comment had died away, an old man, with a bald head, a keen eye, and a very good-humoured face, rose and said "he would make bold to speak a word; bashfulness was suitable to youth, but was not necessary to gray hairs: he was kinder-loath to spoil a young body's pleasure, but he must own he did not like to see so much flourish in borrowed plumes; that, if he read the notice right, the young woman was to speak a piece of her own framing; he had no fault to find with the speaking; she spoke as smart as a lawyer; but he knew them words as well as the catechism, and if the school-master or the minister would please to walk to his house, which was hard by, they might read them out of an old Boston newspaper, that his woman, who had been dead ten years come independence, had pasted up by the side of his bed, to keep off the rheumatis."

The old man sat down; and Mr. Evertson, who had all along been a little suspicious of foul play, begged the patience of the audience, while he himself could make the necessary comparison. Mrs. Wilson, conscious of the possession of a file of old Boston papers, and well knowing the artifice was but too probable, fidgetted from one side of the pew to the other; and the conscience-stricken girl, on the pretence of being seized with a violent tooth-ach, left the church.

The teacher soon returned, and was very sorry to be obliged to say, that the result of the investigation had been unfavourable to the young lady's integrity, as the piece had, undoubtedly, been copied, verbatim, from the original essay in the Boston paper.

"He hoped his school would suffer no discredit from the fault of an individual. He should now, though the young lady had remonstrated against being brought forward under such circumstances, insist on the composition being read, which had been pronounced next best to Miss Wilson's; and which, he could assure the audience, was, unquestionably, original."

The curtain was once more withdrawn, and discovered Jane seated on the throne, looking like the "meek usurper," reluctant to receive the honour that was forced upon her. She presented a striking contrast to the deposed sovereign. She was dressed in a plain black silk frock, and a neatly plaited muslin vandyke; her rich light brown hair was parted on her forehead, and put up behind in a handsome comb, around which one of her young friends had twisted an "od'rous chaplet of sweet summer buds." She advanced with so embarrassed an air, that even Mary Hull thought her triumph cost more than it was worth. As she unrolled the scroll she held in her hand, she ventured once to raise her eyes; she saw but one face among all the multitude—the approving, encouraging smile of her kind patron met her timid glance, and emboldened her to proceed, which she did, in a low and faltering voice, that certainly lent no grace, but the grace of modesty, to the composition. The subject was gratitude, and the remarks, made on the virtue, were such as could only come from one whose heart was warmed by its glow. Mr. Lloyd felt the delicate praise. Mrs. Wilson affected to appropriate it to herself. She whispered to her next neighbour, "It is easy to write about gratitude; but I am sure her conduct is evil and unthankful enough."

As Jane returned to her seat, her face brightened with the relief of having got through. Edward Erskine exclaimed to the young man next him, "By Jove, it is the most elegant composition I ever heard from a girl. Jane Elton has certainly grown very handsome."

"Yes," replied his friend; "I always thought her pretty, but you prefer her cousin."

"I did prefer her cousin," answered Erskine; "but I never noticed Jane much before; she is but a child, and she has always looked so pale and so sad since the change in her family. You know I have no fancy for solemn looks. Elvira is certainly handsome—very handsome; she is a cheating little devil; but, for all that, she is gay, and spirited, and amusing. It is enough to make any body deceitful to live with such a stern, churlish woman, as Mrs. Wilson. The girl has infinite ingenuity in cheating her mother, and her pretty face covers a multitude of faults."

"So I should think," replied his friend, "from the character you have given her. You will hardly applaud the deceits that have led to the disgrace of this morning."

"Oh, no!" answered Erskine; "but I am sorry for her mortification."

The exhibition proceeded; but as our heroine had no further concern with it, neither have we; except to say, that it was equally honourable to the preceptor and pupils. The paraphernalia of the king was exceedingly admired, and some were heard to observe, (very pertinently,) that they did not believe Solomon, in all his glory, was arrayed like him.

Jane's situation, at her aunt's, was rendered more painful than ever, from the events of the school and the exhibition. Mrs. Wilson treated her with every species of vexatious unkindness. In vain Jane tried, by her usefulness to her aunt, to win her favour, and by the most patient

obedience to her unreasonable commands, by silent uncomplaining submission, to sooth her into kindness. It was all in vain; her aunt was more
oppressive than ever; Martha more rude, and Elvira more tormenting. It
was not hearing her called "the just," that provoked their hatred; but it
was the keen and most disagreeable feeling of self-reproach that stung
them, when the light of her goodness fell upon their evil deeds; it was
the "daily beauty of her life that made them ugly."

CHAPTER VII

Pose the cause in justice's equal scales,
Whose beam stands sure.

2 Henry VI.

Jane hoped for some favourable change in her condition, or some slight alleviation of it, from the visit of David Wilson, who had just arrived from college, to pass a six-weeks vacation with his family. At first, he seemed to admire his cousin; and partly to gratify a passing fancy, and partly from opposition to his mother and sisters, he treated her with particular attention. Jane was grateful, and returned his kindness with frankness and affection. But she was soon obliged, by the freedom of his manners to treat him with reserve. His pride was wounded, and he joined the family league against her. He was a headstrong youth of seventeen; his passions had been curbed by the authority of his mother, but never tamed; and now that he was beyond her reach, he was continually falling into some excess; almost always in disgrace at college, and never in favour.

Mr. Lloyd was made acquainted with all the embarrassments in Jane's condition, by Mary Hull. He would have rejoiced to have offered Jane a home, but he had no right to interfere; he was a stranger, and he well knew, that Mrs. Wilson would not consent to any arrangement that would deprive her of Jane's ill-requited services,—such services as money could not purchase.

It was, too, about this period, that Mr. Lloyd went, for the first time, to visit Philadelphia. Jane had passed a day of unusual exertion, and just at the close of it she obtained her aunt's reluctant leave to pay a visit to Mary Hull. It was a soft summer evening; the valley reposed in deep shadow; the sun was sinking behind the western mountains, tinging the light clouds with a smiling farewell ray, and his last beams lingering on the summits of the eastern mountain, as if "parting were sweet sorrow." Jane's spirits rose elastic, as she breathed the open air; she felt like one who has just issued from a close, pent-up, sick room, and inspires the fresh pure breath of morning; she was gayly tripping along, sending an involuntary response to the last notes of the birds that were loitering on "bush and brake," when Edward Erskine joined her; she had often seen him at her aunt's, but, regarding him as the companion of her cousins, she had scarcely noticed him, or had been noticed by him. He joined her, saying, "It is almost too late to be abroad without a companion."

"I am used," replied Jane, "to be without a companion, and I do not need one."

"But, I hope you do not object to one? It would be one of the miseries of human life, to see such a girl as Jane Elton walking alone, and not be permitted to join her."

"Sir?" said Jane, confounded by Edward's unexpected gallantry.

Abashed by her simplicity, he replied, "that he was going to walk, and should be very happy to attend her."

Jane felt kindness, though she knew not how to receive gallantry. She thanked him, and they walked on together. When Edward parted from her, he wondered he had never noticed before how very interesting she was, "and what a sweet expression she has when she smiles; and, oh!" added he, with a rapture quite excusable in a young man of twenty, "her eye is in itself a soul."

"Jane," said Mary Hull to her, as she entered her room, "you look as bright as a May morning, and I have that to tell you, that will make you yet brighter. Mr. Evertson has been here, inquiring for Mr. Lloyd. I had my surmises, that it was something about you, and though Mr. Lloyd was gone, I was determined to find out; and so I made bold to break the ice, and say something about the exhibition, and how much Mr. Lloyd was pleased with the school, &c. &c.—and then he said, he was quite disappointed to find Mr. Lloyd gone; he wanted to consult him about a matter of great importance to himself and to you. Mr. Lloyd was so kind, he said, and had shown such an interest in the school, that he did not like to take any important step without consulting him; and then he spoke very handsomely of those elegant globes that Mr. Lloyd presented to the school. He said, his subscription was so much enlarged, that he must engage an assistant; but, as he wished to purchase some maps, he must get one who could furnish, at least, one hundred dollars. His sick wife and large family, he said, consumed nearly all his profits; and last, and best of all, Jane, he said, that you was the person he should prefer of all others for an assistant."

"Me!" exclaimed Jane.

"Yes, my dear child, you. I told him, you was not quite fifteen; but he said, you knew more than most young women of twenty, and almost all the school loved and respected you."

"But, Mary, Mary," and the bright flush of pleasure died away as she spoke, "where am I to get a hundred dollars?"

"Mr. Lloyd," answered Mary, "I know would furnish it."

"No, Mary," replied Jane, after a few moments consideration, "I never can consent to that."

"But why?" said Mary. "Mr. Lloyd spends all his money in doing good."

Jane could not tell why, but she felt that it was not delicate to incur such an obligation. She merely said, "Mr. Lloyd's means are well employed. If any man does, he certainly will, hear those blessed words, 'I was hungry and ye fed me, naked and ye clothed me, sick and in prison and ye visited me.'"

"I do not eat the bread of idleness, Mary; I think I earn all my aunt gives me; and I am not very unhappy there; indeed, I am seldom unhappy. I cannot tell how it is, but I am used to their ways. I am always busy, and have not time to dwell on their unkindness; it passes me like the tempest from which I am sheltered; and when I feel my temper rising, I remember who it is that has placed me in the fiery furnace, and I feel, Mary, strengthened and peaceful as if an angel were really walking beside me."

"Surely," said Mary, as if but thinking aloud, "The kingdom is come in this dear child's heart."

Both were silent for a few moments. Jane was making a strong mental effort to subdue that longing after liberty, that lurks in every heart. Habitual discipline had rendered it comparatively easy for her to restrain her wishes. After a short struggle, she said, with a smile, "I am sure of one thing, my dear, kind Mary, I shall never lose an opportunity of advantage, while I have such a watchful sentinel as you are, on the look-out for me. Oh! how much have I to be grateful for! I had no reason to expect such favour from Mr. Evertson. Every one, out of my aunt's family, is kind to me; I have no right to repine at the trials I have there; they are, no doubt, necessary to me. Mary, I sometimes feel the rising of a pride in my heart, that I am sure needs all these lessons of humility; and sometimes I feel, that I might be easily tempted to do wrong—to indulge an indolent disposition, for which you often reproved me; but I am compelled to exertion, by necessity as well as a sense of duty. It is good for me to bear this yoke in my youth."

"No doubt, no doubt, my dear child; but then you know if there is a way of escape opened to you, it would be but a tempting of Providence not to avail yourself of it. It is right to endure necessary evils with patience, but I know no rule that forbids your getting rid of them, if you can." Mary Hull was not a woman to leave any stone unturned, when she had a certain benefit in view for her favourite. "Now, dear Jane," said she, "I have one more plan to propose to you, and though it will cost you some pain, I think you will finally see it in the same light that I do. I always thought it was not for nothing Providence moved the hearts of the creditors to spare you all your dear mother's clothes, seeing she had a good many that could not be called necessary; nor was it a blind chance that raised you up such a friend as Mr. Lloyd in a stranger. Now, if you will consent to it, I will undertake to dispose of the articles Mr. Lloyd sent to you, and your mother's lace and shawls, and all the little nick-nacks she left; it shall go hard but I will raise a hundred dollars."

"But, Mary," said Jane, wishing, perhaps, to conceal from herself even the involuntary reluctance she felt to the proposal, "aunt Wilson will never consent to it."

"The consent that is not asked," replied Mary, "cannot be refused. It is but speaking to Mr. Evertson, and he will keep our counsel, for he is not a talking body, and when all is ready, it will be time enough, not to ask Mrs. Wilson's leave, but to tell her your plans; you owe her nothing, my child, unless it be for keeping the furnace hot that purifies the gold. I would not make you discontented with your situation, but I cannot bear to see your mind as well as your body in slavery."

May's long harangue had given Jane a moment for reflection, and she now saw the obvious benefits to result from the adoption of her judicious friend's plan. The real sorrows that had shaded her short life, had taught her not to waste her sensibility on trifles. She doubtless felt it to be very painful to part with any memorials of her mother, but the moment she was convinced it was right and best she should do so, she consented, and cheerfully, to the arrangement. Mary entered immediately upon the execution of her plan.

Those who have been accustomed to use, and to waste, thousands, will smile with contempt at the difficulty of raising a hundred dollars. But let those persons be reduced to want so mean a sum, and they will cease to laugh at the obstacles in the way of getting it. Certain it is, that Mary, anxious and assiduous, spent four weeks in industrious application to those whom she thought most likely to be purchasers in the confined market of ———. The necessity of secrecy increased the difficulty of the transaction; but finally, zeal and perseverance mastered every obstacle, and Mary, with sparkling eyes, and a face that smiled all over in spite of its habitual sobriety, put Jane in possession of the hundred dollars. "This is indeed manna in the wilderness," said Jane, as she received it, "but, dear Mary, I am not the less thankful to you for your exertions for me."

"My child, you are right," replied Mary, "thanks should first ascend to heaven, and then they are very apt to descend in heavenly grace upon the feeble instrument. But something seems to trouble you."

"I am troubled," answered Jane, "I fear, Mary, this sum cannot all have come from the articles you sold; you have added some of your earnings."

"No, my dear child; some, and all of my earnings, would I gladly give to you, but you know my poor blind sister takes all I can earn; while God blesses me with health she shall never want. The town has offered to take her off my hands, as they call it, but this would be a crying shame to me; and besides," she added, smiling, "I can't spare her, for it is more pleasant working for her than for myself. Thanks to Mr. Lloyd, she is now placed in a better situation than I could afford for her. No, Jane, the money is all yours; I have told Mr. Evertson, and you are to enter the school on Monday, and I have engaged a place for you at Mrs. Hervey's, who will be as kind as a mother to you. Between now and Monday you will have time to acquaint your aunt with the fortune you have come to, and to shed all the tears that are necessary on this woful occasion!"

Jane had now nothing to do but to communicate these arrangements; but so much did she dread the tempest she knew the intelligence would produce, that she suffered the day to wear away without opening her lips on the subject. The next day arrived; the time of emancipation was so near, she felt her spirits rise equal to the disagreeable task. The family were assembled in the 'dwelling room;' Mrs. Wilson was engaged in casting up with her son David some of his college accounts, a kind of business that never increased her good humour. Martha and Elvira were seated at a window, in a warm altercation about the piece of work on which they were sewing; the point in controversy seemed to be—to which the mother had assigned the task of finishing it. The two younger children were sitting on little chairs near their mother, learning a long lesson in the 'Assembly's Catechism,' and every now and then crying out—"Please to speak to David, ma'am, he is pinching me;"—"David pulled my hair, ma'am." The complainants either received no notice, or an angry rebuke from the mother. Jane was quietly sewing, and mentally resolving that she would speak on the dreaded subject the moment her aunt had finished the business at which she was engaged. Mrs. Wilson's temper became so much ruffled that she could not understand the accounts; so shuffling the papers all together into her desk, and turning the key, she said angrily to her son, 'her eldest hope,' "you will please to bear in mind, sir, that all these extravagant bills are charged to you, and shall come out of your portion—not a cent of them will I ever pay."

This did not seem to be a very propitious moment for Jane's communication, but she dreaded it so much, that she felt impatient to have it off her mind, and laying down her work, she was fearfully beginning, when she was interrupted by a gentle tap at the door. A mean looking woman entered, who bore the marks of poverty, and sorrow, and sickness. She had a pale, half-starved infant in her arms, and two other little ragged children with her, that she had very considerately left at the outer door. She curtsied very humbly to the lady of the house, 'hoped no offence,' she had a little business with *Miss* Wilson—she believed *Miss* Wilson had forgotten her, it was no wonder—she did not blame her, sickness and trouble made great changes. Mrs. Wilson either did not, or affected not to recognise her. She was aware that old acquaintance might create a claim upon her charity, and she did not seem well-pleased when Jane, who sat near, pushed a chair forward for the poor woman, into which she sunk, as it appeared from utter inability to stand.

"Who do you say you are?" said Mrs. Wilson, after embarrassing the woman by an unfeeling stare.

"I did not say, ma'am, for I thought, may be, when you looked at me so severe, you would know me."

"Let me take your baby, while you rest a little," said Jane.

"Oh miss, he is not fit for you to take, he has a dreadful spell with the whooping-cough and the measles, and they have left him kinder sore and rickety; he has not looked so chirk as he does to-day since we left Buffalo." Jane persisted in her kind offer, and the woman turned again to Mrs. Wilson—"Can't you call to mind, ma'am, Polly Harris, that lived five years at your brother Squire Elton's?"

"Yes, yes, I recollect you now; but you married and went away; and people should get their victuals where they do their work."

"I did not come to beg," replied the woman.

"That may be," said Mrs. Wilson, "but it is a very poor calculation for the people that move into the new countries to come back upon us as soon as they meet with any trouble. I wonder our Select Men don't take it in hand."

"Ah, ma'am!" said the woman, "I guess you was never among strangers; never knew what it was to long to see your own people. Oh it is a heart sickness, that seems to wear away life!"

"Whether I was, or was not, I don't know what that signifies to you; I should be glad to know what your business is with me, if you have any, which I very much doubt."

"I am afraid, ma'am, you will not see fit to make it your business," said the poor woman, and she sighed deeply, and hesitated, as if she was discouraged from proceeding, but the piteous condition of her children stimulated her courage. "Well, ma'am, to begin with the beginning of my troubles, as I was saying, I lived five years with your brother."

"Troubles!" exclaimed Mrs. Wilson, "you had an easy life enough of it there; you was always as plump as a partridge, and your cheeks as red as a rose!"

"I had nothing to complain of but that I could never get my pay when I wanted it. There never was a nicer woman that *Miss* Elton. I believe she saved my life once when I had the typus fever; but then every body knew she never had the use of much money; she never seemed to care any thing about it—when she had any I could always get it; I hope no offence, but every body knows the Squire was always a scheming, and seldom had the money ready to pay his just debts.—I am afraid the child tires you, miss;" she continued, turning to Jane who had walked to the window to hide the emotion the woman's remarks produced.

"No," replied Jane, "I had rather keep him;" and the woman proceeded—

"It lacked but six weeks of the five years I had lived at the Squire's, when I was married to Rufus Winthrop. When Rufus came to a settlement with the Squire, there was a hundred dollars owing to me. We were expecting to move off to a great distance, beyond the Genessee, and Rufus pressed very hard for the payment; the Squire put him off from time to time; Rufus was a peaceable man, and did not want to go to law, and so the upshot of it was, that the Squire persuaded him to take his note—

"That's a very likely story," said Mrs. Wilson impatiently interrupting the narrative—"I don't believe one word of it."

"Well, ma'am," replied Mrs. Winthrop, "I have that must convince you;" and she took from an old pocket book a small piece of paper, and handed it to Mrs. Wilson—"there is the identical note, ma'am, you can satisfy yourself."

Jane cast her eye on the slip of paper in her aunt's hand; it was but too plainly written in her father's large and singular character. Mrs. Wilson coldly returned it, saying, in a moderated tone, "It is as good to you now as a piece of white paper."

"Then I have nothing in this world," said the poor woman, bursting into tears, "but my poor, sick, destitute children."

"How came you in such a destitute condition?" inquired Mrs. Wilson, who, now that she saw the woman had no direct claim on her, was willing to hear her story.

"Oh," answered the poor creature, it seemed as if every thing went cross-grained with us. There was never a couple went into the new countries with fairer prospects; Rufus had tugged every way to save enough to buy him a small farm. When we got to Buffalo, we struck down south, and settled just on the edge of Lake Erie. We had a yoke of oxen, but one of them was pretty much beat out on the road, and died the very day after we got to our journey's end; there was a distemper among the cattle the next winter, and we lost the other ox and our cow. In the spring, Rufus took the long ague, working out in the swampy ground in wet weather, and that held him fifteen months; but he had made some clearings, and we worried through; and for three years we seemed to be getting along ahead a little. Then we both took the lake fever; we had neither doctor nor nurse; our nighest neighbours were two miles off; they were more fore-handed than we, and despot kind, but it was not much they could do, for they had a large sick family of their own. The fever threw my poor husband into a slow consumption, and he died, ma'am, the 20th of last January, and that poor baby was born the next week after he died. It seemed as if nothing could kill me, though I have a weakness in my bones 'casioned by the fever, and distress of mind, that I expect to carry to my grave with me. Sometimes my children and I would almost starve to death, but Providence always sent some relief. Once there was a missionary put up with us; he looked like a poor body, but he left me two dollars; and once a Roman Catholic priest, that was passing over into Canada, gave me a gold piece, and that I saved, till I started on my journey. While my husband was sick, he had great consarn upon his mind about Squire Elton's note; we had heard rumours like that he had broke; but Rufus nor I could not believe but what there would be enough to pay the note, out of all his grandeur, and so Rufus left it in strict charge with me to come back as soon as I could after the spring opened. And so, ma'am, as soon as the roads were a little settled, I pulled up stakes and came off. My good christian neighbours helped me up to Buffalo. I have been nine weeks getting from there, though I was favoured with a great many rides"—

Here Mrs. Wilson interrupted the unfortunate narrator, saying,—"I cannot see what occasion there was for you to be nine weeks on the road; I have known persons to go from Boston to the Falls, and back again, in three weeks."

"Ah, ma'am!" replied the woman, "there is a sight of difference between a gentleman riding through the country for pleasure, with plenty of money in his pocket, and a poor sickly creature, begging a ride now and then of a few miles, and then walking for miles with four little children, and one a baby."

"Four! your story grows—I thought you had but three."

"I have but three, ma'am; I buried my only girl, the twin to the second boy, at *Batavy*. She never was hearty, and the travelling quite overdid her." The afflicted woman wiped away the fast gathering tears with a corner of her apron, and went on. "At *Batavy* I believe I should have gived out, but there was a tender-hearted gentleman from the eastward, going on to see the Falls, and he paid for my passage, and all my children's, in a return stage, quite to *Genevy*. This was a great lift to my spirits, and easement to the children's feet; and so after that, we came on pretty well, and met with a great deal of kindness; but, oh! ma'am, 'tis a wearisome journey."

"And here you are," said Mrs. Wilson; "and I suppose the town must take care of you."

"I did not mean to be a burden to the town," replied the woman. "If it pleased the Lord to restore my health, and if I could have got the hundred dollars, I would not have been a burden to any body. I calculated to hire me a little place, bought a loom, and turned my hand to weaving—I am a master weaver, ma'am."

"I am sorry for you, good woman," said Mrs. Wilson; "here," said she, after rummaging her pocket and taking out a reluctant ninepence; "here is a 'widow's mite' for you. I can't give you the least encouragement about my brother's debt. He left nothing but a destitute child that I have had to support ever since his death."

"Is that little Jane," exclaimed the woman, for the first time recalling to mind the features of our heroine. "Well," added she, surveying her delicate person with a mingled expression of archness and simplicity, "I think it can't have cost you much to support her, ma'am. I wonder I did not know you," she continued, "when you took my baby so kindly. It was just like you. I used to set a great store by you. But you have grown so tall, and so handsome; as to the matter of that, you was always just like a Lon'on doll."

Jane replaced the child in the mother's lap, and said to Mrs. Winthrop, "I recollect you perfectly, Polly. You were very good to me."

"I could not help it, for you was always as pleasant as a little lamb, and as chipper as a bird; but," said she, observing the too evident traces of tears on Jane's cheeks, "I am sorry if I have touched your feelings about the money. I never mistrusted that it was you."

"Do not be uneasy on that account," replied Jane. "I am glad I have heard your story, Polly."

She had listened to the unfortunate woman's history with the keenest anguish. There is no feeling so near of kin to remorse as that which a virtuous child suffers from the knowledge of a parent's vices. The injustice of her father appeared to Jane to have either caused or aggravated every evil the poor woman had suffered. Each particular was sharper than a serpent's tooth to our unhappy orphan. She had not that convenient moral sense, quick to discern and lament the faults of others, but very dull in the perception of our own duties. It was the work of an instant with her to resolve to appropriate her newly acquired treasure to the reparation of her father's injustice; and with the hasty generosity of youth, she left the room to execute her purpose. But, when she took the pocket-book from its hiding-place, and saw again that which she had looked upon with so much joy, as the price of liberty and the means of independence, her heart misgave her; she felt like a prisoner, the doors of whose prison-house have been thrown open to him, who sees the inviting world without, and who is called upon, in the spirit of martyrdom, to close the door, and bar himself from light and hope. Those who have felt the difficulty of sacrificing natural and virtuous wishes to strict justice, will pardon our heroine a few moments' deliberation. She thought that, as the money had been chiefly the avails of the articles given her by Mr. Lloyd, it could not be considered as derived from her father. She thought how much Mary Hull had exerted herself, and how disappointed she would be; the engagement with Mr. Evertson occurred to her, and she was not certain it would be quite right to break it; and, last of all, she thought, that if her present plans succeeded, it could not be very long before she might earn enough to cancel the debt. Jane had not been used to parleying with her duties, or stifling the voice of conscience; and in a moment the recollection of her father's dishonesty, and the poor woman's perishing condition, swept away every selfish consideration. "Oh, Lord!" she exclaimed, "if I have not compassion on my fellow-servant, how can I hope for thy pity."

We would recommend to all persons, placed in similar circumstances, to all who find almost as many arguments for the wrong as for the right, to bring to their aid the certain light of Scripture, and we think they will be altogether persuaded to be like our heroine, not 'saving her bonds.' Sure we are, that she was never more to be envied than when, at the sound of the closing of the parlour door, she flew down stairs, joined Mrs. Winthrop just as she was saying, half sobbing, to her children, "Come, boys—I am poorer than when I came, for my hope is all gone;" and walking a little distance, till a sharp angle in the road concealed them from the house, she said, "Polly, here is a hundred dollars. I know the debt my father owed you amounts to a good deal more now, but this is all I have, take it. It is not probable that I shall ever be able to pay the rest, but I shall never forget that I owe it."

Mrs. Winthrop was for a moment dumb with surprise; then bursting into tears of gratitude and joy, she would have overwhelmed Jane with thanks, but she stopped her, saying, "No, Polly, I have only done what was right. I have two favours to beg of you—say nothing to any body in the world, of your having received this money from me; and," added she, faltering, "do not, again, tell the story of the ———" injustice, she would have said, but the word choked her. "I mean, do not say, to any one, that my parents did not pay you."

"Oh! miss Jane," replied the grateful creature, "I'll mind every thing you tell me, just as much as if it was spoken to me right out of Heaven."

And we have reason to believe, she was quite as faithful to her promise as could have been expected; for she was never known to make any communication on the subject, except that, when some of her rustic neighbours expressed their surprise at the sudden and inexplicable change in her circumstances, she would say, "She came by it honestly, and by the honesty of some people too, who she guessed, though they did it secretly, would be rewarded openly." And when she heard Jane Elton's name mentioned, she would roll up her eyes and say, "That if every body knew as much as she did, they would think that girl was an angel upon earth." These oracular hints were, perhaps, not quite so much heeded as

Polly expected; at any rate, she was never tempted to disclose the grounds of her opinion.

Jane had a difficult task in reconciling her friend Mary to her disappointment. While she felt a secret delight in the tried rectitude of her favourite, she could not deny herself the indulgence of a little repining—"If you had but waited, Jane, till Mr. Lloyd came home, he would have advanced the money with all his heart."

"Yes, but Mary, you must recollect Mr. Lloyd is not to return these six weeks; and, in the mean time, what was to become of the poor woman and her starving children? No, Mary, we must deal justly while we have it in our power. Is it not your great Mr. Wesley who says, 'It is safe to defer our pleasures, but never to delay our duties'?"

"It seems to me, Jane," replied Mary, "you pick fruit from every good tree, no matter whose vineyard it grows in. Well, I believe you have done right; but I shall tell the story to Mr. Evertson and Mrs. Harvey with a heavy heart."

"Tell them nothing," said Jane, "but that I had an unexpected call for the money, and beg them to mention nothing of the past, for I will not unnecessarily provoke aunt Wilson."

"Jane," said Mary earnestly, "you must not deny me the satisfaction of telling how you have laid out the money."

"No," replied Jane, "you cannot have that pleasure without telling *why* I was obliged thus to lay it out.—Oh," added she with more emotion than she had yet shown, "I have never blamed my father that he left me penniless; had he left me the inheritance of a good name, I would not have exchanged it for all the world can give!"

Mary consoled her friend as well as she was able, and then reluctantly parted from her, to perform her disagreeable duty. Mr. Evertson was exceedingly disappointed; he said he had already had an offer of a very good assistant, who could furnish more money than he expected from Jane; he had preferred Jane Elton, for no sum could outweigh her qualifications for the station he wished her to fill. He was, however, obliged to her for so promptly informing him of her determination, as he had not yet sent a refusal to the person who had solicited the place.

Mrs. Harvey, not content with deploring, which she did sincerely, that she could not have Jane for an inmate, wondered what upon earth she could have done with a hundred dollars! and concluded "that it would be just like Jane Elton, though it would not be like any body else in the world, to pay one of her father's old debts with it." Will not our readers pardon

Mary, if Mrs. Harvey inferred from the smile of pleasure that brightened her face, that she had sagaciously guessed the truth. Let that be as it may; all parties promised, and what is much more extraordinary, preserved secrecy; and all that was left of Jane's hopes and plans was the consciousness of having acted right—from right motives. Could any one have seen the peacefulness of her heart, he would have pronounced that consciousness a treasure that has no equivalent.

Thus our heroine, placed in circumstances which would have made some desperate, and most discontented; by 'keeping her heart with all diligence,' proved that 'out of it are the issues of life;' she was first resigned, and then happy. She was on an eminence of virtue, to which the conflicts and irritations of her aunt's family did not reach.

CHAPTER VIII

It may be said of him, that Cupid hath clap'd him o' the shoulder,
but I warrant him heart-whole.

As You Like It.

More than two years glided away without the occurrence of any incident in the life of our heroine that would be deemed worthy of record, by any persons less interested in her history than Mary Hull, or the writer of her simple annals. The reader shall therefore be allowed to pass over this interval, with merely a remark, that Jane had improved in mortal and immortal graces; that the development of her character seemed to interest and delight Mr. Lloyd almost as much as the progress of his own child, and that her uniform patience had acquired for her some influence over the bad passions of her aunt, whose rough points seemed to be a little worn by the continual dropping of Jane's virtues.

In this interval, Martha Wilson had made a stolen match with a tavern-keeper from a neighbouring village, and had removed from her mother's house, to display her character on a new stage, and in a worse light.

Elvira, at eighteen, was much the same as at sixteen, except, that the gayety of her spirits was somewhat checked by the apprehension (that seemed to have grown of late) that Edward Erskine's affections, which had been vacillating for some time between her and her cousin, would finally preponderate in Jane's favour. It may appear singular, that the same person should admire both the cousins; but it must be remembered, that Edward Erskine was not (as our readers are) admitted behind the scenes; and it must be confessed, that he had not so nice a moral sense, as we hope they possess. He neither estimated the purity of Jane's character, as it deserved to be estimated, nor felt for the faults of Elvira the dislike they merited. Edward Erskine belonged to one of the best families in the county of————. His parents had lost several children in their infancy, and this boy alone remained to them—to become the sole object of their cares and fondness. He was naturally what is called 'good-hearted,' which we believe means kind and generous. Flattery, and unlimited indulgence made him vain, selfish, and indolent. These qualities were, however, somewhat modified, by a frank and easy temper, and sheltered by an uncommonly handsome exterior. Some of his college companions thought him a genius, for, though he was seldom caught in the act of studying, he passed through college without disgrace; this (for he certainly was neither a genius nor a necromancer,) might be attributed in part to an aptness at learning, and an excellent memory; but chiefly to an extraordinary facility at appropriating to himself the results of the labours of others. He lounged through the prescribed course of law studies, and entered upon his professional career with considerable *éclat*. He had a rich and powerful voice; and it might be said of him, as of the chosen king of Israel—that 'from the shoulders upwards, he was taller and fairer than any of his brethren.' These are qualifications never slighted by the vulgar; and which are said, but we hope not with truth, to be sure passports to ladies' favour. He had too, for we would do him ample justice, uncommon talents, but not such as we think would justify the remark often made of him, "that the young squire was the *smartest* man in the county." In short, he belonged to that large class of persons who are generous, but not just; affectionate, but not constant; and often kind, though it would puzzle a casuist to assign to their motives their just proportions of vanity and benevolence. He had recently, by the death of his parents, come into possession of a handsome estate; and he was accounted the first match in the county of ———.

Mrs. Wilson could not be insensible to the advantages that she believed might be grasped by Elvira, and she determined to relax the strict rule of her house, and to join her assiduities to her daughter's arts, in order to secure the prize. She was almost as much embarrassed in her manœuvres as the famous transporter of the fox, the geese, and the corn. If she opened her doors to young Erskine, to display her daughter, Jane must be seen too; and though she was sufficiently ingenious in contriving ways and means of employing Jane, and securing a clear field for Elvira, Erskine, with the impatience and perversity of a spoiled child, set a double value on the pleasure that was denied him.

The affairs of Mrs. Wilson's household were in this train, when the following conversation occurred between the cousins:—

"If there is a party made to-morrow, to escort the bride, do you expect to join it, Jane?" said Elvira to her cousin, with an expression of anxiety that was quite as intelligible as her question.

"I should like to," replied Jane.

"Ah, that of course," answered Elvira; "but I did not ask what you would *like*, but what you *expect*."

"You know, Elvira, I am not sure of obtaining your mother's permission."

"For once in your life, Jane, do be content to speak less like an oracle, and tell me in plain English, whether you expect to go, if you can obtain mother's permission."

"In plain English then, Elvira, *yes*," replied Jane, smiling.

"You seem very sure of an invitation," answered Elvira, pettishly. Jane's deep blush revealed the truth to her suspicious cousin, which she did not wish to confess or evade; and Elvira continued, "I was sure I overheard Edward say something to you, about the ride last night, when you parted on the steps." She paused, and then added, her eyes flashing fire, "Jane, Edward Erskine preferred me once, and in spite of your arts, he shall prefer me again. Remember, miss, the fate of lady Euphrasia."

Jane replied, good naturedly, "I do remember her; but if her proud and artful character suits me, the poverty and helplessness of my condition bears a striking resemblance to the forlorn Amanda's. I trust, however, that my fate will resemble neither of your heroines, for you cannot expect me, on account of the honour of being your rival, to be dashed from a precipice, to point the moral of your story; and I am very certain of not marrying a lord."

"Yes, for there is no lord in this vulgar country to marry; but, with all your pretence of modesty, you aspire to the highest station within your reach."

Jane made no reply, and Elvira poured out her spleen in invectives, which neither abated her own ill humour, nor disturbed her cousin's equanimity. She was determined to compass her purposes, and in order to do so, she imparted her conjectures to her mother, who had become as faithful, as she was a powerful auxiliary.

In the evening they were all assembled in the parlour. Edward Erskine entered, and his entrance produced a visible sensation in every member of the little circle. Mrs. Wilson dropped half a needle full of stitches on her knitting work, and gave it to Jane to take them up. Jane seemed to find the task very difficult, for a little girl, who sat by the working stand, observed, "Miss Jane, I could take up the stitches better than you do; you miss them half."

"Give me my spectacles—I'll do it myself," said Mrs. Wilson. "Some people are very easily discomposed."

It was a warm evening in the latter part of September; the window was open; Jane retreated to it, and busied herself in pulling the leaves off a rose-bush. Erskine brought matters to a crisis by saying, "I called, Mrs. Wilson, to ask of you the favour of Miss Elton's company to-morrow on the bridal escort."

"I am sorry," replied Mrs. Wilson, "that any young woman's manners, who is brought up in my house, should authorize a gentleman to believe she will, of course, ride with him if asked."

"I beg your pardon, madam," replied Edward (for he, at least, had no fear of the redoubtable Mrs. Wilson,) "I have been so happy as to obtain Miss Elton's consent, subject to yours."

"Is it possible!" answered Mrs. Wilson, sneeringly—"quite an unlooked-for deference from *Miss Elton*; not unnecessary however, for she probably recollected, that to-morrow is lecture-day; and, indifferent as she is to the privilege of going to meeting, she knows that no pleasures ever prevent my going."

"No, madam," replied Erskine, "the pleasures of *others* weigh very light against your duties."

Before Mrs. Wilson had made up her mind whether or not to resent the sarcasm, Erskine rose, and joining Jane at the window, whispered to her, "Rouse your spirit, for heaven's sake; do not submit to such tyranny."

Jane had recovered her self-possession, and she replied, smiling, "It is my duty to subdue, not rouse my spirit."

"*Duty!*" exclaimed Erskine; "leave all that ridiculous cant for your aunt: I abhor it. I have your promise, and your promise to me is surely as binding as your *duty* to your aunt."

"That promise was conditional," replied Jane, "and it is no longer in my power to perform it."

"Nor in your inclination, Miss Elton?"

Jane was not well pleased that Erskine should persevere, at the risk of involving her with her aunt; and to avoid his importunity, and her aunt's displeasure, she left the room. "The girl wants spirit," said Erskine, mentally; "she is tame, very tame. It is quite absurd for a girl of seventeen to talk about duties."

He was about to take leave, when Mrs. Wilson, who knew none of the skilful tactics of accomplished manœuverers, though her clumsy assaults were often as irresistible, said, "Don't be in such haste, Mr. Erskine. Elvira may go with you."

Edward's first impulse was to decline the offer; but he paused. Elvira was sitting by her mother, and she turned upon him a look of appeal and admiration; his vanity, which had been piqued by Jane, was soothed by this tribute, and he said, "If Miss Wilson is inclined to the party, I will call for her to-morrow."

Miss Wilson confessed her inclination with a glow of pleasure, that consoled him for his disappointment.

Elvira made the most of the advantage she had gained. Mrs. Wilson had of late, though the effort cost her many a groan, indulged Elvira's passion for dress, in the hope that the glittering of the bait would attract the prey. In this calculation she was not mistaken; for, though Erskine affected a contempt for the distinctions of dress, he had been too much flattered for his personal charms, to permit him to be insensible to them; and when he handed Elvira into his gig, he noticed, with pleasure, that she was the best dressed and most stylish looking girl in the party. His vanity was still further gratified, when he overheard his servant say to one of his fellows, "By George, they are a most noble looking pair!" Such is the cormorant appetite of vanity, never satisfied with the quantity, and never nice as to the quality of the food it devours.

Elvira had penetration enough to detect the weakest points in the fortress she had to assail; and so skilfully and successfully did she ply her arts, on this triumphant day, that Erskine scarcely thought of Jane, and we fear not once with regret.

Poor Jane remained at home, mortified that Edward went without her, and vexed with herself that she was mortified. To avoid seeing the party on their return, she went out to walk, and was deliberating whither to direct her steps, when she met her friend Mr. Lloyd. "Ah, Jane," said he, "I just came on an errand from my saucy little girl: she has succeeded for the first time to-day in hitching words together, so as to make quite an intelligible sentence; and she is so much elated, that she has bid me tell thee she cannot go to sleep till "dear Jane" has heard her read."

Jane replied, she "should be glad to hear her;" but with none of the animation with which she usually entered into the pleasures of her little friend. Mr. Lloyd was disappointed; but he thought she had been suffering some domestic vexation, and they walked on silently.

After a few moments he said, "Quaker as I am, I do not like a silent meeting;—though I should be used to it, for, except that I must answer the questions of my Rebecca, and am expected by thy friend Mary to reply to her praises of thee, I have not much more occasion for the gift of speech, than the brothers of La Trappe."

"You forget," replied Jane, who felt her silence gently reproached, "that besides all the use you have for that precious faculty, in persuading the stupid and the obstinate to adopt your benevolent plans of reform, you sometimes condescend to employ it in behalf of a very humble young friend."

"But that young friend must lay aside her humility so far, as to flatter me with the appearance of listening."

Jane was a little disconcerted, and Mr. Lloyd did not seem quite free from embarassment; but as he had roused her from her abstractedness, he began to expatiate on the approach of evening, the charms of that hour when the din of toil has ceased, and no sound is heard but the sweet sounds of twilight breathing the music of nature's evening hymn; he turned his eye to the heavens, which, in their 'far blue arch,' disclosed star after star, and then the constellations in their brightness. He spoke of the power that formed, and the wisdom that directed, them. Jane was affected by his devotion; it was a promethean touch that infused a soul into all nature. She listened with delight, and before they reached the house, her tranquillity was quite restored; and the child and father were both entirely satisfied with the pleasure she manifested in the improvement of her little favourite. But her trials were not over: after the lesson was past—"Dear Jane," said Rebecca, "why did not thee go with the party to-day? I saw them all go past here, and Mr. Erskine and Elvira were laughing, and I looked out sharp for thee; would not any body take thee, Jane?"

Jane did what of all other things she would least have wished to have done—she burst into tears.

The sweet child, whose directness had taken her by surprise, crept up into her lap, and putting her arms around her neck, said affectionately, "I am sorry for thee, dear Jane; don't cry, father would have asked thee, if he had gone." Poor Jane hid her blushes and her tears on the bosom of her kind, but unskilful comforter. She felt the necessity of saying something; but confessions she could not make, and pretences she never made.

Mr. Lloyd saw and pitied her confusion: he rose, and tenderly placing his hand on her head, he said, "My dear young friend, thou hast wisely and safely guided thy little bark thus far down the stream of life; be still vigilant and prudent, and thou wilt glide unharmed through the dangers that alarm thee." He then relieved Jane from his presence, saying, "I am going to my library, and will send Mary to escort thee home."

Jane could not have borne a plainer statement of her case; and though it was very clear that Mr. Lloyd had detected the lurking weakness of her heart, she was soothed by his figurative mode of insinuating his knowledge and his counsel. Persons of genuine sensibility possess a certain tact, that enables them to touch delicate subjects without giving pain. This touch differs as much from a rude and unfeeling grasp as does the management of a fine instrument in the hands of a skilful surgeon, from the mangling and hacking of a vulgar operator.

Mr. Lloyd had heard the village gossip of Edward Erskine's divided attentions to the cousins. Nothing that concerned Jane was uninteresting to him; and he had watched with eager anxiety the character and conduct of Erskine. He had never liked the young man; but he thought that he had probably done him injustice, and he had too fair a mind to harbour a prejudice. 'Perhaps,' he said to himself, 'I have judged him hardly; I am apt to carry my strait-coat habits into every thing; the young man's extravagant way of talking, his sacrifices to popularity, and his indolence and love of pleasure, may all have been exaggerated in my eyes by their opposition to the strict, sober ways in which I have been bred; at any rate, I will look upon the bright side. Jane Elton, pure, excellent as she is, cannot love such a man as Edward Erskine appears to me to be; and she is too noble, I am sure, to regard the advantages which excite the cupidity of her vulgar aunt.'

The result of Mr. Lloyd's investigations was not favourable to Erskine. Still his faults were so specious, that they were often mistaken for virtues; and virtues he had, though none unsullied. There was nothing in his character or history, as far as Mr. Lloyd could ascertain it, that would give him a right to interfere with his advice to Jane; but still he felt as if she was on the brink of a precipice, and he had no right to warn her of her danger. Perhaps this was a false delicacy, considering the amount of the risk; but there are few persons of principle and refinement who do not shrink from meddling with affairs of the heart. Mr. Lloyd hoped— believed that Jane would not marry Edward Erskine; but he did not allow enough for the inexperience of youth, for the liability of a young lady of seventeen to fall in love; for the faith that hopes all things, and believes all things—it wishes to believe.

The fall, the winter, and the spring wore away, and, as yet, no certain indication appeared of the issue of this, to our villagers, momentous affair.

Edward certainly preferred Jane, and yet he was more at his ease with Elvira. He could not but perceive the decided superiority of Jane; but Elvira made him always think more and better of himself; and this most agreeable effect of her flatteries and servility reflected a charm on her. Jane was never less satisfied with herself than during this harassing period of her life. A new set of feelings were springing up in her heart, over which she felt that she had little control. At times, her confidence in Edward was strong; and then, suddenly, a hasty expression, or an unprepared action, revealed a trait that deformed the fair proportions of the hero of her imagination. Elvira's continual projects, and busy rivalry, provoked, at last, a spirit of competition; which was certainly natural, though very wrong; but, alas! our heroine had infirmities. Who is without them?

In the beginning of the month of June, David Wilson came from college, involved in debt and in disgrace. His youthful follies had ripened into vices, and his mother had no patience, no forbearance for the faults, which she might have traced to her own mismanagement, but for which she found a source that relieved her from responsibility. The following was the close of an altercation, noisy and bitter, between this mother and son:—"I am ruined, utterly ruined, if you refuse me the money. Elvira told me you received a large sum yesterday; and 'tis but one hundred dollars that I ask for."

"And I wonder you can have the heart to ask," replied Mrs. Wilson, sobbing with passion, not grief; "you have no feeling; you never had any for my afflictions. It is but two months, yesterday since Martha died, and I have no reason to hope for her. She died without repentance."

"Ha!" replied David, "Elvira told me, that she confessed, to her husband, her abuse of his children, her love of the bottle, (which, by the by, every body knew before,) and a parcel of stuff that, for our sakes, I think she might have kept to herself."

"Yes, yes, she did die in a terrible uproar of mind about some things of that kind; but she had no feeling of her lost state by nature."

"Oh, the devil!" grumbled the hopeful son and brother; "if I had nothing to worry my conscience but my *state by nature*, I might get one good night's sleep, instead of lying from night till morning like a toad under a harrow."

This comment was either unheard or unheeded by the mother, and she went on: "David, your extravagance is more than I can bear. I have been wonderfully supported under my other trials. If my children, though they are my flesh and blood, are not elected, the Lord is justified in their destruction, and I am still. I have done my duty, and I know not 'why tarry His chariot wheels.'"

"It is an easy thing, ma'am," said David, interrupting his mother, "to be reconciled to everlasting destruction; but if your mind is not equally resigned to the temporal ruin of a child, you must lend me the money."

"Lend it! You have already spent more than your portion in riotous living, and I cannot, in conscience, give you any thing."

Mrs. Wilson thus put a sudden conclusion to the conversation, and retreated from the field, like a skilful general, having exhausted all her ammunition.

As she closed the door, David muttered, "curses on her conscience; it will never let her do what she is not inclined to, and always finds a reason to back her inclinations. The money I must have: if fair means will not obtain it, foul must."

CHAPTER IX

Thought, and affliction, passion, Hell itself,
She turns to favour, and to prettiness.
Hamlet.

It was on the evening of the day on which the conversation we have related, had occurred between young Wilson and his mother, that Jane, just as she had parted with Erskine, after an unusually delightful walk, and was entering her aunt's door, heard her name pronounced in a low voice. She turned, and saw an old man emerging from behind a projection of the house. He placed his finger on his lips by way of an admonition to silence, and said softly to Jane, "For the love of Heaven, come to my house to-night; you may save life; tell no one, and come after the family is in bed."

"But, John, I do not know the way to your house," replied Jane, amazed at the strange request.

"You shall have a guide, Miss. Don't be afraid; 'tis not like you to be afraid, when there is good to be done; and I tell you, you may save life; and every one that knows me, knows I never tell a lie for any body."

"Well," said Jane, after a moment's pause, "if I go, how shall I find the way?"

"That's what I am afraid will frighten you most of all; but it must be so. You know where Lucy Willett's grave is, on the side of the hill, above the river; there you will find crazy Bet waiting for you. She is a poor cracked body, but there is nobody I would sooner trust in any trouble; besides, she is in the secret already, and there is no help for it."

"But," said Jane, "may I not get some one else to go with me?"

"Not for the wide world. Nothing will harm you."

Jane was about to make some further protestation, when a sound from the house alarmed the man, and he disappeared as suddenly as he had made his entree.

John was an old man, who had been well known to two or three successive generations in the village. He had never had health or strength for hard labour, but had gained a subsistence by making baskets, weaving new seats into old chairs, collecting herbs for spring beer, and digging medicinal roots from the mountains: miscellaneous offices, which are usually performed by one person where the great principle of a division of labour is yet unknown and unnecessary. A disciple of Gall might, perhaps, have detected in the conformation of the old man's head, certain indications of a contemplative turn of mind, and a feeling heart; but, as we are unlearned in that fashionable science, we shall simply remark, that there was, in the mild cast of his large but sunken eye, and the deep-worn channels of his face, an expression that would lead an observer to think he had felt and suffered; that he possessed the wisdom of reflection, as well as the experience of age; and that he had been accustomed, in nature's silent and solitary places, to commune with the Author of Nature. He inhabited a tenement at some distance from the village, but within the precincts of the town. When the skill of the domestic leeches was at fault, in the case of a sick cow or a wormy child, he was called to a consultation, and the efficacy of the simples he had administered, had sometimes proved so great, as to induce suspicion of a mysterious charm. But the superstitious belief in witches and magic has vanished with the mists of other times; and the awe of 'John of the Mountain,' as he was called, or for brevity's sake, 'John Mountain,' never outlived the period of childhood.

Jane knew John was honest and kind-hearted, and particularly well disposed to her, for he had occasionally brought her a pretty wild-flower, or a basket of berries, and then he would say, "Ah, Miss Jane, I grow old and forgetful, but the old man can't forget the kindness that's been done to him in days past; you was as gay as a lark then. My poor old bald head! it's almost as bare inside as out; but I shall never forget the time—it was a sorrowful year, we had had a hard winter, the snows drifted on the mountains, and for six weeks I never saw the town, and poor Sarah lying sick at home; and when I did get out, I came straight to your mother's, for she had always a pitiful heart, and an open and a full hand too, and she stocked my alms basket full of provisions. Then you came skipping out of the other room, with a flannel gown in your hand, and your very eyes laughed with pleasure, and when you gave it to me, you said, "It is for your wife, and I sewed every stitch of it, John;" and then you was not bigger than a poppet, and could not speak plain yet. When I got home, and told my old woman, she shook her head, and said, you "was not long for this world;" but I laughed at her foolishness, and asked her, if the finest saplings did not live to make the noblest trees? Thanks to Him that is above, you are alive at this day, and many a wanderer will yet find shelter in your branches."

We trust our readers will pardon this digression, and accept the gratitude of the old man, as a proof that all men's good deeds are not 'written in sand.'

After John's departure, Jane remained for a few moments where he had left her, ruminating on his strange request, when her attention was called to a noise in her aunt's sleeping apartment, and she heard, as she thought, crazy Bet's voice raised to its highest pitch. She passed hastily through the passage, and on opening her aunt's door, she beheld a scene of the greatest confusion. The bed-clothes had been hastily stripped from the bed and strewed on the floor, and Bet stood at the open window with the bed in her right hand. She had, by sudden exertion of her strength, made an enormous rent in the well-wove home-made tick, and was now quite leisurely shaking out the few feathers that still adhered to it. In her left hand she held a broom, which she dexterously brandished, to defend herself from the interference of Sukey, the coloured servant girl, who stood panic-struck and motionless; her dread of her mistress' vengeance impelling her forward, and her fear of the moody maniac operating upon her locomotive powers, like a gorgon influence. Her conflicting fears had not entirely changed her ethiopian skin, but they had subtracted her colour in stripes, till she looked like Robin Hood's willow wand.

"Why did you not stop her?" exclaimed Jane, hastily passing the girl.

"Stop her, missy? the land's sake! I could as easy stop a flash of lightning! missy must think me a 'rac'lous creature, respecting me to hold back such a harricane."

At Jane's approach Bet dropped the broom, and threw the empty bed-tick at poor Sukey, who shook it off, not, however, till her woolly pate was completely powdered with the lint. "Now, Sukey," screamed Bet with a wild peal of laughter, "look in the glass, and you'll see how white you'll be in heaven; the black stains will all be washed out there!"

"But, Bet, said Jane, "where are the feathers?"

"Where? child," she replied, smiling with the most provoking indifference, "where are last year's mourners? where is yesterday's sunshine, or the morning's fog?"

"Why did you do this, Bet?"

"Do you ask a *reason* of me?" she replied, with a tone in which sorrow and anger were equally mingled, and then putting her finger to her forehead, she added, "the light is quite out, there is not a glimmering left."

Jane felt that the poor woman was not a subject for reproach; and turning away, she said, "Aunt will be very angry."

"Yes," replied Bet, "she will weep and howl, but she should thank me for silencing some of the witnesses."

"Witnesses, Bet?"

"Yes, child, witnesses; are not moth-eaten garments and corrupted riches witnesses against the rich, the hard-hearted, and close-handed? She should not have denied a bed to my aching head and weary body. She should not have told me, that the bare ground and hard boards were soft and easy enough for a "rantipole beggar.""

The recollection of the promise she had given to John now occurred to Jane, and she was deliberating whether or not to speak to Bet about it, when Mrs. Wilson, who had been absent on a visit to one of her neighbours, came in. In her passage through the kitchen, Sukey had hinted to her her loss, and she hastened on to ascertain its extent. Inquiries were superfluous; the empty tick was lying where Sukey had left it, and the feathers which had swelled it almost to bursting, were not. Mrs. Wilson darted forwards towards Bet, on whom she would have wreaked her hasty vengeance, but Bet, aware of her intention, sprang through the window, quick as thought, and so rapid, and as it were, spiritual, was her flight, that a minute had scarcely passed, when the shrill tones of her voice were heard rising in the distance, and they were just able to distinguish the familiar words of her favourite methodist hymn—

> "Sinners stand a trembling,
> Saints are rejoicing."

Mrs. Wilson turned to Jane, and with that disposition which such persons have when any evil befals them, to lay the blame on somebody, she would have vented her spite on her, but it was too evident that the only part Jane had had in the misfortune was an ineffectual effort to avert it, and the good lady was deprived of even that alleviation of her calamity. This scene, notwithstanding the pecuniary loss sustained by Mrs. Wilson, occasioned Jane a good deal of diversion. Still it was not at all calculated to inspire her with confidence in the guide, whose wild and fantastic humours she knew it to be impossible for any one to control. Her resolution was a little shaken; but, after all, she thought, "It is possible I may find the house without her. I know the course I should take. At any rate, I should be miserable if any evil should come of my neglect of the old man's request. There can be no real dangers, and I will not imagine any."

Still, after the family were all hushed in repose, and Jane had stolen from her bed and dressed herself for her secret expedition, she shrunk involuntarily from the task before her. "I do not like this mystery," said she, mentally; "I wish I had told my aunt, and asked David to go with me, or I might have told Mary Hull. There could be no harm in that. But it is now too late. John said, I might save life, and I will think of nothing else."

She rose from the bed, where she had seated herself to ponder, for the last time, upon the difficulties before her, crept softly down stairs, passed her aunt's room, and got clear of the house unmolested, except by a slight growl from Brutus, the house-dog, whose dreams she had broken, but, at her well-known kindly patting, and "Lie down Brutus, lie down," he quietly resumed his sleeping posture. Her courage was stimulated by having surmounted one obstacle. The waning moon had risen, and shed its mild lustre over the peaceful scene. "Now," thought Jane, "that I have stirred up my womanish thoughts with a manly spirit, I wonder what I could have been afraid of."

Anxious to ascertain whether she was to have the doubtful aid of crazy Bet's conduct, or trust solely to her own, she pressed onward. To shorten her way to Lucy's grave, and to avoid the possibility of observation, she soon left the public road, and walked along under the shadow of a low-browed hill, which had formerly been the bank of the river, but from which it had receded and left an interval of beautiful meadow between the hill and its present bed. The deep verdure of the meadow sparkled with myriads of fire-flies, that seemed, in this hour of their dominion, to be keeping their merry revels by the music of the passing stream. The way was, as yet, perfectly familiar to Jane. After walking some distance in a straight line, she crossed the meadow by a direct path to a large tree, which had been, in part, uprooted by a *freshet*, and which now laid across the river, and supplied a rude passage to the adventurous, the tenacity of some of its roots still retaining it firmly in the bank. Fortunately the stream was unusually low, and when our heroine reached the further extremity of the fallen trunk, she sprang without difficulty over the few feet of water between her and the dry sand of the shore.

"That's well done!" exclaimed crazy Bet, in a voice that made the welkin ring, and starting up from the mound. "Strong of heart, and light of foot, you are a fit follower for one that hates the broad and beaten road, and loves the narrow straight way and the high rock. Sit down and rest you," she continued, for Jane was out of breath from ascending the steep bank where crazy Bet stood; "sit down, child; you may sit quiet. It is not time for her to rise yet."

"Oh, Bet," said Jane, "if you love me, take those greens off your head; they make you look so wild."

A stouter heart than Jane's would have quailed at Bet's appearance. She had taken off her old bonnet and tied it on a branch of the tree that shaded the grave, and twisted around her head a full leaved vine, by which she had confined bunches of wild flowers, that drooped around her pale brow and haggard face; her long hair was streaming over her shoulders; her little black mantle thrown back, leaving her throat and neck bare. The excitement of the scene, the purpose of the expedition, and the moonlight, gave to her large black eyes an unusual brightness.

To Jane's earnest entreaty she replied, "Child, you know not what you ask. Take off these greens, indeed! Every leaf of them has had a prayer said over it. There is a charm in every one of them. There is not an imp of the evil one that dares to touch me while I wear them. The toad with his glistening eye, springs far from me; and the big scaly snake, that's coiled and ready to dart, glides away from me."

"But," said Jane, in a tone of more timid expostulation, "what have I to guard me, Bet?"

"You!" and as she spoke she stroked Jane's hair back from her pure smooth brow; "have not you innocence? and know you not that is 'God's seal in the forehead' to keep you from all harm. Foolish girl! sit down— I say, she will not rise yet."

Jane obeyed her command, and rallying her spirits, replied, "No, Bet, I am not afraid she will rise. I believe the dead lie very quiet in their graves."

"Yes, those may that die in their beds and are buried by the tolling of the bell, and lie with a merry company about them in the church yard; but, I tell you, those that row themselves over the dark river, never have a quiet night's rest in their cold beds."

"Come," said Jane, impatiently rising, "for mercy's sake, let us go."

"I cannot stir from this spot," replied Bet, "till the moon gets above that tree; and so be quiet, while I tell you Lucy's story. Why, child, I sit here watching by her many a night, till her hour comes, and then I always go away, for the dead don't love to be seen rising from their beds."

"Well, Bet, tell me Lucy's story, and then I hope you will not keep me any longer here; and you need not tell me much, for, you know, I have heard it a thousand times."

"Ah! but you did not see her as I did, when Ashley's men went out, and she followed them, and begged them on her knees, for the love of God, not to fire upon the prisoners; for the story had come, that Shay's men would cover their front with the captives; and you did not see her when he was brought to her shot through the heart, and dead as she is now. She did not speak a word—she fell upon his neck, and she clasped her arms round him; they thought to cut them off, it was so hard to get them loose;—and when they took her from him, (and the maniac laid her hand on Jane's head) she was all gone here. The very day they put him under the green sod, she drowned herself in that deep place, under the mourning willow, that the boys call Lucy's well. And they buried her here, for the squires and the deacons found it against law and gospel too, to give her Christian burial."

Bet told all these circumstances with an expression and action that showed she was living the scene over, while her mind dwelt on them. Jane was deeply interested; and when Bet concluded, she said, "Poor Lucy! I never felt so much for her."

"That's right, child; now we will go on—but first let that tear-drop that glistens in the moonbeam, fall on the grave, it helps to keep the grass green—and the dead like to be cried for;" she added mournfully.

They now proceeded; crazy Bet leading the way, with long and hasty strides, in a diagonal course still ascending the hill, till she plunged into a deep wood, so richly clothed with foliage as to be impervious to the moon-beams, and so choked with underbrush, that Jane found it very difficult to keep up with her pioneer. They soon, however, emerged into an open space, completely surrounded and enclosed by lofty trees. Crazy Bet had not spoken since they began their walk; she now stopped, and turning abruptly to Jane, "Do you know," said she, "who are the worshippers that meet in this temple? the spirits that were 'sometime disobedient,' but since *He* went and preached to them, they come out from their prison house, and worship in the open air, and under the light of the blessed heavens."

"It is a beautiful spot," said Jane; "I should think all obedient spirits would worship in this sanctuary of nature."

"Say you so;—then worship with me." The maniac fell on her knees— Jane knelt beside her: she had caught a spark of her companion's enthusiasm. The singularity of her situation, the beauty of the night, the novelty of the place, on which the moon now riding high in the heavens poured a flood of silver light, all conspired to give a high tone to her feelings. It is not strange she should have thought she never heard any thing so sublime as the prayer of her crazed conductor—who raised her arms and poured out her soul in passages of scripture the most sublime and striking, woven together by her own glowing language. She concluded suddenly, and springing on her feet, said to Jane, "Now follow me: fear not, and falter not; for you know what awaits the fearful and unbelieving."

Jane assured her she had no *fear* but that of being too late. "You need not think of that; the spirit never flits til I come."

They now turned into the wood by a narrow pathway, whose entrance laid under the shadow of two young beech trees: crazy Bet paused—"See ye these, child," said she, pointing to the trees, "I knew two, who grew up thus on the same spot of earth;—so lovingly they grew," and she pointed to the interlacing of the branches—"young and beautiful; but the axe was laid to the root of one—and the other (and she pressed both her hands on her head, and screamed wildly) perished here." A burst of tears afforded her a sudden relief.

"Poor broken-hearted creature!" murmured Jane.

"No, child; when she weeps, then the band is loosened: for" added she, drawing closer to Jane and whispering, "they put an iron band around her head, and when she is in darkness, it presses till she thinks she is in the place of the Tormentor; by the light of the moon it sits lightly. Ye cannot see it; but it is there—always there."

Jane began now to be alarmed at the excitement of Bet's imagination; and turning from her abruptly, entered the path, which, after they had proceeded a few yards, seemed to be leading them into a wild trackless region. "Where are we going Bet?" she exclaimed. "Through a pass, child, that none knows but the wild bird and the wild woman. Have you never heard of the "caves of the mountain?"

"Yes," replied Jane; "but I had rather not go through them to-night. Cannot we go some other way?"

"Nay, there is no other way; follow me, and fear not."

Jane had often heard of the pass called the 'Mountain-Caves,' and she knew it had only been penetrated by a few rash youths of daring and adventurous spirit. She was appalled at the thought of entering it in the dead of night, and with such a conductor; she paused, but she could see no way of escape, and summoning all her resolution to her aid, she followed Bet, who took no note of her scruples. They now entered a defile, which had been made by some tremendous convulsion of nature, that had rent the mountain asunder, and piled rock on rock in the deep abyss. The breadth of the passage, which was walled in by the perpendicular sides of the mountain, was not in any place more than twenty feet; and sometimes so narrow, that Jane thought she might have extended her arms quite across it. But she had no leisure for critical accuracy; her wayward guide pressed on, heedless of the difficulties of the way. She would pass between huge rocks, that had rolled so near together, as to leave but a very narrow passage between them; then grasping the tangled roots that projected from the side of the mountain, and placing her feet in the fissures of the rocks, or in the little channels that had been worn by the continual dropping from the mountain rills, she would glide over swiftly and safely, as if she had been on the beaten highway. They were sometimes compelled, in the depths of the caverns, to prostrate themselves and creep through narrow apertures in the rocks, it was impossible to surmount; and Jane felt that she was passing over immense masses of ice, the accumulation perhaps of a hundred winters. She was fleet and agile, and inspired with almost supernatural courage; she, 'though a woman, naturally born to fears,' followed on fearlessly; till they came to an immense rock, whose conical and giant form rested on broken masses below, that on every side were propping this 'mighty monarch of the scene.'

For the first time, crazy Bet seemed to remember she had a companion, and to give a thought to her safety. "Jane," said she, "go carefully over this lower ledge, there is a narrow foot-hold there; let not your foot slip on the wet leaves, or the soft moss. I am in the spirit, and I must mount to the summit."

Jane obeyed her directions, and when, without much trouble, she had attained the further side of the rock, she looked back for crazy Bet, and saw her standing between heaven and earth on the very topmost point of the high rock: she leant on the branch of a tree she had broken off in her struggle to reach that lofty station. The moon had declined a little from the meridian; her oblique rays did not penetrate the depths where Jane stood, but fell in their full brightness on the face of her votress above. Her head, as we have noticed, was fantastically dressed with vines and flowers; her eyes were in a fine 'frenzy, rolling from earth to heaven, and heaven to earth;' she looked like the wild genius of the savage scene, and she seemed to breathe its spirit, when, after a moment's silence, she sang, with a powerful and thrilling voice, which waked the sleeping echoes of the mountain, the following stanza:

> "Tell them 'I AM,' Jehovah said
> To Moses, while earth heard in dread,
> And smitten to the heart;
> At once above, beneath, around,
> All nature, without voice or sound,
> Replied, Oh Lord, Thou art!"

In vain Jane called upon her. In vain she entreated her to descend. She seemed wrapt in some heavenly vision; and she stood mute again and motionless, till a bird, that had been scared from its nest in a cleft of the rock, by the wild sounds, fluttered over her and lit on the branch she still held in her hand. "Oh!" exclaimed she, "messenger of love, and omen of mercy, I am content;" and she swiftly descended the sloping side of the rock, which she hardly seemed to touch.

"Now," said Jane, soothingly, "you are rested, let us go on."

"Rested! yes, my body is rested, but my spirit has been the way of the eagle in the air. You cannot bear the revelation now, child. Come on, and do your earthly work."

They walked on for a few yards, when Bet, suddenly turned to the left and ascended the mountain, which was there less steep and rugged than at any place they had passed. At a short distance before her Jane perceived, glimmering through the trees, a faint light. "Heaven be praised!" said she, "that must be John's cottage."

As they came nearer the dog barked; and the old man, coming out of the door, signed to Jane to sit down on a log, which answered the purpose of a rude door-step; and then speaking to crazy Bet, in a voice of authority, which, to Jane's utter surprise, she meekly obeyed—"Take off," said he, "you mad fool, those ginglements from your head, and stroke your hair back like a decent Christian woman; get into the house, but mind you, say not a word to her."

Crazy Bet entered the house, and John, turning to Jane, said, "You are an angel of goodness for coming here to-night, though I am afraid it will do no good; but since you are here, you shall see her."

"See her! See what, John?" interrupted Jane.

"That's what I must tell you, Miss; but it is a piercing story to tell to one that looks like you. It's telling the deeds of the pit to the angels above." He then went on to state, that a few days before he had been searching the mountains for some medicinal roots, when his attention was suddenly arrested by a low moaning sound, and on going in the direction from whence it came, he found a very young looking creature, with a new-born infant, wrapped in a shawl, and lying in her arms. He spoke to the mother, but she made no reply, and seemed quite unconscious of every thing, till he attempted to take the child from her; she then grasped it so firmly, that he found it difficult to remove it. He called his wife to his assistance, and placed the infant in her arms. Pity for so young a sufferer nerved the old man with unwonted strength, and enabled him to bear the mother to his hut. There he used the simple restoratives his skill dictated; but nothing produced any effect till the child, with whom the old woman had taken unwearied pains, revived and cried. "The sound," he said, "seemed to waken life in a dead body." The mother extended her arms, as if to feel for her child, and they gently laid it in them. She felt the touch of its face, and burst into a flood of tears, which seemed greatly to relieve her; for after that she took a little nourishment, and fell into a sweet sleep, from which she awoke in a state to make some explanations to her curious preservers. But as the account she gave of herself was, of necessity, interrupted and imperfect, we shall take the liberty to avail ourselves of our knowledge of her history, and offer our readers a slight sketch of it.

CHAPTER X

Death lies on her like an untimely frost,
Upon the sweetest flower of all the field.
                                    Romeo and Juliet.

The name of the stranger was Mary Oakley. Her parents had gone out adventurers to the West Indies, where, at the opening of flattering prospects, they both died victims to the fever of the climate, which seldom spares a northern constitution. Mary, then in her infancy, had been sent home to her grand-parents, who nursed this only relict of their unfortunate children with doating fondness. They were in humble life; and they denied themselves every comfort, that they might gratify every wish, reasonable and unreasonable, of their darling child. She, affectionate and ardent in her nature, grew up impetuous and volatile. Instead of 'rocking the cradle of reposing age,' she made the lives of her old parents resemble a fitful April day, sunshine and cloud, succeeding each other in rapid alternation. She loved the old people tenderly—passionately, when she had just received a favour from them; but, like other spoiled children, she never testified that love by deferring her will to theirs, or suffering their wisdom to govern her childish inclinations. She grew up

> "Fair as the form that, wove in fancy's loom,
> Floats in light vision round the poet's head."

Most unhappily for her, there was a college in the town where she lived, and she very early became the favourite belle of the young collegians, whose attentions she received with delight, in spite of the remonstrances and entreaties of her guardians, who were well aware that a young and beautiful creature could not, with propriety or safety, receive the civilities of her superiors in station, attracted by her personal charms.

David Wilson, more artful, more unprincipled than any of his companions, addressed her with the most extravagant flattery, and lavished on her costly favours. Giddy and credulous, poor Mary was a victim to his libertinism. He soothed her with hopes and promises, till in consequence of the fear of detection in another transaction, where detection would have been dangerous, he left—and returned to his mother's, without giving Mary the slightest intimation of his departure.

She took the desperate resolution of following him. She felt certain she should not survive her confinement, and hoped to secure the protection of Wilson for her infant. Her tenderness, we believe, more than her pride, induced her to conceal her miseries from her only true friends. She thought any thing would be easier for them to bear than a knowledge of her misconduct; and for the few days she remained under their roof, and while she was preparing a disguise for her perilous journey, she affected slight sickness and derangement. They were alarmed and anxious, and insisted on making a bed for her in their room: this somewhat embarrassed her proceedings; but, on the night of her escape, she told them, with a determined manner, that she could only sleep in her own bed, and alone in her own room. They did not resist her; they never had. Mary kissed them when she bade them good-night with unusual tenderness. They went sorrowing to their beds. She wrote a few incoherent lines, addressed to them, praying for their forgiveness; expressing her gratitude and her love; and telling them, that life before her seemed a long and a dark road, and she did not wish to go any further in it; and begging them not to search for her, for in one hour the waves would roll over her. She placed the scroll on her table, crept out of her window, and left for ever the protecting roof of her kind old parents.

When they awoke to a knowledge of their loss, they were overwhelmed with grief. Their neighbours flocked about them, to offer their assistance and consolation; and though some of the most penetrating among them, suspected the cause of the poor girl's desperation, more forbearing and kind than persons usually are, in such circumstances, they spared the old people the light of their conjectures.

Poor Mary persevered in her fatiguing and miserable journey, which was rendered much longer by her fearfully shunning the public road. She obtained a kind shelter at the farmers' houses at night, where she always contrived to satisfy their curiosity by some plausible account of herself. At the end of a week she arrived wearied and exhausted in the neighbourhood of Wilson. She watched for him in the evening, near his mother's house, and succeeded in obtaining an interview with him. He was enraged that she had followed him, and said that it was impossible for him to do any thing for her. She told him, she asked nothing for herself; but she entreated him not to add to his guilt the crime of suffering their unhappy offspring to die with neglect. Utterly selfish and hard-hearted, the wretch turned from her without one word of kindness: and then recollecting that if she was discovered, he should be involved in further troubles, he returned, and gave her a direction, which he believed would enable her to find John's cottage on the mountain. If she gets there, thought he as he left her, whether she lives or dies, she will be far out of the way for the present—and the future must take care of itself.

Mary with a faint heart followed his direction, and the next day she was discovered by old John in the situation we have mentioned. Perhaps there are some who cannot believe that any being should be so utterly depraved as David Wilson. But let them remember, that he began with a nature more inclined to evil than to good, that his mother's mismanagement had increased every thing that was bad in him, and extinguished every thing that was good—that the continual contradictions of his mother's professions and life, had led him to an entire disbelief of the truths of religion, as well as a contempt of its restraints.

After the old man had finished Mary's story, or rather so much of it as he had been able to gather from her confessions, Jane asked him "Why she had been sent for?"

"Why Miss," he replied, "after the poor thing had come to herself, all her trouble seemed to be about her baby, and I did not know what to advise her; my woman and I might have done for it for the present, but our sun is almost set, and we could do but a little while. I proposed to her to go for Wilson, and I was sure the sight of her might have softened a heart of flint; but she shivered at the bare mention of it: she said, "No, no; I cannot see that cruel face upon my death-bed." And then I thought of you, and I told her if there was any body could bring him to a sense of right it was you, and that at any rate you might think of some comfort for her; for I told her every body in the village knew you for the wisest and discreetest, and gentlest. At first she relucted, and then the sight of her baby seemed to persuade her, and she bade me go, but she gave me a strict charge that no one should come with you; for she said she wished her memory buried with her in the grave. When I left her to go to you, I hoped you might speak some words of comfort to her that would be better than medicine for her, and heal the body as well as the mind; but when I came back, there was a dreadful change—the poor little one had gone into a fit, and she would take it from my wife into her arms, and there it died more than an hour ago; and she sits up in the bed holding it yet, and she has not spoken a word, nor turned her eyes from it; her cheeks look as if there was a living fire consuming her. Oh, Miss Jane, it is awful to look upon such a fallen star! Now you are prepared—come in—may be the sight of you will rouse her."

Jane followed John into his little habitation. The old couple had kindly resigned their only bed to the sufferer. She was sitting as John had described her, fixed as a statue. Her beautiful black glossy curls, which had been so often admired and envied, were in confusion, and clustered in rich masses over her temples and neck. A tear that had started from the fountain of feeling, now sealed for ever, hung on the dark rich eye-lash that fringed her downcast eye. Jane wondered that any thing so wretched could look so lovely. Crazy Bet was kneeling at the foot of the bed, and apparently absorbed in prayer, for her eyes were closed, and her lips moved, though they emitted no sound. The old woman sat in the corner of the fire-place, smoking a broken pipe, to sooth the unusual agitation she felt.

Jane advanced towards the bed. "Speak to her," said John. Jane stopped, and laid her hand gently on Mary's. She raised her eyes for the first time, and turned them on Jane with a look of earnest inquiry, and then shaking her head, she said in a low mournful voice—"No, no; we cannot be parted; you mean to take her to heaven, and you say I am guilty, and must not go. They told me you were coming—you need not hide your wings—I know you—there is none but an angel would look upon me with such pity."

"Oh!" exclaimed Jane in an agony, "can nothing be done for her? at least let us take away this dead child, it is growing cold in her arms." She attempted to take the child, and Mary relaxed her hold; but as she did so, she uttered a faint scream—became suddenly pale as 'monumental marble,'—and fell back on the pillow.

"Ah, she is gone!" exclaimed John.

Crazy Bet sprang on her feet, and raised her hand—"Hush!" said she, "I heard a voice saying, 'Her sins are forgiven'—she is one 'come out of great tribulation.'"

There were a few moments of as perfect stillness as if they had all been made dumb and motionless by the stroke of death. Jane was the first to break silence—"Did she," she inquired of the old man, "express any penitence—any hope?"

John shook his head. "Them things did not seem to lay on her mind; and I did not think it worth while to disturb her about them. Ah, Miss, the great thing is how we live, not how we die."

Jane felt the anxiety, so natural, to obtain some religious expression, that should indicate preparation in the mind of the departed.

"Surely," said she, "it is never too late to repent—to beg forgiveness."

"No, Miss;" replied John, who seemed to have religious notions of his own—"especially when there has been such a short account as this poor child had; but the work must be all between the creature and the Creator, and for my part, I don't place much dependance on what people say on a death-bed. I have lived a long life, Miss Jane, and many a one have I seen, and heard too, when sickness and distress were heavy upon them, and death staring them in the face, and they could not sin any more— they would seem to repent, and talk as beautiful as any saint; but if the Lord took his hand from them, and they got well again, they went right back into the old track. No, Miss Jane, it is the life—it is the life, we must look to. This child," he added, going to the bed, and laying his brown and shrivelled hand upon her fair young brow, now 'chill and changeless,' "this child was but sixteen, she told me so. The Lord only knows what temptations she has had; He it is, Miss Jane, that has put that in our hearts that makes us feel sorry for her now; and can you think He is less pitiful than we are? I think she will be beaten with few stripes; but," he concluded solemnly, covering his face with his hands,—"we are poor ignorant crea- tures; it is all a mystery after this world; we know nothing about it."

"Yes," said Jane, "we do know, John, that all will be right."

"True," he replied; "and it is that should make us lay our fingers on our mouths and be still."

Jane had been so much absorbed in the mournful scene, that the necessity of her return before the breaking of day had not occurred to her mind, and would not, perhaps, if John had not, after a few moments pause, reminded her of it, by saying, "I am sorry Miss Jane, you have had such a walk for nothing; but," added he, "to the wise nothing is vain, and you are of so teachable a make, that you may have learned some good lessons here; you may learn, at least, that there is nothing to be much grieved for in this world but guilt; and some people go through a long life without learning that. You had better return now; I will go round the hill with you, and show you the path this crazy creature should have led you. She is in one of her still fits now; there is nothing calms her down like seeing death; she will not move from here till after the burying."

Jane looked for the last time on the beautiful form before her, and with the ingenuous and keen feeling of youth, wept aloud.

"It is indeed a sore sight," said John; "it makes my old eyes run over as they have not for many a year. The Lord have mercy on her destroyer! Oh, Miss! it is sad to see this beautiful flower cut down in its prime; but who would change her condition for his? He may go rioting on, but there is that gnawing at his heart's core that will not be quieted."

Jane told the kind old man that she was now ready to go, and they left the hut together. He led her by a narrow foot path around the base of the mountain, till they came to a part of the way that was known to Jane. She then parted from her conductor, after inquiring of him if he could inter the bodies secretly? He replied, that he could without much difficulty; and he certainly should, for he had given his promise to the young creature, who seemed to dread nothing so much as a discovery which might lead to her old parents knowing her real fate.

Anxious to reach home in time to avoid the necessity of any disclosures, Jane hastened forward, and arrived at her aunt's before the east gave the slightest notice of the approach of day. She entered the house carefully, and turned into the parlour to look for some refreshment in an adjoining pantry. A long walk, and a good deal of emotion, we believe, in real life, are very apt to make people, even the most refined, hungry and thirsty.

Jane had entered the parlour, and closed the door after her, before she perceived that she was not the only person in it; but she started with alarm, which certainly was not confined to herself, when she saw standing at Mrs. Wilson's desk, which was placed at one corner of the room, her son David, with his mother's pocket-book in his hand, from which he was in the act of subtracting a precious roll of bank bills that had been deposited there the day before. Jane paused for a moment, and but for a moment, for as the truth flashed on her, she sprang forward, and seizing his arm, exclaimed, "For heaven's sake, David, put back that money! Do not load yourself with any more sins."

He shook her off, and hastily stuffing the money in his pocket, said, that he must have it; that his mother would not give him enough to save him from destruction; that he had told her, ruin was hanging over his head; that she had driven him to help himself; and, "as to sin," he added fiercely, "I am in too deep already to be frightened by that thought."

It occurred to Jane that he might have been driven to this mode of supplying himself, in order to relieve the extreme need of Mary Oakley; and she told him, in a hurried manner, the events of the night. For a moment he felt the sting of conscience, and, perhaps, a touch of human feeling; for, he staggered back into a chair, and covering his face with his hands, muttered, "*dead*! Mary *dead*! Good God! Hell has no place bad enough for me;" and then rousing himself, he said, with a deep tone, "Jane Elton, I am a ruined, desperate man. You thought too well of me, when you imagined it was for that poor girl I was doing this deed. No, no! her cries did not trouble me; but there are those whose clamours must be hushed by money—curse on them!"

"But," said Jane, "is there no other way, David? I will entreat your mother for you."

"You! yes, and she will heed you as much as the vulture does the whining of his prey. I tell you, I am desperate, Jane, and care not for the consequences. But," he added, "I will run no risk of discovery," and as he spoke, he drew a pistol from beneath his surtout, and putting the muzzle to his breast, said to Jane, "give me your solemn promise, that you will never betray me, or I will put myself beyond the reach of human punishment."

"Oh!" said Jane, "I will promise any thing. Do not destroy your soul and body both."

"Do you promise then?"

"I do, most solemnly."

"Then," said he, hastily replacing the pistol, and locking the desk with the false key he had obtained; "then all is as well as it can be. My mother will suspect, but she will not dare to tell whom; and your promise, Jane, makes me secure."

Jane saw he was so determined, that any further interposition would be useless, and she hurried away to her own apartment, where she threw herself upon her bed, sorrowing for the crimes and miseries of others. Quite exhausted with the fatigues of the night, she soon fell asleep.

She was too much distressed and terrified, to reflect upon the bad effects that might result from the exacted promise. She had, doubtless, been unnecessarily alarmed by David's threat of self-slaughter; for, confused and desperate as he was, he would hardly have proceeded to such an outrage; and, besides, we have reason to believe the pistol was neither primed nor loaded; but, that he had provided himself with it for emergencies which might occur in the desperate career in which he had engaged. He had been concerned with two ingenious villains in changing the denomination of bank bills. His accomplices had been detected and imprisoned, and they were now exacting money from him by threatening to disclose his agency in the transaction.

Always careless of involving himself in guilt, and goaded on by the fear of the state-prison, he resolved, without hesitation, on this robbery, which would not only give him the means of present relief, but would supply him with a store for future demands, which he had every reason to expect from the character of his comrades.

CHAPTER XI

There is no terror, Cassius, in your threats;
For I am armed so strong in honesty,
That they pass by me as the idle wind,
Which I respect not.

Julius Cæsar.

Jane, exhausted by the agitations of the night, contrary to her usual custom, remained in bed much longer than the other members of the family, and did not awake from deep and unquiet slumbers, till the bell called the household to prayers.

Mrs. Wilson was scrupulous in exacting the attendance of every member of her family at her morning and evening devotions. With this requisition Jane punctually and cheerfully complied, as she did with all those that did not require a violation of principle. But still she had often occasion secretly to lament, that where there was so much of the form of worship, there was so little of its spirit and truth; and she sometimes felt an involuntary self-reproach, that her body should be in the attitude of devotion, while her mind was following her aunt through earth, sea, and skies, or pausing to wonder at the remarkable inadaptation of her prayers to the condition and wants of humanity, in general, and especially to their particular modification in her own family.

Mrs. Wilson was fond of the bold and highly figurative language of the prophets; and often identified herself with the Psalmist, in his exultation over his enemies, in his denunciations, and in his appeals for vengeance.

We leave to theologians to decide, whether these expressions from the king of Israel are meant for the enemies of the church, or whether they are to be imputed to the dim light which the best enjoyed under the Jewish dispensation. At any rate, such as come to us in 'so questionable a shape,' ought not to be employed as the medium of a Christian's prayer.

When Jane entered the room, she found her aunt had begun her devotions, which were evidently more confused than usual; and when she (her voice wrought up to its highest pitch) "Lo! thine enemies, O Lord! lo, thine enemies shall perish; all the workers of iniquity shall be scattered; but my horn shalt thou exalt like the horn of a unicorn: I shall be anointed with fresh oil: mine eye also shall see my desire on my enemies, and my ears shall hear my desire of the wicked that rise up against me;" Jane perceived, from her unusual emotion, that she must allude to something that touched her own affairs, and she conjectured that she had already discovered the robbery. Her conjectures were strengthened when she observed, that, during the breakfast, her aunt seemed very much agitated; but she was at a loss to account for the look she darted on her, when one of the children said, "How your hair looks, Jane; this is the first time I ever saw you come to breakfast without combing it."

Jane replied, that she had over-slept.

"You look more," said Elvira, "as if you had been watching all night, and crying too, I should imagine, from the redness of your eyes—and now I think of it," she added, regardless of Jane's embarrassment, "I am sure I heard your door shut in the night, and you walking about your room."

Jane was more confused by the expression of her aunt's face, than by her cousin's observations. What, thought she, can I have done to provoke her? I certainly have done nothing; but there is never a storm in the family, without my biding some of its pitiless pelting.

After breakfast, the family dispersed, as usual, excepting Mrs. Wilson, David, and Jane, who remained to assist her aunt in removing the breakfast apparatus. Mrs. Wilson, neither wishing nor able any longer to restrain her wrath; went up to her desk, and taking hold of a pocket handkerchief which appeared to lie on the top of it, but which, as she stretched it out, showed one end caught and fastened in the desk—"Do you know this handkerchief, Jane Elton?" she said in a voice choking with passion.

"Yes, ma'am," replied Jane, turning pale—"it is mine." She ventured, as she spoke, to look at David. His eyes were fixed on a newspaper he seemed to be reading; not a muscle of his face moved, nor was there the slightest trace of emotion.

"Yours," said Mrs. Wilson; "that you could not deny, for your name is at full length on it; and when did you have it last?"

"Last night, ma'am."

"And who has robbed me of five hundred dollars? Can you answer to that?"

Jane made no reply. She saw, that her aunt's suspicions rested on her, and she perceived, at once, the cruel dilemma in which she had involved herself by her promise to David.

"Answer me that," repeated Mrs. Wilson, violently.

"That I cannot answer you, ma'am."

"And you mean to deny that you have taken it yourself?"

"Certainly I do, ma'am," replied Jane, firmly, for she had now recovered her self-possession. "I am perfectly innocent; and I am sure that, whatever appearances there may be against me, you cannot believe me guilty—you do not."

"And do you think to face me down in this way. I have evidence enough to satisfy any court of justice. Was not you heard up in the night—your guilty face told the story, at breakfast, plainer than words could tell it. David," she continued to her son, who had thrown down the paper and walked to the window, where he stood with his back to his mother, affecting to whistle to a dog without; "David, I call you to witness this handkerchief, and what has now been said; and remember, she does not deny that she left it here."

One honest feeling had a momentary ascendancy in David's bosom; and he had risen from his seat with the determination to disclose the truth, but he was checked by the recollection that he should have to restore the money, which he had not yet disposed of. He thought, too, that his mother knew, in her heart, who had taken the money; that she would not dare to disclose her loss, and if she did, it would be time enough for him to interpose when Jane should be in danger of suffering otherwise than in the opinion of his mother, whose opinion, he thought, not worth caring for. Therefore, when called upon by his mother, he made no reply, but turning round and facing the accuser and the accused, he looked as composed as any uninterested spectator.

Mrs. Wilson proceeded, "Restore me my money, or abide the consequences."

"The consequences I must abide, and I do not fear them, nor shrink from them, for I am innocent, and God will protect me."

At this moment they were interrupted by the entrance of Edward Erskine; and our poor heroine, though the instant before she had felt assured and tranquil in her panoply divine, burst into tears, and left the room. She could not endure the thought of degradation in Erskine's esteem; and she was very sure that her aunt would not lose such an opportunity of robbing her of his good opinion. She did not mistake. Mrs.

Wilson closed the door after Jane; and seating herself, all unused as she was to the melting mood, gave way to a passion of tears and sobs, which were, as we think, a sincere tribute to the loss she had experienced.

"For heaven's sake, tell me what is the matter!" said Erskine to young Wilson; for his impatience for an explanation became irrepressible, not on account of the old woman's emotion, for she might have wept till she was like Niobe, all tears, without provoking an inquiry, but Jane's distress had excited his anxiety.

"The Lord knows," replied David; "there is always a storm in this house;" and he flung out of the room without vouchsafing a more explicit answer.

Erskine turned to Mrs. Wilson: "Can you tell me, madam, what has disturbed Miss Elton?"

Mrs. Wilson was provoked that he did not ask what had disturbed her, and she determined he should not remain another moment without the communication, which she had been turning over in her mind to get it in the most efficient form.

"Oh! Mr. Erskine," she said, with a whine that has been used by all hypocrites from Oliver Cromwell's time down; "oh! my trial is more than I can endure. I could bear, they should devour me and lay waste my dwelling place; I could be supported under that; but it is a grief too heavy for me, to reveal to you the sin, and the disgrace, and the abomination, of one that I have brought up as my own—who has fed upon my children's bread."

"Madam," interrupted Erskine, "you may spare yourself and me any more words. I ask for the cause of all this uproar."

Mrs. Wilson would have replied angrily to what she thought Erskine's impertinence, but, remembering that it was her business to conciliate not offend him, she, after again almost exhausting his patience by protestations of the hardship of being obliged to uncover the crimes of her relation, of the affliction she suffered in doing her duty, &c.&c. told him, with every aggravation that emphasis and insinuation could lend to them, the particulars of her discovery.

With unusual self-command he heard her through; and though he was unable to account for the suspicious circumstances, he spurned instinctively the conclusion Mrs. Wilson drew from them.

Her astonishment, that he neither expressed horror, nor indignation, nor resentment towards the offender, was not at all abated when he only replied by a request to speak alone with Miss Elton.

Mrs. Wilson thought he might intend the gathering storm should burst on Jane's head; or, perhaps, he would advise her to fly; at any rate, it was not her cue, to lay a straw in his way at present. She even went herself and gave the request to Jane, adding to it a remark, that as she "was not very fond of keeping out of Erskine's way, she could hardly refuse to come when asked."

"I have no wish to refuse;" replied Jane, who, ashamed of having betrayed so much emotion, had quite recovered her self-possession, and stood calm in conscious integrity.—"But hear me, ma'am," said she to her aunt, who had turned and was leaving the room—"all connexion between us is dissolved for ever; I shall not remain another night beneath a roof where I have received little kindness, and where I now suffer the imputation of a crime, of which I cannot think you believe me guilty."

Mrs. Wilson was for a moment daunted by the power of unquestionable innocence.—"I know not where I shall go, I know not whether your persecutions will follow me; but I am not friendless—nor fearful."

She passed by her aunt, and descended to the parlour. 'No thought infirm altered her cheek;' her countenance was very serious, but the peace of virtue was there. Her voice did not falter in the least, when she said to Edward, as he closed the door on her entrance into the parlour—"Mr. Erskine, you have no doubt requested to see me in the expectation that I would contradict the statement my aunt must have made to you. I cannot, for it is all true."

Edward interrupted her—"I do not wish it, Jane; I believe you are perfectly innocent of that and of every other crime; I do not wish you even to deny it. It is all a devilish contrivance of that wicked woman."

"You are mistaken, Edward; it is not a contrivance; the circumstances are as she has told them to you.—Elvira did not mistake in supposing she heard me up in the night; and my aunt did find my handkerchief in her desk. No, Edward; she is right in all but the conclusion she draws from these unfortunate circumstances; perhaps," she added after a moment's pause, "a kinder judgment would not absolve me."

"A saint," replied Edward cheeringly, "needs no absolution. No one shall be permitted to accuse you, or suspect you; you can surely explain these accidental circumstances, so that even your aunt, malicious—venemous as she is, will not dare to breathe a poisonous insinuation against you, angel as you are."

"Ah," replied Jane, with a sad smile, "there are, and there ought to be, few believers in earth-born angels. No, Mr. Erskine, I have no explanation to make; I have nothing but assertions of my innocence, and my general character to rely upon. Those who reject this evidence must believe me guilty."

She rose to leave the room. Erskine gently drew her back, and asked if it was possible she included him among those who could be base enough to distrust her; and before she could reply he went on to a passionate declaration of his affections, followed by such promises of eternal truth, love, and fidelity, as are usual on such occasions.

At another time, Jane would have paused to examine her heart, before she accepted the professions made by her lover, and she would have found no tenderness there that might not be controlled and subdued by reason. But now, driven out from her natural protectors by suspicion and malignant accusation, and touched by the confiding affection that refused to suspect her; the generosity, the magnanimity that were presented in such striking contrast to the baseness of her relations—she received Edward's declarations with the most tender and ingenuous expressions of gratitude; and Erskine did not doubt, nor did Jane at that moment, that this gratitude was firmly rooted in love.

Edward, ardent and impetuous, proposed an immediate marriage: he argued, that it was the only, and would be an effectual, way of protecting her from the persecutions of her aunt.

Jane replied, that she had very little reason to fear that her aunt would communicate to any other person her suspicions. "She had a motive towards you," she added, "that overcame her prudence. I have found a refuge in your heart, and she cannot injure me while I have that asylum. I have too much pride, Edward, to involve you in the reproach I may have to sustain. I had formed a plan this morning, before your generosity translated me from despondency to hope, which I must adhere to, for a few months at least. An application has been made to me to teach some little girls who are not old enough for Mr. Evertson's school: my aunt, as usual, put in her veto; I had almost made up my mind to accept the proposal in spite of it, when the events of the morning came to my aid, and decided me at once, and I have already announced to my aunt my determination to leave her house. I trust that in a few months something will occur, to put me beyond the reach of suspicion, and reward as well as justify your generous confidence."

Edward entreated—protested—argued—but all in vain; he was obliged at length to resign his will to Jane's decision. Edward's next proposal was to announce the engagement immediately. On this he insisted so earnestly, and offered for it so many good reasons, that Jane consented. Mrs. Wilson was summoned to the parlour, and informed of the issue of the conference, of which she had expected so different a termination. She was surprised—mortified—and most of all, wrathful—that her impotent victim, as she deemed Jane, should be rescued from her grasp. She began the most violent threats and reproaches; Edward interrupted her by telling her that she dare not repeat the first; and from the last her niece would soon be for ever removed, as he should require they should in future be perfect strangers. Mrs. Wilson felt like a wild animal just encaged; she might lash herself to fury, but no one heeded her.

Edward left the room, saying, that he should send his servant to convey Jane's baggage wherever she would order it to be sent. Jane went quietly to her own apartment, to make the necessary arrangements; there she soon overheard the low growlings of Mrs. Wilson's angriest voice, communicating, as she inferred from the loud responsive exclamations and whimpering, her engagement to Elvira. Mrs. Wilson's perturbed spirit was not quieted even by this outpouring; and after walking up and down, scolding at the servants and the children, she put on her hat and shawl, and sallied out to a shop, to pay a small debt she owed there. No passion could exclude from her mind for any length of time the memory of so disagreeable a circumstance as the necessity of paying out money. After she had discharged the debt, and the master of the shop had given her the change, he noticed her examining one of the bills he had handed her with a look of scrutiny and some agitation. He said, "I believe that is a good bill, Mrs. Wilson; I was a little suspicious of it too at first; I took it, this morning, from your son David, in payment of a debt that has been standing more than a year. I thought myself so lucky to get any thing, that I was not very particular."

Mrs. Wilson's particularity seemed to have a sudden quietus, for she pushed the bill into the full purse after the others, muttering something about the folly of trusting boys being rightly punished by the loss of the debt.

The fact was, that Mrs. Wilson recognised this bill the moment she saw it, as one of the parcel she had received the day before, and which she had marked, at the time, for she was eagle-eyed in the detection of a spurious bill. There is nothing more subtle, more inveterate than a habit of self-deception. It was not to the world alone that Mrs. Wilson played the hypocrite, but before the tribunal of her own conscience she appeared with hollow arguments and false pretences. From the moment she had discovered her loss in the morning, she had, at bottom, believed David guilty; she recollected the threats of the preceding day, and her first impulse was to charge him with the theft, and to demand the money; but then, she thought, he was violent and determined, and that, without exposing him, (even Mrs. Wilson shrunk from the consequences of exposure to her son) she could not regain her money. She was at a loss how to account for the appearance of Jane's handkerchief; but neither that, nor Jane's subsequent emotion at the breakfast table, nor her refusal to make any explanation of the suspicious circumstances, enabled Mrs. Wilson to believe that Jane had borne any part in the dishonesty of the transaction. Such was the involuntary tribute she paid to the tried, steadfast virtue of this excellent being. Still she could not restrain the whirlwind of her passion; and it burst, as we have seen, upon Jane. She was at a loss to account for Jane's refusal to vindicate herself. It was impossible for her to conceive of the reasons that controlled Jane, which would have been no more to Mrs. Wilson, than were to Sampson the new ropes he snapped asunder at the call of Delilah. She felt so fearful, at first, that any investigation would lead to the discovery of the real criminal, that she had not communicated the fact of the handkerchief to any one, even to Elvira, whose discretion, indeed, she never trusted; but, after she found that Jane was in a dilemma, from which she would not extricate herself by any explanations, she thought herself the mistress of her niece's fate; and the moment she saw Erskine, she determined to extract good out of the evil that had come upon her, to dim the lustre of Jane's good name, that 'more immediate jewel of her soul,' and thus to secure for her daughter the contested prize. But Mrs. Wilson, it seems, was destined to experience, on this eventful day, how very hard is the way of the transgressor. Her niece's fortunes were suddenly placed beyond her control or reach; and nothing remained of all her tyranny and plots, but the pitiful and malignant pleasure of believing, that Jane thought herself in some measure in her power, though she knew that she was not.

After the confirmation of her conjecture at the shop, she saw that secrecy was absolutely necessary; and she was too discreet to indulge herself with telling Elvira of any of the particulars, about which she had been so vociferous to the young lovers.

Perhaps few ladies, old or young, were ever less encumbered with baggage than Jane Elton, and yet, so confused was she with the events of the night and morning, that the labour of packing up, which at another time she would have despatched in twenty minutes, seemed to have no more tendency to a termination than such labours usually have in dreams. In the midst of her perplexities one of the children entered and said Mr. Lloyd wished to speak to her. She was on the point of sending him an excuse, for she felt an involuntary disinclination to meet his penetrating eye at this moment, when recollecting how much she owed to his constant, tender friendship, she subdued her reluctance, and obeyed his summons. When she entered the room, "I am come," said he, "Jane, to ask thee to walk with me. I am an idler and have nothing to do, and thou art so industrious thou hast time to do every thing. Come, get thy hat. It is 'treason against nature' sullenly to refuse to enjoy so beautiful a day as this." Jane made no reply. He saw she was agitated, and leading her gently to a chair, said, "I fear thou art not well, or, what is much worse, not happy."

Jane would have replied, "I am not;" but she checked the words, for she felt as if the sentiment they expressed, was a breach of fidelity to Erskine; and instead of them she said, hesitatingly, "I ought not to be perfectly happy till my best (I should say one of my best) friends knows and approves what I have done this morning."

"What hast thou done, Jane?" exclaimed Mr. Lloyd, anticipating from her extraordinary embarrassment and awkwardness the communication she was about to make; "hast thou engaged thyself to Erskine?"

She faltered out, "Yes."

Mr. Lloyd made no reply; he rose and walked up and down the room, agitated, and apparently distressed. Jane was alarmed; she could not account for his emotion; she feared he had some ground for an ill opinion of Edward, that she was ignorant of. "You do not like Edward?" said she; "you think I have done wrong?"

The power of man is not limited in the moral as in the natural world. Habitual discipline had given Mr. Lloyd such dominion over his feelings, that he was able now to say to their stormy wave, 'thus far shalt thou come, and no farther.' By a strong and sudden effort he recovered himself, and turning to Jane, he took her hand with a benignant expression—"My dear Jane, thy own heart must answer that question. Dost thou remember a favourite stanza of thine?

"Nae treasures nor pleasures
    Could make us happy lang;
The heart aye's the part aye
    That makes us right or wrang."

Jane imagined that Mr. Lloyd felt a distrust of her motives. "Ah!" she replied, "the integrity of my heart will fail to make me happy, if I have fallen under your suspicion. If you knew the nobleness, the disinterestedness of Erskine's conduct, you would be more just to him, and to me."

"It is not being very unjust to him, or to any one, to think him unworthy of thee, Jane. But since these particulars would raise him so much in my opinion, why not tell them to me? May not 'one of your best friends' claim to know, that which affects, so deeply, your happiness?"

Jane began to reply, but hesitated, and faltered out something of its being impossible for her to display to Mr. Lloyd, Erskine's generosity in the light she saw it.

"Dost thou mean, Jane, that the light of truth is less favourable to him than the light of imagination?"

"No," answered Jane, "such virtues as Edward's shine with a light of their own; imagination cannot enhance their value."

"Still," said Mr. Lloyd, "they shine but on one happy individual. Well, my dear Jane," he continued, after a few moments pause, "I will believe without seeing. I will believe thou hast good reasons for thy faith, though they are incommunicable. If Erskine make thee happy, I shall be resigned."

Happily for both parties, this very unsatisfactory conference was broken off by the entrance of Erskine's servant, who came, as he said, for Miss Elton's baggage. Jane explained, as concisely as possible, to Mr. Lloyd, her plans for the present, and then took advantage of this opportunity to retreat to her own apartment, where she had no sooner entered than she gave way to a flood of tears, more bitter than any her aunt's injustice had cost her. She had, previous to her interview with Mr. Lloyd, determined not to disclose to him, or Mary Hull, the disagreeable affair of the robbery. She wished to spare them the pain, the knowledge of a perplexity from which they could not extricate her, must give to them. She was sure Mary, whose discernment was very quick, and who knew David well, would, at once, suspect him; and therefore, she thought, that in telling the story, she should violate the spirit of her promise; and, at bottom, she felt a lurking fearfulness that Mr. Lloyd might think there was more of gratitude than affection in her feelings to Erskine; she thought it possible, too, he might not estimate Edward's magnanimity quite as highly as she did; for "though," she said, "Mr. Lloyd has the fairest mind in the world, I think he has never liked Erskine. They are, certainly, very different"—and she sighed as she concluded her deliberations.

Mr. Lloyd, after remaining for a few moments in the posture Jane had left him, returned to his own home, abstracted and sad. 'The breath of Heaven smelt as wooingly,' and the sun shone as brightly as before, but there was now no feeling of joy within to vibrate to the beauty without; and he certainly could not be acquitted of the 'sullen neglect of nature,' that he had deemed treason an hour before.

"I knew," thought he, "she was fallible, and why should I be surprised at her failure? It cannot be Erskine, but the creature of her imagination, that she loves. She is too young to possess the Ithuriel touch that dissolves false appearances: she could not detect, under so specious a garb, the vanity and selfishness that counterfeit manly pride and benevolence. If he were but worthy of her, I should be perfectly happy."

Mr. Lloyd was mistaken; he would not, even in that case, have been perfectly happy. He did not, though he was very much of a self-examiner, clearly define all his feelings on this trying occasion. He had loved Jane first as a child, and then as a sister; and of late he had thought if he could love another woman, as a wife, it would be Jane Elton. But his lost Rebecca was more present to his imagination than any living being. He had formed no project for himself in relation to Jane; yet he would have felt disappointment at her appropriation to any other person, though, certainly, not the sorrow which her engagement to Erskine occasioned him. Mr. Lloyd was really a disinterested man. He had so long made it a rule to immitate the Parent of the universe, in still educing good from evil, that, in every trial of his life, it was his first aim to ascertain his duty, and then to perform it. He could weave the happiness of others, even though no thread of his own was in the fabric. In the present case, he resolved still to watch over Jane; to win the friendship of Erskine, to endeavour to rectify his principles, to exert over him an insensible influence, and, if possible, to render him more worthy of his enviable destiny.

In the course of the day, Mary Hull heard the rumours that had already spread through the village, of Jane's removal to Mrs. Harvey's, and her engagement. She ran to the library door, and in the fulness of her heart, forgetful of the decorum of knocking, she entered and found Mr. Lloyd sitting with his little girl on his knee. "Mary, I am glad to see thee," said the child; "I cannot get a word from father; he is just as if he was asleep, only his eyes are wide open."

Mary, regardless of the child's prattle, announced the news she had just heard. Mr. Lloyd coldly replied, that he knew it already; and Mary left the room, a little hurt that he had not condescended to tell her, and wondering what made him so indifferent, and then wondering whether it was indifference; but as she could not relieve her mind, she resolved to go immediately to Jane, with whom the habits of their early lives, and her continued kindness, had given and established the right of free intercourse.

She found Jane alone, and not looking as happy as she expected. "You have come to give me joy, Mary," she said, smiling mournfully as she extended her hand to her friend.

"Yes," replied Mary, "I came with that intention, and you look as if joy was yet to be given. Well," she continued after a pause, "I always thought you and Mr. Lloyd were different from every body else in the world, but now you puzzle me more than ever. I expected to see your aunt Wilson look grum—that's natural to her, when any good befalls any one else; and Elvira, who every body knows has been setting her cap every way for Erskine, ever since she was old enough to think of a husband; she has a right to have her eyes as red as a ferret's. But there is Mr. Lloyd, looking as sorrowful as if he had seen some great trouble, and could not relieve it; and you, my dear child, I have seen you pass through many a dark passage of your life with a happier face than you wear now, when you are going to have the pride of the county for your husband, to be mistress of the beautiful house on the hill, and have every thing heart can desire."

Jane made no explanation, nor reply, and after a few moments consideration Mary proceeded—"To be sure, I could wish Erskine was more like Mr. Lloyd; but then he is six or eight years younger than Mr. Lloyd, and in that time, with your tutoring, you may make him a good deal like Mr. Lloyd (Mr. Lloyd was Mary's beau-ideal of a man); that is, if your endeavours are blessed. It is true, I always thought you would not marry any man that was not religious; not but what 'tis allowable, for even professors do it; but then, Jane, you are more particular and consistent than a great many professors; and, I know, you think there is nothing binds hearts together like religion—that bond endures where there is neither marrying nor giving in marriage."

Poor Jane had listened to Mary's pros and cons with considerable calmness; but now she laid her head in her friend's lap, and gave vent to the feelings, she had been all day arguing down, by a flood of tears. "Ah! my dear Jane, is it *there* the shoe pinches? I an't sorry to find you have thought of it though. If the 'candle of the Lord' is lighted up in the heart, we ought to look at every thing by that light. But now you have decided, turn to the bright side. I don't know much about Mr. Erskine; he is called a nice young man, and who knows what he may become, when he sees how good and how beautiful it is to have the whole heart and life ordered and governed by the christian rule. I often think to myself, Jane, that your life, and Mr. Lloyd's too, are better than preaching. Don't take on so, my child," she continued, soothingly, "you have Scripture for you; for the Bible says, 'the believing wife may sanctify the unbelieving husband;' and that must mean that her counsel and example shall win him back to the right way, and persuade him to walk in the paths of holiness. Cheer up, my child, there is a good ministry before you; and I feel as if you had many happy days to come yet. Those that sow in tears, shall reap with joy. It is a load off my mind, at any rate, that you are away from your aunt's, and under good Mrs. Harvey's roof. I stopped at your aunt's on my way here, and she raised a hue and cry about your leaving her house so suddenly: she said, your grand fortune had turned your head; 'she was not disappointed, she had never expected any gratitude from you! but 'twas not for worldly hire she did her duty!' Poor, poor soul! I would not judge her uncharitably; but I do believe she has the 'hope that will perish.' I just took no notice of her, and came away. As I was passing through the kitchen, Sukey says to me, "Mrs. Wilson may look out for other *help*, for now Miss Jane, the only righteous one, is gone out from us, I sha'nt stay to hear nothing but disputings, and scoldings, and prayers." But, says I, Sukey, you don't object to the prayers? Yes, says she, I don't like lip-prayers—it is nothing but a mockery."

"Sukey has too much reason," replied Jane. "But now, Mary, you must not think from what you have seen that I am not happy, for I have reason to be grateful, and I ought to be very, very happy."

'*Ought*,' thought Mary, 'she may be *contented*, and *resigned*, and even *cheerful*, because she *ought*—but happiness is not duty-work.' However, she had discretion enough to suppress her homely metaphysics; and patting Jane's head affectionately, she replied, "Yes, my child, and if you wish it, I will set these tears down for tears of joy, not sorrow." Jane smiled at her friend's unwonted sophistry, and they parted: Mary, confirmed in a favourite notion, that every allotment of Providence is designed as a trial for the character; that all will finally work together for good; and that Jane was going on in the path to perfection, which, though no methodist, she was not (in her partial friend's opinion,) far from attaining. Jane was very much relieved by Mary's wise suggestions and sincere sympathy.

A sagacious observer of human nature and fortunes has said, that "if there were more knowledge, there would be less envy." The history of our heroine is a striking exemplification of the truth of this remark: when all was darkness without, she had been looked upon by the compassionate as an object of pity, for they could not see the sunshine of the breast; and now that she was considered as the chief favourite of the fickle goddess, there was not one that would have envied her, if the internal conflict she suffered—if that most unpleasant of all feelings, disagreement with herself, had been as visible, as her external fortunes were.

Erskine was in too good humour with himself, and with Jane, to find fault with any thing: yet he certainly was a little disappointed, that in spite of his earnest persuasions to the contrary, she firmly persisted in the plan of the school; and we fear he was surprised, perhaps slightly mortified, that she showed no more joy at having secured a station, to which he knew so many had aspired.

CHAPTER XII

The world is still deceived with ornament.
In law, what plea so tainted and corrupt,
But, being season'd with a gracious voice,
Obscures the show of evil?

Merchant of Venice

Jane entered upon the duties of her new vocation with more energy and interest than could have been reasonably expected from a young lady who had so recently entered into an engagement, and one which opened upon her the most flattering prospects. She already felt the benefits resulting from the severe discipline she had suffered in her aunt's family. She had a rare habit of putting *self* aside: of deferring her own inclinations to the will, and interests, and inclinations of others. A superficial survey of the human mind in all its diversity of conditions, will convince us that it may be trained to any thing; else, how shall we account for the proud exultation of a savage amidst the cruellest tortures his triumphant enemy can inflict; or for any of the wonderful phenomena of enterprise, of fortitude, of patience, in beings whose physical natures are so constituted, that they instinctively shrink from suffering?

Our fair young readers (if any of that class condescend to read this unromantic tale) will smile at the idea that Jane had any further occasion for the virtues of adversity; but she was far from being happy; she had not that firm confidence in the character of her lover that could alone have inspired the joy of hope, and secured a quiet spirit. Since her engagement, and even before, and ever since she had been interested in Erskine, she had not dared to sound the depths of her heart. Though quite a novice in the experience of love, she would have been able to detect its subtleties; she would have been able to ascertain the nature, and amount of her affection for Erskine, had she not been driven by his apparent magnanimity, and the oppression of her relations, to a sudden decision.

We appeal then once more to our fair young readers, and trust their justice will aware to our heroine some praise, for her spirited and patient performance of her duties to her young pupils, who were very far from imagining that their kind and gentle teacher had any thing in the world to trouble her, or to engage her mind, but their wants and pursuits.

Her disquietude did not escape the quickened vision of her vigilant friend Mr. Lloyd; he observed the shadows of anxiety settling on her usually bright and cheerful countenance, but even he had no conception of the extent of her busy apprehensions and secret misgivings.

Week after week passed away, and there seemed to be no prospect that any thing would occur to free Jane from the very unpleasant situation in which her aunt's accusations had placed her. Erskine became restless and impatient, derided all Jane's arguments in favour of delaying their marriage, and finally affected to distrust her affection for him. If the undefined, and undefinable sentiment which was compounded in Jane's heart of youthful preference and gratitude, was not love. Jane believed it was, and she at last yielded a reluctant consent, that the marriage should take place at the end of three months, even though nothing should occur to release her from her aunt's power.

It was a few days after this promise had been given, that as she was one day returning from her school, Erskine joined her.—"Your friend Robert Lloyd," said, he, "has taken a mighty fancy to me of late, I cannot conceive what is the reason for it."

Jane blushed, for she thought he might have guessed the reason. "I am glad of it," she replied, "for he seems to have withdrawn his friendship from me, and you are the only person, Edward, to whom I should be resigned to have it transferred."

"Ah, Jane! you need not be alarmed; he and I should never mix, any more than oil and vinegar."

"I am sorry for that; but which is the oil, and which the vinegar?"

"Oh, he is the oil, soft—neutralizing—rather tasteless; while I, you know, have a character of my own—am positive—am—but perhaps it would not be quite modest for me to finish the parallel. To confess the truth to you, Jane, I have always had an aversion to Quakers; they are a very hypocritical sect, depend upon it; pretending, sly, cheating rogues."

"That's a harsh judgment," replied Jane, with some warmth, "and a prejudice, I think; is not Mr. Lloyd the only Quaker you know?"

"Why—ye—yes, the only one I know much of."

"And does he justify your opinion?"

"I don't know; it takes a great while to find them out; and even if Lloyd should be what he would seem, the exception only proves the rule. I have always disliked Quakers. I remember a story my father used to tell, when I was a child, about his being over-reached in a most ingenious, practised manner, by one of the scoundrels, as he called the whole race. It was not an affair of any great moment; but no man likes to be outwitted in a bargain, and my father used to say it gave him an antipathy to the very name of a Quaker." ⸱

"I think your father was in fault," replied Jane, "so carelessly to implant a prejudice, which, as it seems to have had very slight ground, I trust has not taken such deep root that it cannot be easily eradicated."

"There is more reason in my judgment than you give me credit for," replied Edward pettishly. "If they are an upright, frank people, why is the world kept in ignorance of their belief? The Quakers have no creed; and though I have no great faith in the professors of any sect, yet they ought to let you know what they do think: it is fair and above board. You may depend upon it, Jane, the Quakers are a jesuitical people."

"Have you ever read any of their books?" inquired Jane.

"I read them!" he replied, laughing; "why, my dear girl, do you take me for a theologian? No—I never read the books of any sect; and Quaker books, I believe there are not. Quaker books!" he continued, still laughing, "no, no—I shall never addict myself to divinity, till Anne Ratcliffe writes sermons, and Tom Moore warbles hymns."

Jane did not join in his laugh; but replied, "There is a book, Edward, that contains the creed of the Quakers; a creed to which they have never presumed to add any thing, nor have they taken any thing from it; the only creed to which they think it right to require the assent of man, and from which no rational man can dissent—that book is *the Bible*! and," she continued, earnestly, "their faith in this creed is shown by their works. My dear Edward, examine their history for their vindication."

"That I shall not, while their cause has so fair a champion."

"Spare me your sarcasms, Edward, and let me entreat you to look at the life of their wise and excellent Penn. See him patiently and firmly enduring persecution, and calumny, and oppression at home; giving up his time, his fortune, his liberty, to the cause of suffering humanity, in every mode of its appeal to his benevolence. Follow him with his colony to the wilderness, and see him the only one of all the colonial leaders (I grieve that I cannot except our fathers, the pilgrims) the only one who treated the natives of the land with justice and mercy. Our fathers, Edward, refused to acknowledge the image of God in the poor Indian. They affected to believe they were the children of the evil one, and hunted them like beasts of prey, calling them 'worse than Scythian wolves;' while Penn, and his peaceful people, won their confidence, their devotion, by treating them with even-handed justice, with brotherly kindness; and they had their reward; they lived unharmed among them, without forts, without a weapon of defence. Is it not the Friends that have been foremost and most active in efforts for the abolition of slavery? Among what people do we find most reformers of the prisons—guardians of the poor and the oppressed—most of those who 'remember the forgotten, and attend to the neglected—who dive into the depths of dungeons, and plunge into the infection of hospitals'?"

There was a mingled expression of archness and admiration in Edward's smile as he replied, "My dear Jane, you are almost fit to speak in meeting. All that your defence wants in justness, is made up by the eloquence of your eye and your glowing cheek. I think friendship is a stronger feeling in your heart than love, Jane," he continued, with a pene-trating look that certainly did not abate the carnation of her cheek. "If I, and all my ancestors had gone on crusades and pilgrimages, the spirit would not have moved you to such enthusiasm in our cause, as you manifest for the broad-brimmed, straight-coated brethren of *friend Lloyd*."

"Edward, have you yet to learn of me, that I speak least of what I feel most?"

The gentleness of Jane's manner, and the tenderness of her voice, soothed her lover; and he replied, "Forgive me, dear Jane, a little jealousy; you know jealousy argues love. To confess to you the honest truth, I felt a little more ticklish than usual, this evening, on the subject of quakerism. I had just parted with Mr. Lloyd; and he has been earnestly recommending to me, to undertake a reform in our poor-laws, by which, he thinks, that we should rid ourselves of the burden of supporting many who are not necessarily dependant on us, and improve the condition of those who are. The plan seems to me to be good and feasible."

"And what then, Edward, provoked your displeasure?"

"Why, he wished me to take the whole conduct of it. He preferred the plan should appear to originate with me; that I should head a petition to the Legislature; and, if we succeeded, that I should superintend the execution of the plan."

"Still, dear Edward, I see any thing but offence in all this."

"Because your eye-sight is a little dimmed by your partiality. Do you believe, Jane, that any man would be willing to transfer to another all the merit and praise of a scheme, which, if it succeeds, will be a most important benefit to the community; will be felt, and noticed, and applauded by every body? No—there is some design lurking under this specious garb of disinterestedness—disinterestedness! it only exists in the visions of poets, or the Utopian dreams of youth; or, perhaps, embodied in the fine person of a hero of romance."

"Oh! my dear Edward, it does exist; it is the principle, the spirit of the Christian!"

"*Par exemple*—of your aunt Wilson, and of sundry other staunch professors I could mention, who,

> "If *self* the wavering balance shake,
> It's *never* right adjusted."

"Is it fair," replied Jane, "to condemn a whole class because some of its members are faithless and disloyal? A commander does but *decimate* a mutinous corps; and you exclude the whole from your confidence, because a few are treacherous. I allow," continued Jane, "there are few, very few, who are perfectly disinterested; but every Christian, in proportion to his fidelity to the teachings and example of his Master, will be moved and governed by this principle."

Perhaps Edward felt a passing conviction of the truth of Jane's assertions; at any rate, he made no reply, and afterwards he shunned the subject; and even Jane seemed to shrink from it as one upon which they had no common feeling.

The day before entering on the duties of her second school-term, Jane determined to indulge herself in a solitary walk to the cottage of old John of the Mountain. She had purchased some comforts for the old people, with a part of her small earnings, and she knew if she carried them herself she should double their value. She found the way without difficulty, for her night-walk had indelibly impressed it on her memory. On her approach to the cottage, and as she emerged from the wood, she perceived just on its verge a slight rising in the form of a grave; a wild rose-bush grew beside it. Jane paused for a moment, and plucking one of the flowers, she said, 'fragrant and transient, thou art a fit emblem of the blasted flower below!' As she turned from the grave, she perceived that a magical change had been wrought upon John's hut. Instead of a scarcely habitable dwelling, of decayed logs, filled in with mud, she saw a neat little framed house, with a fence around it, and a small garden annexed to it, enclosed by the logs of the former building. Jane hastened forward, and entered the cottage with the light step of one who goes on an errand of kindness.

"Who would have thought," said the good dame, as she dusted a chair and offered it to Jane, "of your coming all this way to see whether we were above ground yet?"

"Ah," said John, "there are some in this world, a precious few, who remember those that every body else forgets."

"I could not forget you, my good friends," replied Jane, "though John does not come any more to put me in mind of you."

"Why, Miss Jane," said John, "I grow old, and I have been but twice to the village since that mournful night you was here, and then I was in such a worrying matter that I did not think even of you."

"What have you had to disturb you?" inquired Jane. "I hoped from finding you in this nice new house that all had gone well since I saw you."

"Ah," replied John, "I have been greatly favoured; but the storm came before the calm. Miss Jane, did you never hear of my *law-suit*? the whole town was alive with it."

Jane assured John that she had never heard a word of it; that she had a little school to take care of; and that she saw very few persons, and heard little village news, even when it was so important as his law suit.

"Then, Miss Jane," said John, "if you have time and patience to hear an old man's story, I will tell you mine.—It is fifty years since my old woman and I settled down in these woods. Like all our fellow-creatures, we have had our portion of storms and sunshine: it has pleased the Lord to lop off all our branches, to cut down the little saplings that grew up at our feet, and leave us two lonely and bare trunks, to feel, and resist the winds of heaven as we may: two old evergreens," he continued, with a melancholy smile, "that flourish when every thing has faded about them. Yes, fifty years I have seen the sun come over that mountain every morning; and there is not a tree in all these thick woods but it seems like an old friend to me. Here my sons and daughters have been born to me, and here I have buried them, all but poor Jem, who you know was lost at sea. They died when they were but little children, and nobody remembers them but us; but they are as fresh in our minds as if it was but yesterday they were playing about us, with their laughing eyes and rosy cheeks. This has not much to do with my law-suit," continued John, after a pause, and clearing his voice, "only that I shall want some excuse for loving the old rookery so well before I get through with my story. I hired this bit of land of a man that's been dead twenty years, and it has changed hands many a time since, but I have always been able to satisfy for the rent; it was but a trifle, for no one but I would fancy the place. Lately it's come into the hands of the two young Woodhulls, by the death of the Deacon their father. They are two hard-favoured, hard-hearted, wild young chaps, Miss Jane, that think all the world was made for them, and their pleasure. If my memory serves me, it was just one week after you was here, that they were hunting up in these woods with young Squire Erskine. John, the oldest, took aim at a robin that was singing on the tree just before my door: it had built its nest there early in the summer; we had fed it with crumbs from our table, and it was as tame as a chicken. I told this to them, and begged the little innocent's life so earnestly, that the boys laughed, but Erskine said, "Let the old fool have his way." They said it was nonsense to give up to my whims, and told me to take away my hand, (for I had raised it up to protect the nest) or they would fire through it. I did take it away, and the nest with it, and brought it into the house. They came swearing in, and demanded the bird. I refused to give it up; they grew more and more angry: may be Erskine might have brought them to reason, but he had walked away. They said it was their land, and their bird, and they would not be thwarted by me; and they called me, and my wife too, many a name that was too bad for a decent person's ear. They worked themselves up to a fury, and then warned me off the ground. I made no reply; for I thought when they got over their passion they'd forget it. But they returned the next day with handspikes, and threatened to pull the house down on our heads, if we did not come out of it. I have had a proud spirit in my day, Miss Jane, but old age and weakness have tamed it. I begged them to spare us our little dwelling, with tears in my eyes; and my poor old woman prayed she might bring out the few *goods* we had; but oh! 'a fool in his folly is like a bear robbed of her whelps.' They said they would dust our *goods* for us; and so we came out and turned away our faces; but we heard the old house that had sheltered us so long crumble to pieces, as you'd crush an egg-shell in your hand; yes, and we heard their loud deriding laugh; but thank the Lord, we were too far off, to hear the jokes they passed between every peal of laughter. Ah, there is more hope of any thing than of a hard heart in a young body."

"Can it be possible," interrupted Jane, "that for so slight a cause the Woodhulls could do you such an injury?"

"It is even so," replied John; "youth is headstrong, and will not bear crossing."

"But where did you find a shelter?"

"I led my wife down the other side of the mountain, to one Billy Downie's, a soft feeling creature, who has more goodness in his heart than wit in his head, and he made us kindly welcome. I left my wife there, and the next day I came over to the village, to see if the law would give me justice of those that had no mercy. I should have gone to Squire Erskine with my case, for I knew he was called a fine pleader, though he is too wordy to suit me—but he was a friend of the Woodhulls, and so I applied to the stranger that's lately moved in: he proved a raw hand. The trial was appointed for the next Saturday. The day came; and all the men in the village were collected at the tavern, for Erskine was to plead for the Woodhulls, and every body likes to hear his silver tongue."

"Erskine plead for the Woodhulls!" exclaimed Jane.

"Oh yes, Miss Jane; for, as I told you, they are very thick. My attorney was a kind of a 'prentice-workman at the law; he was afraid of Erskine too; and he stammered, and said one thing and meant another, and made such a jingle of it, I could not wonder the justice and the people did not think I had a good claim for damages. But still, the plain story was so much against the Woodhulls, and the people of the village are so friendly-like to me, that it is rather my belief, I should have been righted if Erskine had not poured out such a power of words, that he seemed to take away people's senses. He started with what he called a proverb of the law, and repeated it so many times, I think I can never forget it, for it seemed to be the hook he hung all his arguifying upon. It was '*cujus est solum, ejus est usque ad cœlum*, (we have taken the liberty slightly to correct the old man's quotation of the Latin); which, if I rightly understood, it means, that whoever owns the soil, owns all above it to the sky; and though it stands to reason it can't be so, yet Erskine's fine oration put reason quite out of the question; and so the justice decided that the Woodhulls had a right to do what seemed good in their own eyes with my furniture; and then he gave me a bit of an exhortation, and told me I should never make out well in the world, if I did not know more of the laws of the land! and concluded with saying, I ought to be very thankful I had so little to be destroyed. I said nothing; but I thought it was late in the day for me to study the laws of the land; and my mite was as much to me as his abundance to him. When the trial was over, Erskine and the Woodhulls invited the justice and the company into the bar-room to treat them; and through the open door I heard Erskine propose a bumper to those who knew how to maintain their rights. "No," Woodhull said, "it should be to him who knew how to defend a friend"—right or wrong, thought I. But," said John, pausing, "my story is too long for you, Miss Jane."

Jane had turned away her head; she now assured John, she was listening to every word he said, and begged him to go on.

"Well, Miss, I thought I was alone in the room, and I just let out my heart, as you know a body will when he thinks there is no eye, but His that's above, sees him. I saw nothing before Sarah and I, but to go upon the town, and that's what I always had a dread of; for, though I have been a poor man all my life, Miss Jane, what I had was my own. I have been but weakly since I was a boy, but my woman and I have been sober and industrious. We have always had a shelter for ourselves; and sometimes, too, for a poor houseless creature that had not a better; and we wanted but little, and we were independent: and then you know, what the town gives is neither given nor taken with a good will. Well, as I said, I thought I was alone in the room; but I heard a slight noise behind me, and there was one who had not followed the multitude; he had a clear open face, and *that look*—I can't justly describe it, Miss Jane, but it seems as if it was the light of good deeds sent back again; or, may be, the seal the Lord puts upon his own children—and pity and kindness seemed writ in every line of his face. Do you know who I mean?"

"Mr. Lloyd," she replied, in a scarcely audible voice.

"Yes, yes—any body that had ever seen him would guess. He beckoned to me to shut the door, and asked me if I had any particular attachment to this spot; and I owned to him, as I have to you, my childishness about it; and he smiled, and said, he was afraid I was too old to be cured of it; and then asked, if I believed I could persuade the young men to sell as much of the land as I should want. I was sure I could, for I know they are wasteful and ravenous for money, and besides they had had their will, and the land was of no use to them. And then he told me, Miss Jane, that he would give me the money for the land, if I could make a bargain with the Woodhulls, and enough besides to build me a comfortable little house. I could not thank him—I tried, but I could not; and so he just squeezed my hand, and said, he understood me—and charged me to keep it a secret where I got help; and I have minded him till this day, but I could not keep it from you."

"You'd better stop now, John," said the old woman, "for the long walk, and the long story, have quite overdone Miss Jane; she has had the flushes this half hour."

Jane was obliged to own she did not feel well; but after drinking some water, she made an effort to compose herself, and asked the old man, "What reason he had to think the Woodhulls and Erskine were intimate friends?"

"Why, did you never hear, Miss, that it was Erskine that got John Woodhull clear when Betsy Davis sued him for breach of promise? I was summoned to court as a witness. It was a terrible black business; but Erskine made it all smooth; and after the trial was past, I overheard these chaps flattering Erskine till they made him believe he was more than mortal. At any rate, they put such a mist before his eyes, that he could not see to choose good from evil, else he never would have chosen them for his companions; he never would have been led to spend night after night with them at the gambling club."

"At the gambling club, John!—where—what do you mean?" and poor Jane clasped her hands together, and looked at him with an expression of such wretchedness, that the old man turned his eyes from her to his wife and back again to Jane, as if he would, but dared not, inquire the reason of her emotion.

"I have done wrong," he stammered out, "old fool that I was. Erskine is your friend, Miss Jane. The Lord forgive me," he added, rising and walking to the door. Jane had risen also, and with a trembling hand was tying on her hat. "And the Lord help thee, child," he continued, turning again towards her, "and keep thee from every snare. Well, well!—I never should have thought it."

Jane felt humbled by the old man's sympathy; and yet it was too sincere, too kindly felt, to be repressed. She was hastening away, when Sarah said, "You have forgotten your bundle, Miss."

"It is for you, my good friend," she replied; and, without awaiting their thanks, she bade them farewell, and was soon out of sight of the old man, whose eyes followed her quick footsteps till she was hid by the adjoining wood. He then turned from the door, and raised his hands and his faded eye, glistening with the gathering tears, to Heaven—"Oh Lord!" he exclaimed, "have mercy on thy young servant. Suffer not this child of light to be yoked to a child of darkness."

We believe that, in all classes and conditions, women are more inclined to look on the bright side of matrimony than men. In this case Sarah, after a little consideration, said, "I'm a thinking, John, you take on too much;

you are a borrowing trouble for Miss Jane. She is a wise, discreet young body, and she may cure Mr. Erskine of his faults. Besides, he may have his vagaries, and that's no uncommon thing for a young man; but then he is not wicked and hard-hearted like the Woodhulls."

"No, no, Sarah, he an't so bad as the Woodhulls, but he has been a wilful spoilt child from the beginning: he is a comely man to look to, and he has a glib tongue in his head; but he is all for self—all for self, Sarah. You might as well undertake to make the stiff branches of that old oak tender and pliable as the sprouts of the sapling that grows beside it, as to expect Miss Jane can alter Erskine. No—he alone can do it with whom all things are possible. We have no right to expect a miracle. She has no call to walk upon the sea, and we cannot hope a hand will be stretched out to keep her from sinking. It is the girl's beauty has caught him; and when that is gone, and it is a quickly fading flower, she will have no hold whatever on him."

We know not how long the old man indulged in his reflections, for he was not again interrupted by Sarah, whose deference for her husband's superior sagacity seems to have been more habitual than even her namesake's of old.

Our unhappy heroine pursued her way home, her mind filled with 'thick-coming' and bitter fancies, revolving over and over again the circumstances of John's narrative. He had thrown a new light on the character of her lover; and she blamed herself, that faults had seemed so dim to her, which were now so glaring. She was not far from coming to the result, which, we trust, our readers have expected from the integrity and purity of her character. "If I had remained ignorant of his faults," she thought, "I should have had some excuse; I might then have hoped for assistance and blessing in my attempts to reform him. It would be presumption to trust, now, in any efforts I could make; and what right have I, with my eyes open, to rush into a situation where my own weak virtues may be subdued by trials—must be assailed by temptation? Oh! when I heard him speak lightly of religion, how could I hope he would submit to its requisitions and restraints? I started at the first thought, that he was unprincipled; and yet I have always known there was no immoveable basis for principle, but religion. Selfish—vain—how could I love him! And yet—and she looked at the other side of the picture— his preference of me was purely disinterested—an orphan—destitute— almost an outcast—liable to degradation—and he has exposed himself to all the obloquy I may suffer—and does he not deserve the devotion of my life?" A moment before, she would have answered her self-interrogation in the negative; but now she seemed losing herself in a labyrinth of opposing duties. She thought that she ought not to place implicit reliance in John's statements. He might have exaggerated Erskine's faults. In his situation, it was natural he should; but he had such a calm, sober way with him, every word bore the impress of truth. The story of the gambling club had turned the scale; but John might have been misinformed.

Thus, after all her deliberations, Jane re-entered her home, without having come to any decision. Though we believe the opinion of a great moralist is against us, we doubt if "decision of character" belongs to the most scrupulously virtuous.

CHAPTER XIII

It is religion that doth make vows kept,
But thou hast sworn against religion;
Therefore, thy latter vow against thy first
Is in thyself rebellion to thyself:
And better conquest never canst thou make
Than arm thy constant and thy nobler parts
Against these busy loose suggestions.

King John.

As Jane entered Mrs. Harvey's door she met her kind hostess just returning from a walk, her face flushed with recent pleasure. "Where upon earth have you been?" she exclaimed. "Ah! if you had gone with me, you would not have come home with such a wo-begone face. Not a word! Well—nothing for nothing is my rule, my dear; and so you need not expect to hear where I have been, and what superb papers have come from New-York, for the front rooms; and beautiful china, and chairs, and carpets, and a fine work-table, for an industrious little lady, that shall be nameless; all quite too grand for a sullen, silent, deaf and dumb schoolmistress." She added, playfully, "if our cousin Elvira had been out in such a shower of gold, we should have been favoured with sweet smiles and sweet talk for one year at least. But there comes he that will make the bird sing, when it won't sing to any one else; and so, my dear, to escape chilling a lover's atmosphere, or being melted in it, I shall make my escape."

Jane would gladly have followed her, but she sat still, after hastily throwing aside her hat, and seizing the first book that she could lay her hands upon, to shelter her embarrassment. She sat with her back to the door.

Edward entered, and walking up to her, looked over her shoulder as if to see what book had so riveted her attention. It chanced to be Penn's

"Fruits of Solitude." "Curse on all quakers and quakerism!" said he, seizing the book rudely and throwing it across the room; "wherever I go, I am crossed by them."

He walked about, perturbed and angry. Jane rose to leave him, for now, she thought, was not the time to come to an explanation; but Erskine was not in a humour to be opposed in any thing. He placed his back against the door, and said, "No, Jane, you shall not leave me now. I have much to tell you. Forgive my violence. There is a point beyond which no rational creature can keep his temper. I have been urged to that point; and, thank Heaven, I have not learnt that smooth-faced hypocrisy that can seem what it is not."

Jane trembled excessively. Erskine had touched the 'electric chain;' she sunk into a chair, and burst into tears.

"I was right," he exclaimed, "it is by your authority, and at your instigation, that I am dogged from place to place by that impertinent fellow; you have entered into a *holy league*; but know, Miss Elton, there is a tradition in our family, that no Erskine was ever ruled by his wife; and the sooner the lady who is destined to be mine learns not to interfere in my affairs, the more agreeable it will be to me, and the more safe for herself."

Jane's indignation was roused by this strange attack; and resuming her composure, she said, "If you mean that I shall understand you, you must explain yourself, for I am ignorant and innocent of any thing you may suspect me of."

"Thank heaven!" replied Erskine, "I believe you, Jane; you know in the worst of times I have believed you; and it was natural to be offended that you should distrust me. You shall know the 'head and front of my offending.' The sins that have stirred up such a missionary zeal in that body of quakerism, will weigh very light in the scales of love."

"Perhaps," said Jane gravely, "I hold a more impartial balance than you expect."

"Then you do not love me, Jane, for love is, and ought to be, blind; but I am willing to make the trial, I will never have it repeated to me, that 'if you knew all, you would withdraw your affections from me.' No one shall say that you have not loved me, with all my youthful follies on my head. I know you are a little puritanical; but that is natural to one who has had so much to make her miserable: the unhappy are apt to affect religion. But you are young and curable, if you can be rescued from this quaker climate and influence."

Edward still rattled on, and seemed a little to dread making the promised communication; but at last, inferring from Jane's seriousness that she was anxious, and impatient himself to have it over, he went on to tell her—that from the beginning of their engagement Mr. Lloyd had undertaken the *surveillance* of his morals; that if he had not been fortified by his antipathy to Quakers, he should have surrendered his confidence to him.

"No gentleman," he said, "no man of honourable feeling—no man of proper sensibility—would submit to the interference of a stranger—a man not much older than himself—in matters that concerned himself alone; it was an intolerable outrage. If Jane was capable of a fair judgment, she would allow that it was so."

Jane mildly replied, that she could only judge from the facts; as yet she had heard nothing but accusations. Erskine said, he had imagined he was stating his case in a court of love and not of law; but he had no objection, since his judge was as sternly just as an old Roman father, to state facts. He could pardon Mr. Lloyd his eagerness to make him adopt his plans of improvement in the natural and moral world: to the first he might have been led by his taste for agriculture, (which he believed was unaffected) and to the second he was pledged by the laws of holy quaker church. Still he said none but a Quaker would have thought of meddling with the affairs of people who were strangers to him—however, that might be pardonable: as he said before, he supposed every Quaker was bound to that officiousness, by an oath, or an *affirmation*, for tender conscience' sake. "But my sweet judge, you do not look propitious," Erskine continued after this misty preamble, from which Jane could gather nothing but that his prejudices and pride had thrown a dark shadow over all the virtues of Mr. Lloyd.

"I cannot, Erskine, look propitious on your sneers against the principles of my excellent friend."

"Perhaps," replied Erskine tartly, "his practice will be equally immaculate in your eyes. And now, Jane, I beseech you for once to forget that Mr. Lloyd is your *excellent friend*; a man who bestowed some trifling favours on your childhood, and remember the rights of one to whom you at least owe your love—though he would neither accept that, nor your gratitude, as a debt."

Jane assured him she was ready to hear any thing and every thing impartially that he would tell her. He replied, that he detested stoical impartiality; that he wished her to enter into his loves and his hates, without expecting a reason in their madness. But since you must have the reason, I will not withhold it. As I told you, I submitted to a thousand vexatious, little impertinences: he is plausible and gentlemanly in his manners, so there was nothing I could resent, till after a contemptible affair between John the old basketmaker and the Woodhulls, in which I used my humble professional skill to extricate my friends, who had been perhaps a little hasty in revenging the impertinence of the foolish old man. Lloyd was present at the trial before the justice: I fancied from the expression on his face that he wished my friends to be foiled, and this quickened my faculties. I succeeded in winning my cause in spite of law and equity, for they were both against me; and this you know is rather flattering to one's talents. The Woodhulls overwhelmed me with praises and gratitude. I felt sorry for the silly old fool, whom they had very unceremoniously unhoused, and I proposed a small subscription to enable him to pay the bill of costs, &c. which was his only receipt from the prosecution. I headed it, and it was soon made up; but the old fellow declined it with as much dignity as if he had been a king in disguise. It was an affair of no moment, and I should probably never have thought of it again, if Lloyd had not the next day made it the text upon which he preached as long a sermon as I would hear, upon the characters of the Woodhulls; he even went so far as to presume to remonstrate with me upon my connexion with them, painted their conduct on various occasions in the blackest colours, spoke of their pulling down the old hovel, which had in fact been a mere cumberer of the ground for twenty years, as an act of oppression and cruelty; said their habits were all bad; their pursuits all either foolish or dangerous. I restrained myself as long as possible, and then I told him, that I should not submit to hear any calumnies against my friends; friends who were devoted to me, who would go to perdition to serve me. If they had foibles, they were those that belonged to open, generous natures; they were open-handed, and open-hearted, and had not smothered their passions, till they were quite extinguished. I told him, they were honourable young men, not governed by the fear that 'holds the wretch in order.' He might have known that I meant to tell him they were what he was not; but he seemed quite unmoved, and I spoke more plainly. I had never, I told him, been accustomed to submit my conduct to the revision of any one; that he had no right, and I knew not why he presumed, to assume it, to haunt me like an external conscience; that my 'genius was not rebuking by his,' neither would it be, if all the marvelous light of all his brethren was concentrated in his luminous mind."

"Oh, Erskine, Erskine!" exclaimed Jane, "was this your return for his friendly warning?"

"Hear me through, Jane, before you condemn me. He provoked me more than I have told you. He said that I was responsible to you for my virtue; that I betrayed your trust by exposing myself to be the companion, or the prey, of the vices of others. Would you have had me borne this, Jane? Would you thank me for allowing, that he was more careful of your happiness than I am?"—"Well," added he, after a moment's pause, "as you do not reply, I presume you have not yet decided that point. We separated, my indignation roused to the highest pitch, and he cold and calm as ever. When we next met, there was no difference in his manners to me that a stranger would have observed; but I perceived his words were all weighted and measured, as if he would not venture soon again to disturb a lion spirit."

"Is that all?" asked Jane.

"Not half," replied Erskine; and after a little hesitation he continued, "I perceive that it is impossible for you to see things in the light I do. Your aunt with her everlasting cant, your methodist friend with her old maid notions, and this precise quaker, above all, have made you so rigid, have so bound and stiffened every youthful indulgent feeling, that I have as little hope of a favourable judgment, as a heretic could have had in the dark ages, from his triple-crowned tyrant."

"Then," said Jane, rising, "it is as unnecessary as painful for me to hear the rest."

"No, you shall not go," he replied; "I expect miracles from the touch of love. I think I have an advocate in your heart, that will plead for me against the whole 'privileged order,' of professors—of every cast. Do not be shocked, my dear Jane; do not, for your own sake, make mountains of mole-hills, when I tell you, that the young men of the village instituted a club, three or four months since, who meet once a week socially, perhaps a little oftener, when we are all about home: and"—he hesitated a moment, as one will when he comes to a ditch and is uncertain whether to spring over, to retreat, or to find some other way; but he had too much pride to conceal the fact, and though he feared a little to announce it, yet he was determined to justify it. Jane was still mute, and he went on—"We play cards; sometimes we have played later and higher perhaps than we should if we had all been in the leading-strings of prudence; all been bred quakers. Our club are men of honour and spirit, high-minded gentlemen; a few disputes, misunderstandings, might arise now and then, as they will among people who do not weigh every word, lest they should chance to have an idle one to account for; but, till the last evening, we have, in the main, spent our time together as whole-souled fellows should, in mirth and jollity. As I said, last evening unfortunately—"

"Tell me nothing more, Mr. Erskine; I have heard enough," interrupted Jane.

"What! you will not listen to friend Lloyd's reproaches; not listen to what most roused his holy indignation?"

"I have no wish to hear any thing further," replied Jane. "I have heard enough to make my path plain before me. I loved you, Edward; I confessed to you that I did."

"And you do not any longer?"

"I cannot; the illusion has vanished. Neither do you love me." Edward would have interrupted her, but she begged him to hear her, with a dignified composure, that convinced him this was no sudden burst of resentment, no girlish pique that he might sooth with flattery and professions. "A most generous impulse, Edward, led you to protect an oppressed orphan; and I thought the devotion of my heart and my life were small return to you. It is but a few months since. Is not love an engrossing passion? But what sacrifices have you made to it? Oh, Edward! if in the youth and spring of your affection, I have not had more power over you, what can I hope from the future?"

"Hope!—believe every thing, Jane. I will be as plastic as wax, in your hands. You shall mould me as you will."

"No, Edward; I have tried my power over you, and found it wanting. Broken confidence cannot be restored."

"Jane, you are rash; you are giving up independence—protection. If you reject me, who will defend you from your aunt? Do you forget that you are still in her power?"

"No," replied Jane; "but I have the defence of innocence, and I do not fear her. It was not your protection, it was not independence I sought, it was a refuge in your affection;—that has failed me. Oh, Edward!" she continued, rising, "examine your heart as I have examined mine, and you will find the tie is dissolved that bound us; there can be no enduring love without sympathy; our feelings, our pursuits, our plans, our inclinations, are all diverse."

"You are unkind, ungrateful, Jane."

"I must bear that reproach as I can; but I do not deserve it, Mr. Erskine."

Erskine imagined he perceived some relenting in the faltering of her voice, and he said, "Do not be implacable, Jane; you are too young, too beautiful, to treat the follies of youth as if they were incurable; give me a few months probation, I will do any thing you require; abandon the club, give up my friends."

Jane paused for a moment, but there was no wavering in her resolution—"No, Mr. Erskine; we must part now; if I loved you, I could not resist the pleadings of my heart."

Erskine entreated—promised every thing; till convinced that Jane did not deceive him or herself, his vanity and pride, mortified and wounded, came to his relief, and changed his entreaties to sarcasms. He said the rigour that would immolate every human feeling, would fit her to be the Elect Lady of a Shaker society; he assured her that he would emulate her stoicism.

"I am no stoic," replied Jane; and the tears gushed from her eyes. "Oh, Erskine! I would make any exertions, any sacrifices to render you what I once thought you. I would watch and toil to win you to virtue—to heaven. If I believed you loved me, I could still hope, for I know that affection is self-devoting, and may overcome all things. Edward," she continued, with a trembling voice, "there is one subject, and that nearest to my heart, on which I discovered soon after our engagement we were at utter variance. When I first heard you trifle with the obligations of religion, and express a distrust of its truths, I felt my heart chill. I reproached myself bitterly for having looked on your insensibility on this subject as the common carelessness of a gay young man, to be expected, and forgiven, and easily cured. These few short months have taught me much; have taught me, Erskine, not that religion is the only sure foundation of virtue—that I knew before—but they have taught me, that religion alone can produce unity of spirit; alone can resist the cares, the disappointments, the tempests of life; that it is the only indissoluble bond—for when the silver chord is loosed, this bond becomes immortal. I have felt that my most sacred pleasures and hopes must be solitary." Erskine made no reply; he felt the presence of a sanctified spirit. "You now know all, Erskine. The circumstances you have told me this evening, I partly knew before."

"From Lloyd?" said Edward. "He then knew, as he insinuated, why the 'treasure of your cheek had faded.'"

"You do him wrong. He has never mentioned your name since the morning I left my aunt's. I heard them, by accident, from John."

"It is, in truth, time we should part, when you can give your ear to every idle rumour;" he snatched his hat, and was going.

Jane laid her hand on his arm, "Yes, it is time," she said, "that we should part; but not in anger. Let us exchange forgiveness, Edward." Erskine turned and wept bitterly. For a few gracious moments his pride, his self-love, all melted away, and he felt the value, the surpassing excellence of the blessing he had forfeited. He pressed the hand Jane had given him, to his lips fervently, "Oh, Jane," he said, "you are an angel; forget my follies, and think of me with kindness."

"I shall remember nothing of the past," she said, with a look that had 'less of earth in it than heaven,' "but your goodness to me—God bless you, Edward; God bless you," she repeated, and they separated—for ever!

For a few hours Erskine thought only of the irreparable loss of Jane's affections. Every pure, every virtuous feeling he possessed, joined in a clamorous tribute to her excellence, and in a sentence of self-condemnation that could not be silenced. But Edward was habitually under the dominion of self-love, and every other emotion soon gave place to the dread of being looked upon as a rejected man. He had not courage to risk the laugh of his associates, or what would be much more trying, their affected pity; and to escape it all, he ordered his servant to pack his clothes, and make the necessary preparations for leaving the village in the morning, in the mail-stage for New-York. He was urged to this step too, by another motive, arising from a disagreeable affair in which he had been engaged— the affair which had induced Mr. Lloyd to make a second attempt to withdraw him from his vicious associates. At a recent meeting of the club, the younger Woodhull had introduced a gentleman who pretended to be a Mr. Rivington, from Virginia. Woodhull had met him at Saratoga Springs. They were kindred spirits, and, forming a sudden friendship, Rivington promised Woodhull that, after he had exhausted the pleasures of the Springs, he would come to ———, and pass a few days with him before his return to Virginia. Rivington was a fit companion for his new friend; addicted to a score of vices; gambling high, and out-drinking, out-swearing, and out-bullying his comrades. Edward was certainly far better than any other member of this precious association. He was, from the first, disgusted with the stranger, with his gross manners, and with his manifest indisposition to pay to him the deference he was accustomed to receive from the rest of the company. The club sat later than usual. Rivington's passions became inflamed by the liquor he had drank. A dispute arose about the play. Erskine and John Woodhull were partners. Rivington accused Woodhull of unfair play. Edward defended his partner. A violent altercation ensued between them. The lie was given and retorted in so direct a form as to afford ample ground for an honourable adjustment of the dispute.

Rivington said, "If he had to deal with a Virginian—a man of honour—the quarrel might be settled in a gentlemanly way; but a snivling cowardly Yankee had no honour to defend. Edward was provoked to challenge him; and arrangements were made for the meeting at day-light in the morning, in a neighbouring wood, which had never been disturbed by a harsher sound than a sportman's gun. The brothers were to act as seconds.

The parties were all punctual to their appointment. The morning of which they were going to make so unhallowed a use, was a most beautiful one. Nature was in a poetic mood; in a humour to give her votaries an opportunity to diversify her realities with the bright creations of their imaginations. The vapour had diffused itself over the valley, so that from the hill, which was the place of rendezvous, it appeared like a placid lake, that no 'breeze was upon;' from whose bosom rose the green spires of the poplar, rich masses of maple foliage, and the graceful and widely spreading boughs of the elm—

——————— "Jocund day
Stood tip-toe on the misty mountain's top,"

and sent her morning greetings to the white cliffs of the southern mountain,—brightened the mist that filled the deep indenting dells between the verdant heights, resembling them to island hills, and sending such a flood of light upon the western slopes, that they shone as if there had been a thousand streams there rejoicing in the sunbeams. But this appeal of Nature was unheeded and unnoticed by these rash young men. Her sacred volume is a sealed book to those who are inflamed by passion, or degraded by vice.

The ground was marked out, the usual distance prescribed by the seconds, and the principals were just about to take their stations, when they were interrupted by Mr. Lloyd, who, in returning from his morning walk, passed through this wood, which was within a short distance of his house. On emerging from the thick wood, into the open space selected by the young men, they were directly before him, so that it was impossible for him to mistake the design of their meeting.

"Confusion!" exclaimed Edward; mortified that Mr. Lloyd, of all men living, should have witnessed this scene; and then turning to him, for Mr. Lloyd was approaching him, "To what, Sir," said he haughtily, "do we owe the favour of your company?"

"Purely to accident, Mr. Erskine, or, I should say, to Providence, if I may be so happy as to prevent a rash violation of the laws of God and man."

"Stand off, Sir!" said Edward, determined now to brave Mr. Lloyd's opposition, "and witness, if you will, for you shall not prevent a brave encounter."

Mr. Lloyd had interposed himself between Edward and his adversary, and he did not move from his station. "Brave encounter!" he replied, pointing with a smile of contempt to Rivington, who was shaking as if he had an ague; "that young man's pale cheeks and trembling limbs do not look like 'imposters to true fear;' they do not promise the merit of bravery to your encounter, Mr. Erskine."

"The devil take the impertinent fellow!" exclaimed the elder Woodhull, (Edward's second); "proceed to your business, gentlemen."

Erskine placed himself in an attitude to fire, and raised his arm. Mr. Lloyd remained firm and immoveable. "Do you mean to take my fire, Sir?" asked Erskine. "If you continue to stand there, the peril be upon yourself; the fault rests with you."

"I shall risk taking the fire, if you dare risk giving it," replied Mr. Lloyd, coolly.

"Curse him!" said Woodhull, "he thinks you are afraid to fire."

This speech had the intended effect upon Erskine. "Give us the signal," he said, hastily.

The signal was given, and Edward discharged his pistol. The ball grazed Mr. Lloyd's arm, and passed off without any other injury. "It was bravely done," said he, with a contemptuous coolness, that increased, if any thing could increase the shame Erskine felt, the moment he had vented his passion by the rash and violent act. "We have been singularly fortunate," he continued, "considering thou hadst all the firing to thyself, and two fair marks. Poor fellow!" he added, turning to Rivington, "so broad a shield as I furnished for thee, I should have hoped would have saved some of this fright."

John Woodhull had perceived that his friend's courage, which, the preceeding evening, had been stimulated by the liquor, had vanished with the fog that clouded his reason; and ever since they came on the battle-ground, he had been vainly endeavouring to screw him up to the sticking point, by suggesting, in low whispers, such motives as he thought might operate upon him; but all his efforts were ineffectual. Rivington was, to use a vulgar expression, literally 'scared out of his wits.' When the signal was given for firing, he had essayed to raise his arm, but it was all unstrung by fear, and he could not move it. The sound of Erskine's pistol completed his dismay; he sunk on his knees, dropped his pistol, said he was willing to own he was no gentleman; he would beg Mr. Erskine's pardon, and all the gentlemen's pardon; he would do any thing almost the gentlemen would say.

John Woodhull felt his own reputation implicated by his principal's cowardice; and passionate and reckless, he seized the pistol, and would have discharged the contents at Rivington; but Mr. Lloyd, seeing his intention, caught hold of his arm, wrenched the pistol from him, fired it in the air, and threw it from him. "Shame on thee, young man!" he exclaimed, "does the spirit of murder so possess thee, that it matters not whether thy arm is raised against friend or foe?"

"He is no friend of mine," replied Woodhull, vainly endeavouring to extricate himself from Mr. Lloyd's manly grasp; he is a coward, and by my life and sacred honour!"——

"Oh, Mr. Woodhull! sir," interrupted Rivington, "I am your friend, sir, and all the gentlemen's friend, sir. I am much obliged to you, sir," turning to Mr. Lloyd, who could not help laughing at the eagerness of his cowardice; "I am sorry for the disturbance, gentlemen, and I wish you all a good morning, gentlemen!" and so saying, he walked off the ground as fast as his trembling limbs could take him.

Mr. Lloyd now released young Woodhull from his hold; and winding his handkerchief around his arm, which was slightly bleeding, he said, "I perceive, gentlemen, there is no further occasion for my interposition. I think the experience of this morning will not tempt you to repeat this singular disturbance of the peace of this community."

The party were all too thoroughly mortified to attempt a reply, and they separated. Erskine felt a most humiliating consciousness of his disgrace, but he had not sufficient magnanimity to confess it, nor even to express a regret that he had wounded a man, who exposed his life to prevent him from committing a crime. The Woodhulls were deprived of the pitiful pleasure of sneering at Mr. Lloyd's want of courage. The younger brother's arm still ached from his experience of Mr. Lloyd's physical strength; and they all felt the inferiority of their boastful, passionate, and reckless fool-hardiness, to the collected, disinterested courage of a peaceful man, who had risked his life in their quarrel.

To fill up the measure of their mortification, Rivington had not left the village two hours, before several persons arrived there in pursuit of him. They informed his new friends, that he was not a Virginian, a name that passes among our northern bloods as synonymous with gentility, high-mindedness, noble-daring, and other youthful virtues, but that he was a countryman of their own, a celebrated swindler, who had lived by his wits, ascending by regular gradations through the professions of hostler, dancing-master, and itinerant actor; and that having lately, by cleverness in managing the arts of his vocation, possessed himself of a large sum of money, he had made his debût as gentleman at the Springs.

After the events of the morning, Mr. Lloyd felt more anxiety than ever on Jane Elton's account; and never weary in well-doing, he determined to make one more effort to rescue Erskine from the pernicious society and influence of the Woodhulls. He solicited an interview with him; and without alluding to the events of the morning, he remonstrated warmly and kindly against an intimacy, of which the degradation and the danger were too evident to need pointing out. He trusted himself to speak of Jane, of her innocence, her purity, her trustful affection, her solitariness, her dependance.

At any other time, we cannot think Edward would have been unmoved by the eloquence of his appeal; but now he was exasperated by the mortifications of the morning; and when Mr. Lloyd said, "Erskine, if Jane Elton knew all, would she not withdraw her affections from thee?" he replied, angrily, "She shall know all. I have a right to expect she will overlook a few foibles; such as belong to every man of spirit. She owes me, at least, so much indulgence. She is bound to me by ties that cannot be broken—that she certainly cannot break." He burst away from Mr. Lloyd, and went precipitately to Mrs. Harvey's, where the explanation we have related ensued, and put a final termination to their unequal alliance.

The speculations of villagers are never at rest till they know the *wherefore* of the slightest movements of the prominent personages that figure on their theatre. Happily for our heroine, who was solicitous for a little while to be sheltered from the scrutiny and remarks of her neighbours, the affair of the duel soon became public, and sufficiently accounted for Erskine's abrupt departure.

Jane would have communicated to Mary, her kind, constant friend Mary Hull, the issue of her engagement; but it so happened, that she was at this time absent on a visit to her blind sister. She felt it to be just, that she should acquaint Mr. Lloyd with the result of an affair, in which he had manifested so benevolent and vigilant a care for her happiness. Perhaps she felt a natural wish, that he should know his confidence in her had not been misplaced. She could not speak to him on the subject, for their intercourse had been suspended of late; and besides, she was habitually reserved about speaking of herself. She sat down to address a note to him; and, after writing a dozen, each of which offended her in some point—either betrayed a want of delicacy towards Erskine, or a sentiment of self-complacency—either expressed too much, or too little— she threw them all into the fire, and determined to leave the communication to accident.

CHAPTER XIV

Oh, wad some pow'r the giftie gie us,
To see oursels as others see us!
It wad frae monie a blunder free us,
          And foolish notion:
What airs in dress an' gait wad lea'e us,
          And e'on devotion!

A few days after Erskine's departure, Mrs. Harvey entered Jane's room hastily,—"Our village," she exclaimed, "is the most extraordinary place in the world; wonders cease to be wonderful among us."

"What has happened now?" inquired Jane, "I know not from your face whether to expect good or evil."

"Oh evil, my dear, evil enough to grieve and frighten you. Your wretched cousin David Wilson has got himself into a scrape at last, from which all the arts of all his family cannot extricate him. You know," she continued, "that we saw an account in the New-York paper of last week, of a robbery committed on the mail-stage: the robbers have been detected and taken, and Wilson, who it seems had assumed a feigned name, is among them."

"And the punishment is death!" said Jane, in a tone of sorrow and alarm.

"Yes; so Mr. Lloyd says, by the laws of the United States, against which he has offended. Mr. Lloyd has been here, to request that you, dear Jane, will go to your aunt, and say to her that he is ready to render her any services in his power. You know he is acquainted in Philadelphia, where David is imprisoned, and he may be of essential use to him."

"My poor aunt, and Elvira! what misery is this for them!" said Jane, instinctively transfusing her own feelings into their bosoms.

"For your aunt it may be," replied Mrs. Harvey, "for I think nothing can quite root out the mother; but as for Elvira, I believe she is too much absorbed in her own affairs to think of David's body or soul."

"I will go immediately to my aunt; but what has happened to Elvira?"

"Why Elvira, it seems, during her visit to the west, met with an itinerant french dancing-master, who became violently enamoured of her, and who did not sigh or hope in vain. She probably knew his vocation would be an insuperable obstacle to her seeing him at home; and so between them they concerted a scheme to obviate that difficulty, by introducing him to Mrs. Wilson as a french physician, from Paris, who should volunteer his services to cure her scrofula, which, it is said, has lately become more troublesome than ever. By way of a decoy, he was to go upon the usual quack practice of 'no cure no pay.'"

"And this," exclaimed Jane, "is the sick physician we heard was at my aunt's?"

"Yes, poor fellow, and sick enough he has been. He arrived just at twilight, last week on Monday, and having tied his horse, he was tempted, by seeing the door of the chaise-house half open, to go in there to arrange his dress previous to making his appearance before Miss Wilson. He had hardly entered, before old Jacob coming along, saw the door open, and giving the careless boys (whom he supposed in fault) a reversed blessing, he shut and fastened it. It was chilly weather, you know, but there the poor fellow was obliged to stay the live-long night, and till Jacob, sallying forth to do his morning chores, discovered him half-starved and half-frozen. But," said Mrs. Harvey, "you are prepared to go to your aunt, and I am detaining you—you may ask the sequel of Elvira."

"Oh no, let me hear the rest of it; only be short, dear Mrs. Harvey, for if any thing is to be done for that wretched young man, not a moment should be lost."

"My dear, I will be as short as possible, but my words will not all run out of my mouth at once, as they melted out of Gulliver's horn. Well, this poor french doctor, dancer, or whatever he is, effected an interview with Elvira, before he was seen by the mother; and though no doubt she was shocked by his unsentimental involuntary vigil, she overlooked it, and succeeded in palming him off on the old lady as a foreign physician, who had performed sundry marvellous cures in his western progress. Mrs. Wilson submitted her disease to his prescription. In the meanwhile, he, poor wretch, as if a judgment had come upon him for his sins, has been really and seriously sick, in consequence of the exposure to the dampness of a September night, in his nankins; and Elvira has been watching and nursing him according to the best and most approved precedents to be found in ballads and romances."

"Is it possible," asked Jane, "that aunt Wilson should be imposed on for so long a time? Elvira is ingenious, and ready, but she is not a match for her quick-sighted mother."

"No, so it has proved in this case. The doctor became better, and the patient worse; his prescriptions have had a dreadful effect upon the scrofula; and as the pain increased, your aunt became irritable and suspicious. Last evening, she overheard a conversation between the hopeful lovers, which revealed the whole truth to her."

"And what has she done?"

"What could she do, my dear, but turn the good for nothing fellow out of doors, and exhaust her wrath upon Elvira. The dreadful news she received from David late last evening, must have driven even this provoking affair out of her troubled mind. But," said Mrs. Harvey, rising and going to the window, "who is that coming through our gate? Elvira, as I live!—what can she be after here?"

"Aunt has probably sent for me," replied Jane; and she hastened to open the door for her cousin, who entered evidently in a flutter. "I was just going to your mother's," said Jane.

"Stay a moment," said Elvira; "I must speak with you. Come into your room," and she hastened forward to Jane's apartment. She paused a moment on seeing Mrs. Harvey, and then begged she would allow her to speak with her cousin alone.

Mrs. Harvey left the apartment, and Elvira turned to Jane, and was beginning with great eagerness to say something, but she paused—unpinned her shawl, took it off, and then put it on again—and then asked Jane, if she had heard from Erskine; and, without waiting a reply, which did not seem to be very ready, she continued, "How glad I was he fought that duel; it was so spirited. I wish my lover would fight a duel. It would have been delightful if he had only been wounded."

Jane stared at her cousin, as if she had been smitten with distraction. "Elvira," she said, with more displeasure than was often extorted from her, "you are an incurable trifler! How is it possible, that at this time you can waste a thought upon Erskine or his duel?"

"Oh! my spirits run away from me, dear Jane; but I do feel very miserable," she replied, affecting to wipe away the tears from her dry eyes. Poor David!—I am wretched about him. He has disgraced us all. I suppose you have heard, too, about Lavoisier. Every body has heard of mother's cruelty to him and to me. Oh, Jane! he is the sweetest creature—the most interesting being"——

"Elvira," replied Jane, coldly, "I do not like to reproach you in your present affliction; but you strangely forget all that is due to your sex, by keeping up such an intercourse with a stranger—by ranting in this way about a wandering dancing-master—a foreigner."

"A foreigner, indeed! as if that was against him. Why, my dear, foreigners are much more genteel than Americans; and besides, Lavoisier is a Count in disguise. Oh! if you could only hear him speak French; it is as soft as an Eolian harp. Now Jane, darling, don't be angry with me. I am sure there never was any body so persecuted and unfortunate as I am. Nobody feels for me."

"It is impossible, Elvira, to feel for those who have no feeling for themselves."

"Oh, Jane! you are very cruel," replied Elvira, whimpering; "I have been crying ever since I received poor David's latter, and it was about that I came here; but you do not seem to have any compassion for our sorrows, and I am afraid to ask for what I came for."

"I cannot afford to waste any compassion on unnecessary or imaginary sorrows, Elvira. The real and most horrible calamity that has fallen upon you, requires all the exertions and feelings of your friends."

"That's spoken like yourself, dear, blessed Jane," said Elvira, brightening; "now I am sure you will not refuse me—you are always so generous and kind."

"I have small means to be generous," replied Jane; "but let me know, at once, what it is you want, for I am in haste to go to your mother."

"You are a darling, Jane—you always was."

"What is it you wish, Elvira?" inquired Jane again, aware that Elvira's endearments were always to be interpreted as a prelude to the asking of a favour.

"I wish, dear Jane," she replied, summoning all her resolution to her aid; "I wish you to lend me twenty dollars. If you had seen David's piteous letter to me, you could not refuse. It is enough to make any body's heart ache; he is down in a dark disagreeable dungeon, with nothing to eat, from morning to night, but bread and water. He petitions for a little money so earnestly, it would make your heart bleed to read his letter. Mother declares she will not send him a dollar."

"How do you intend sending the money to him?" asked Jane, rising and going to her bureau.

"Oh!" replied Elvira, watching Jane's movements, "you are a dear soul. It is easy enough getting the money to him. I heard, this morning, that

Mr. Harris is going on to the south; he starts this afternoon. I shall not mind walking to his house, though it is four miles from here; I shall go immediately, and I shall charge him to deliver the money himself. It will be such a relief and comfort to my unfortunate brother."

There seemed to be something in Elvira's eagerness to serve her brother, and in her newly awakened tenderness for him, that excited Jane's suspicions; for she paused in the midst of counting the money, turned round, and fixed a penetrating look upon her cousin. Elvira, without appearing to notice any thing peculiar in her expression, said (advancing towards her,) "Do be quick, dear Jane; it is a great way to Mr. Harris's; I am afraid I shall be late."

Jane had finished counting the money.

"Twenty dollars, is it, dear?" said Elvira, hastily and with a flutter of joy seizing it. "There are five dollars more," she continued, looking at a single bill Jane had laid aside; "let me have that too, dear; it will not be too much for David."

"I cannot," replied Jane; "that is all I have in the world, and that I owe to Mrs. Harvey."

"La, Jane! what matter is that; you can have as much money as you want of Erskine; and besides, you need not be afraid of losing it; I shall soon be of age, and then I shall pay you, for mother can't keep my portion from me one day after that. Then I will have a cottage. Lavoisier says, we can have no idea, in this country, how beautiful, a cottage is, *à la Française*. Do, dearest, let me have the other five."

"No," said Jane, disgusted with Elvira's importunity and levity, and replacing the note in her drawer; "I have given you all I possess in the world, and you must be contented with it."

Elvira saw that she should obtain no more. She hastily kissed Jane; and after saying, "Good bye, my dear, go to mother's, and stay till I come," she flew out of the house, exulting that her false pretences had won so much from her cousin. At a short distance from Mrs. Harvey's she joined her lover, according to a previous arrangement between them.

Lavoisier had procured a chaise from a neighbouring farmer, which was principally devoted to the transportation of its worthy proprietor and the partner of his joys to and from the meeting-house on Sundays and lecture days, but was occasionally hired out *to oblige* such persons as might stand in need of such an accommodation, and could afford to pay what was 'consistent' for it.

"Allons—marche donc!" said the dancing philosopher to his horse, after seating Elvira; and turning to her, he pressed one of her hands to his lips, saying, "Pardonnez-moi,"—adding, as he dropt it, "tout nous sourit dans la nature."

Elvira pointed out the road leading to the dwelling of a justice of the peace, a few miles beyond the line which divides the State of Massachusetts from that of New-York. They arrived at this temple of Hymen, and of petty litigation, about eleven in the morning. The justice was at work on his farm; a messenger was soon despatched for him, with whom he returned in about thirty minutes, which seemed as many hours to our anxious lovers.

"Dey say," said Lavoisier, "l'amour fait passer le temps, but in l'Amerique it is very differente."

The justice took Lavoisier aside, and inquired whether there were any objections to the marriage, on the part of the lady's friends.

"Objections!" said Lavoisier, "it is the most grande félicité to every body. You cannot conceive."

On being further interrogated, Lavoisier confessed that they came from Massachusetts; and being asked why they were not married at the place of the lady's residence, he said that "some personnes without sensibilité may wait, but for mademoiselle and me, it is impossible."

Elvira being examined apart, in like manner, declared that her intended husband's impatience and her own dislike to the formality of a publishment, had led them to avoid the usual mode and forms of marriage.

The justice, who derived the chief profits of his office from clandestine matches, and who had made these inquiries more because it was a common custom, than from any scruples of conscience, or sense of official duty, was perfectly satisfied; and after requiring from the bridegroom the usual promise to love and cherish; and from the bride, to love, cherish, and obey; pronounced them man and wife, and recorded the marriage in a book containing a record of similar official acts, and of divers suits and the proceedings therein.

The bride and bridegroom immediately set out for the North River, intending to embark there for New-York.

"These things do manage themselves better in France," said Lavoisier. "Les nôces qui se font ici—the marriages you make here—are as solemn que la sepulture—as to bury. Le Cupidon ici a l'air bien sauvage; if de little god was paint here, they would make him work as de justice. Eh bien!" said he, after a pause, "chacun a son métier; without some fermiers there should not be some maîtres-de-danse, some professeurs of de elegant arts: et sans les justices, you would not be mon ange—you would not be Madame Lavoisier."

Elvira was so occupied with the change in her condition, and the prospect before her, that she did not observe the direction in which they were travelling; and by mistake they took the road leading back through a cleft in the mountain towards a village in the vicinity of the one they had left.

As they ascended the top of a hill, their steed began to prick his ears at the distant sound of a drum and fife, which the fugitives soon perceived to be part of the pride, pomp, and circumstance of a militia training. The village tavern was in full view, and within a short distance, and the company was performing some marching evolutions a little beyond. An election of captain had just taken place; and the suffrages of the citizen soldiers had fallen upon a popular favourite, who had taken his station as commanding officer, and was showing his familiarity with the marches and counter-marches of Eaton's Manual. He had been just promoted from the rank of first lieutenant; and previous to the dismissal of his men, which was about to take place, he drew them up in front of the village store, when, according to custom, and with due regard to economy, which made the store a more eligible place for his purposes than the tavern, he testified his gratitude for the honour which had been done him by copious libations of cherry rum, and of St. Croix, which was diluted or not, according to the taste of each individual. The men soon began to grow merry; and some of them swore that they would not scruple to vote for the captain for major-general, if they had the choosing of that officer. The venders of ginger-bread felt the influence of the good fellowship and generosity which the captain had set in motion. A market for a considerable portion of their commodity was soon furnished by the stimulated appetites of the men, and a portion was distributed by the more gallant among them, to some spectators of the softer sex, who were collected upon the occasion.

The happy pair in the mean time had arrived at the tavern. Elvira's attention had not been sufficiently awakened by any thing but the conversation of her husband, to notice where she was, until she was called to a sense of her embarrassing situation by the landlord's sign, as it was gently swinging in the wind between two high posts, and exhibited a successful specimen of village sign-painting, the distinguished name of the host, and the age of his establishment.

Elvira directed the Frenchman to stop and turn his horse, which he did immediately, without understanding the object.

"Eh bien!" said he, his eyes still fixed on the young soldiers; "Il me vient une idée. I shall tell you." He went on to signify that he would immediately offer to teach the art of fencing and of using the broad-sword; that he would instruct them "dans l'art militaire, à la mode de Napoleon;" and that, after giving a few lessons, he would make a tournament, in which he would let them see, among other things, how Bonaparte conquered the world; how the cavalry could trample down flying infantry; and how the infantry, in such circumstances, could defend themselves; and that he would, in this way, make himself "bien riche."

During all this time, Elvira was collecting her wits to know what the emergency required; and as soon as Lavoisier's volley ceased, she begged him to turn again, thinking she might best avoid observation by seeking shelter in the tavern till dark.

They immediately alighted, and Lavoisier, after showing his bride to her apartment, descended to give some orders about his horse; when, to his astonishment, he was accosted by the jolly landlord, whose name was Thomas, "Ha, mounsheer, I guess you are the man who staid with me a fortnight two years ago, when I kept house in York state, and borried my chaise to go a jaunting, and told me to take care of your trunk, that had nothing but a big stone in it, till you came back. I got my horse and chaise agin," continued he, seizing the astounded professor of the dancing and military arts by the collar, "and now I'll take my recknin out of your skin, if I can't get it any other way."

At this moment the new captain and a considerable number of his merry men entered the house. After they had learned the circumstances of the case, from what passed between monsieur and the landlord, one of them cried out, "ride him on a rail—let him take his steps in the air!"

"He ought to dance on nothing, with a rope around his neck," said Thomas.

"No, no," said a third, "he has taken steps enough; that flashy jacket had better be swapped for one of tar and feathers."

"Messieurs, messieurs," said Lavoisier, "je suis bien malheureux. I am very sorry. Il etoit mon malheur—it was my misère to not pay monsieur Thomas, and it was his malheur not to be paid. I shall show you my honneur, when I shall get de l'argent. Il faut se soumettre aux circonstances. De honesty of every body depend upon what dey can do. I am sure, every body is gentleman in dis country. C'est un beau pays."

By this time one of the corporals had set a skillet of tar on the fire, and another, at the direction of the lieutenant, who seemed to take upon himself the command of the party, had brought a pillow from a bed in an adjoining room. The pillow was very expeditiously uncased, and a sufficient rent made in the ticking. The astonished Français stood aghast, as his bewildered mind caught a faint notion of the purpose of these preparations. He changed his tones of supplication to those of anger. "Vous êtes des sauvages!" he exclaimed. "You are monstres, diables! You do not merit to have some gentiman to teach la belle danse in dis country."

"He'll cackle like a blue jay," said the corporal, "by the time we get the feathers on him."

"They are hen's feathers," said the lieutenant, "but they'll do. Now ensign Sacket get on to the table, and corporal you hand him the skillet of tar. You Mr. Le Vosher, or whatever your name is, stand alongside of the table."

Monsieur believed his destiny to fixed—"Oh, mon Dieu!" he exclaimed; "le diable! qu'est que c'est que ça? Vat you do—vat is dat?"

"Tar, tar, nothing but tar—stand up to the table," was the reply.

"Sacristie! put dat sur ma tête—on my head et sur mes habits—my clothes; mes beaux habits de noces—my fine clothes for de marriage! Oh, messieurs, de grace, pardonnez moi; vous gaterez—you will spoil all my clothes."

"Blast your clothes!" said the corporal; "pull them off."

"Je vous remercie, tank you gentlemen;" and he very deliberately divested himself of a super-fine light blue broad-cloth coat, an embroidered silk vest, a laced cravat, and an under cravat of coarser fabric. He prolonged the operation as much as possible, making continued efforts to conciliate the compassion of his persecutors, which only added to their merriment.

At last all pretences for delay was over; every voice was hushed. The ensign began to uplift the fatal skillet, when all composure of mind forsook the affrighted bridegroom, and he uttered a loud hysteric shriek. Favoured by the general stillness, Elvira distinctly heard his voice, and knew at once that it betokened the extremity of distress. She rushed to the rescue, screaming for mercy. The men fell back, leaving their trembling victim in the centre of the room. "Ah! ma chère, quels bêtes!" he exclaimed, with a grimace that produced a peal of laughter. One of the men threw him his coat, another his vest; while the corporal set down the skillet, saying, "If it had not been for his *gal*, I'd have given him a wedding suit."

But we rather think monsieur would have been released without the interposition of his distressed bride, for a yankey mob is proverbially good-natured, and the merry men had enlisted in the landlord's cause, for the sake of a joke, rather than with the intention of inflicting pain. After the ludicrous adventure was over—ludicrous to the jolly trainers, but sad enough to the fugitive pair—Elvira deemed it expedient to press their retreat. Monsieur brought the chaise to the door, and they drove away, amidst the loud huzzas and merry clappings of the jovial company.

CHAPTER XV

————————Even-handed justice
Commends the ingredients of our poison'd
Chalice, to our own lips.

Macbeth

David Wilson, not long after the affair of the robbery of his mother's desk, went to New-York, in order to see his comrades, who were imprisoned there, and, if possible, to abate their demands on his purse. He succeeded in doing this; but having fallen in (attracted doubtless by natural affinities) with other companions as wicked, and more desperate, he soon spent in that city, which affords remarkable facilities for ridding men of their money, all that remained of the five hundred dollars. He preyed on others for a little time, as he had been their prey; and, finally reduced to extreme want, he joined two of his new associates in the attempt on the southern mail, which ended in his detection and commitment to jail in Philadelphia, where he was now awaiting a capital trial. A particular account of the whole affair, accompanied with letters from her son, was transmitted to Mrs. Wilson, who seemed now to be visited on every side with the natural and terrible retribution of her maternal sins.

After Elvira's departure, with all the profits of her little school, Jane did not delay another moment to go to her aunt's, in order to communicate to her Mr. Lloyd's kind offer of assistance, and to extend to her any aid or consolation in her own power.

She found Mrs. Wilson alone, but not in a frame of mind that indicated any just feelings. She received her niece coldly. After a silence of a few moments, which Jane wished but knew not how to break, she inquired of Mrs. Wilson, whether she had any more information respecting David than was public?

Her aunt replied, she had not. She understood the particulars were all in the paper, even to his name; she thought that might have been omitted; but people always seemed to delight in publishing every one's misfortunes.

Jane asked if the letters expressed any doubt that David would be convicted?

"None," Mrs. Wilson said. "To be sure," she added, "I have a letter from David, in which he begs me to employ counsel for him; so I suppose he thinks it possible that he might be cleared; but a drowning man catches at straws."

"Do you know," inquired Jane, "the names of the eminent lawyers in Philadelphia? Mr. Lloyd will be best able to inform you whom to select among them. I will go to him immediately."

"No, no, child; I have made up my mind upon that subject. It would be a great expense. There is no conscience in city lawyers; they would devour all my substance, and do me no good after all. No, no—I shall leave David entirely in the hands of Providence."

"And can you, aunt," said Jane, "acquiesce in your son's being cut off in the spring of life, without an effort to save him—without an effort to procure him a space for repentance and reformation?"

"Do not presume, Jane Elton," replied Mrs. Wilson, "to instruct me in my duties. A space for repentance! A day—an hour—a moment is as good as an eternity for the operations of the Spirit. Many, at the foot of the gallows, have repented, and have died exulting in their pardon and new-born hope."

"Yes," replied Jane; "and there have been many who have thus repented and rejoiced, and then been reprieved; and have they then shown the only unquestionable proof of genuine penitence—a renewed spirit? Have they kept the commandments, for by this shall ye know that they are disciples of Christ? No; they have returned to their old sins, and been tenfold worse than at first."

"I tell you," said Mrs. Wilson, impatiently, "you are ignorant, child; you are still in the bond of iniquity; you cannot spiritually discern. There is more hope, and that is the opinion of some of our greatest divines, of an open outrageous transgressor, than of one of a moral life."

"Then," replied Jane, "there is more hope of a harvest from a hard bound, neglected field, than from that which the owner has carefully ploughed and sowed, and prepared for the sun and the rains of heaven."

"The kingdom of grace is very different from the kingdom of nature," answered Mrs. Wilson. "The natural man can do nothing towards his own salvation. Every act he performs, and every prayer he offers, but provokes more and more the wrath of the Almighty."

Jane made no reply; but she raised her hands and eyes as if she deprecated so impious a doctrine, and Mrs. Wilson went on: "Do not think my children are worse than others; you, Jane, are as much a child of wrath, and so is every son and daughter of Adam, as he is—all totally depraved—totally corrupt. You may have been under more restraint, and not acted out your sins; but no thanks to you;" and she continued, fixing her large gray eyes stedfastly on Jane, "there are beside my son who would not *seem* better, if they had not friends to keep their secrets for them." Mrs. Wilson had, for very good reasons, never before alluded to the robbery of her desk, since the morning it was committed; but she was now provoked to foul means to support her argument, tottering under the assault of facts.

Jane did not condescend to notice the insinuation; she felt too sincere a pity for the miserable self-deluded woman; but, still anxious that some effort should be made for David, she said to Mrs. Wilson, "Is there, then, nothing to be done for your unhappy son?"

"Nothing, child, nothing; he has gone out from me, and he is not of me; his blood be upon his own head; I am clear of it. My 'foot standeth on an even place.' My case is not an uncommon one," she continued, as if she would by this vain babbling, silence the voice within. "The saints of old—David, and Samuel, and Eli, were afflicted as I am, with rebellious children. I have planted and I have watered, and if it is the Lord's will to withhold the increase, I must submit."

"Oh, aunt!" exclaimed Jane, interrupting and advancing towards her, "do not—do not, for your soul's sake, indulge any longer this horrible delusion. You have more children," she continued, falling on her knees, and taking one of her aunt's hands in both hers, and looking like a rebuking messenger from Heaven, "be pitiful to them; be merciful to your own soul. You deceive yourself. You may deceive others; but God is not mocked."

Mrs. Wilson was conscience stricken. She sat as motionless as a statue; and Jane went on with the courage of an Apostle to depicture, in their true colours, her character and conduct. She made her realize, for a few moments at least, the peril of her soul. She made her feel, that her sound faith, her prayers, her pretences, her meeting-goings, were nothing—far worse than nothing in his sight, who cannot be deceived by the daring hypocrisies, the self-delusions, the refuges of lies, of his creatures. She described the spiritual disciple of Jesus; and then presented to Mrs. Wilson so true an image of her selfishness, her pride, her domestic tyranny, and her love of money, that she could not but see that it was her very self.

There was that in Jane's looks, and voice, and words, that was not to be resisted by the wretched woman; and like the guilty king, when he saw the record on the wall, her "countenance was changed, her thoughts were troubled, and her knees smote one against the other."

At this moment they were interrupted by the entrance of Mr. Lloyd. Jane rose, embarrassed for her aunt and herself, and walked to the window. Mrs. Wilson attempted to speak, to rise; she could do neither, and she sunk back on her chair, convulsed with misery and passion. Mr. Lloyd mistook her agitation for the natural wailings of a mother, and with instinctive benevolence he advanced to her, and kindly taking her hand, said, "Be composed, I pray; I have intelligence that will comfort thee."

"What is it?" inquired Jane, eager to allay the storm she had raised.

Mrs. Wilson was still unable to speak.

"Thy son has escaped, Mrs. Wilson, and is, before this, beyond the reach of his country's laws. Here is a letter addressed to thee, which came enclosed in one to me." Mr. Lloyd laid the letter on Mrs. Wilson's lap, but she was unable to open it or even to hold it. Her eyes were fixed, her hands firmly closed, and she continued to shiver with uncontrollable emotion. "She is quite unconscious," he said, "she does not hear a word I say to her."

Jane flew to her assistance, spoke to her, entreated her to answer, bathed her temples and her hands—but all without effect. "Oh!" she exclaimed, terrified and dismayed, "I have killed her."

"Do not be so alarmed," said Mr. Lloyd, "there is no occasion for it; the violence of her emotion has overcome her, it is the voice of nature; let us convey her to her bed."

Jane called assistants, and they removed her to her own room, and placed her on her bed.

"See," whispered Mr. Lloyd to Jane, after a few moments, "she is becoming composed already; leave her for a little time with this domestic—I have much to say to thee."

Jane followed him to the parlour. He took both her hands, and said, his face radiant with joy, "Jane, many daughters have done virtuously, but thou excellest them all. Nay, do not tremble, unless it be for the sin of having kept from me so long the blessed intelligence of this morning."

Poor Jane tried to stammer out an apology for her reserve, but Mr. Lloyd interrupted her by saying playfully, "I understand it all; I am too old, too rigid, too—quakerish, to be a young lady's confidant."

"Oh, say not so," exclaimed Jane, gathering courage from his kindness; "you have been my benefactor, my guardian, my kindest friend; forgive my silence—I feel it all—I have always felt it; perhaps most, when I seemed most insensible, most reckless. Mr. Lloyd looked gratified beyond expression; it cost him an effort to interrupt her, for there is perhaps nothing more delightful than the merited praises of those we love. But he said, "Nay, my sweet friend, it will be my turn next, if thou dost not stop, and we shall indeed be, as the French name my brethren, a house of Trembleurs. I have a great deal to tell thee; our joys have clustered. What sayest thou Jane, to another walk to old John's, with as strange, and a more welcome guide, than your fitful wanderer? I have no time to lose in enigmas; our despatches were brought by a sailor, a fine good-natured, hardy looking fellow, who came to my house this morning. I was wondering what he could be doing so far from his element, when Mary, who returned to us yesterday, opened the door for him, and exclaimed, with a ludicrous mixture of terror and joy, "The Lord have mercy on us! is it you, or your ghost, Jemmy?" The sailor gave her a truly professional, and most unghostly, smack, and replied between crying and laughing, "I am no ghost, Mary, as you may see; but excuse me, Mary, (for Mary had stepped back, a little embarrassed by the involuntary freedom of her friend) I was so glad, I could not help it. No, no, Mary, I am no ghost, but a prodigal that's come back, thanks to the Lord! a little better than I went." James, who is indeed the long lost son of our good friend John of the Mountain, went on to detail his experiences to Mary, who by turns raised her hands and eyes in wonder and devout thankfulness. The amount of it is, for their joy overflowed all barriers of reserve, he left here ten years ago in despair, because Mary would not marry him, and sailed to the Mediterranean; the poor fellow was taken by the Algerines, and after suffering almost incredibly for six years, he was so happy as to procure his freedom along with some English captives. After his release, he said he could not endure the thought of coming to his father and mother quite destitute; for, as he said to Mary, though he was a wild lad, and had a fancy to follow the sea, her cruelty would not have driven him to leave them, if he had not hoped to get something to comfort their old age with. He wrote them an account of his sufferings, and of an engagement he had made to go to Calcutta in the service of an English merchantman. The letters it seems never reached here. He went to India; many circumstances occurred to advance him in the favour of his employer; his integrity, which, he said, the tears streaming from his eyes, was "all owing to the teachings and examples of his good old parents," and his intelligence, "thanks to his country, which took care to give the poor man learning," occasioned his being employed in the company's service, and sent with some others into the interior of India on business of great hazard and importance, the success of which his employers attributed to him, and rewarded him most liberally. All these facts came out inevitably in the course of his narrative, for he spoke not boastfully, but with simplicity and gratitude. He has returned with enough to purchase a farm, and give to his parents all that they want of this world; and, what our friend Mary thinks best of all, he has come home a Methodist, having been made one by a missionary of that zealous sect in India. If I have not misinterpreted Mary's glistening eye, this fact will cost me my housekeeper."

"Dear, dear Mary!" exclaimed Jane, brushing away the tears of sympathy and joy that Mr. Lloyd's narrative had brought to her eyes, "and John, and old Sarah. Oh, it is as beautiful a conclusion of their lives, as if it had been conjured up by a poet."

"Ah, Jane," replied Mr. Lloyd, "there are realities in the kind dispositions of Providence more blessed than a poet can dream of; and there are virtues in real life," he continued, smiling, "that might lend a persuasive grace to the page of a moralist, it is of those I must now speak."

"Not now," said Jane, hastily rising, "I must go to my aunt."

"At least then, take these letters with thee, the levity of one will give thee some pain; in the other, the wretched Wilson has done thee late justice. Now go, my blessed friend, to thy aunt; would that thou couldst minister to her mind, distracted by these terrible events. Oh that power might be given to thy voice to awaken her conscience from its deep, oblivious sleep!"

It was a remarkable proof of Mr. Lloyd's habitual grace, that he did not forget, at this moment, that Jane could not work miracles without supernatural assistance.

There is not a happier moment of existence than that which a benevolent being enjoys, when he knows that the object of his solicitude and love has passed safely through trial, is victorious over temptation, and has overcome the world. This was the joy that now a thousand fold requited Mr. Lloyd for all his sufferings in the cause of our heroine. Would Mr. Lloyd have been equally happy in the proved virtue of his favourite, if hope had not brightened his dim future with her sweetest visions? Certainly not. He who hath wonderfully made us, has, in wisdom, implanted the principle of self-love in our bosoms; and let the enthusiast rave as he will, it is neither the work of grace nor of discipline to eradicate it; but it may, and if we would be good, it must be modified, controlled, and made subservient to the benefit and happiness of others.

Mr. Lloyd had no very definite plans for the future; but his horizon was brightening with a coming day; and, without vanity or presumption, he trusted all would be well.

Jane returned to her aunt's apartment, and found her in a sullen stupor. She did not seem to notice; at any rate, she made no reply to Jane's kind inquiries, and she, after drawing the curtains and dismissing the attendant, sat down to the perusal of the letters Mr. Lloyd had given to her. The first she read was from Erskine to Mr. Lloyd, and as it was not long, and was rather characteristic, we shall take the liberty to transcribe it for the benefit of our readers.

"Dear Sir,

"In returning to my lodgings, late last evening, I was accosted by a man, muffled in a cloak. I recognised his voice at once. It was our unfortunate townsman, Wilson. He has succeeded à merveille in an ingenious plan of escape from durance, and sails in the morning for one of the West India islands, where he will, no doubt, make his debût as pirate, or in some other character for which his training has equally qualified him. A precious rascal he is indeed; but, allow me a phrase of your fraternity, Sir, I had no *light* to give him up to justice, after he had trusted to me; and more than that, for he informs me, that he had, since his confinement, written to the Woodhulls to engage me as counsel, and through them he learnt the fact of my being in this city. This bound me, in some sort, to look upon the poor devil as my client; and, as it would have been my duty to get him out of the clutches of the law, it would have been most ungracious to have put him into them you know, since his own cleverness, instead of mine, has extricated him. He has explained to me, and he informs me has communicated to you, (for he says he cannot trust his mother to make them public,) the particulars of the sequestration of the old woman's money. I think Miss Elton never imparted to you the event that led to the sudden engagement, from which she has chosen to absolve me; and you have yet to learn, that there is generosity, disinterestedness in the world, that may rival the virtue which reposes under the shadow of the broad-brim. But, your pardon. I have wiped out all scores. The reception I have met with in this finest of cities, has been such as to make me look upon the incidents of an obscure village as mere bagatelles, not worthy of a sigh from one who can bask in the broad sunshine of ladies favour and fortune's gifts. One word more, en passant, of Wilson's explanation. I rejoice in it sincerely, on Miss Elton's account. She deserved to have suffered a little for her childishness in holding herself bound by an exacted promise, for having put herself in a situation in which her guilt would have seemed apparent to any one but a poor dog whom love had hood-winked—pro tempore. She is too young and too beautiful a victim for the altar of conscience. However, I forgive her, her scruples, her fanaticism, and her cruelties; and wish her all happiness in this world and the next, advising her not to turn anchorite here, for the sake of advancement there.

"I know not when I shall return to village life: stale, flat, and unprofitable. This gay metropolis has cured me of my rural tastes; and, as I flatter myself, fashion's cannie hand has quite effaced my rusticity.

"By a lucky chance I met the son of your protegé, John, yesterday. The poor dog's 'hairbreadth 'scapes' will make the villagers stare, all unused as they are to the marvellous. I told him, by way of a welcome to his country, I should pay his expenses home. This I hope you, Sir, will accept in expiation of all my sins against the old basket-maker.

"With many wishes that you may find a new and more pliant subject for your mentor genius, I remain, Sir, your most obedient,

"humble servant,

"E. Erskine.

"N. B. My regards to Miss Elton. Tell her I look at the windows of our print shops every day, in the expectation of seeing, among their gay show, her lovely figure chosen by one of the sons of Apollo, to personate the stern lady, Justice, (whom few seek and none love) poising her scales in solitary dignity."

"And is this the man," thought Jane, as she folded the letter, "that I have loved—that I fancied loved me?"—and her heart rose in devout thankfulness for the escape she had made from an utter wreck of her happiness.

She next read Wilson's letter to Mr. Lloyd. It began with the particulars of his late escape, which seemed to possess his mind more than any thing else. He then said, that being about to enter on a new voyage, he wished to lighten his soul of as much of its present cargo of sin as possible. He stated, and we believe with sincerity, that he had intended, if it ever became necessary, to assert Jane's innocence; but that, as long as no one believed her guilty, he had thought it fair to slip his neck out of the yoke; and now, that every body might know how good she was, he wished Mr. Lloyd to make known all the particulars of the transaction. He then went on to detail as much as he knew of her visit to the mountain, which had led to her subsequent involvement. He expressed no remorse for the past, no hope of the future. His wish to exculpate Jane had arisen from a deep feeling of her excellence, and seemed to be the last ray of just or kindly feeling that his dark, guilty spirit emitted.

Jane had scarcely finished reading the letters, when her attention was called to her aunt, who had been thrown into a state of agitation almost amounting to frenzy, by the perusal of her son's farewell letter to herself, which Mr. Lloyd had placed on the pillow beside her, believing that it merely contained such account of David's escape and plans, as would have a tendency to allay the anguish of her mind, which he still supposed arose solely from her apprehensions for her son's life. But Mr. Lloyd was too good even to conceive of the bitterness of a malignant exasperated spirit, wrought to madness, as Wilson's was, by his mother's absolute refusal to make any effort to save his life.

The letter was filled with execrations. "If I have a soul," he said, "eternity will be spent in cursing her who has ruined it;" but he did not fear the future—hell was a bugbear to frighten children. "You," he continued, "neither fear it, nor believe it; for if you did, your religion would be something besides a cloak to hide your hard, cruel heart. Religion! what is it but a dream, a pretence? I might have believed it, if I had seen more like Jane Elton—whom you have trodden on, wrongfully accused, when *you knew* her innocent. Mother, mother! oh, that I must call you so!—as I do it, I howl a curse with every breath—you have destroyed me. You, it was, that taught me, when I scarcely knew my right hand from my left, that there was no difference between doing right and doing wrong, in the sight of the God you worship; you taught me, that I could do nothing acceptable to him. If you taught me truly, I have only acted out the nature totally depraved, (your own words,) that he gave to me, and I am not to blame for it. I could do nothing to save my own soul; and according to your own doctrine, I stand now a better chance than my moral cousin, Jane. If you have taught me falsely, I was not to blame; the peril be on your own soul. My mind was a blank, and you put your own impressions on it; God (if there be a God) reward you according to your deeds!"

This horrible letter, of which we have given a brief and comparatively mild specimen; and subtracted from that the curses that pointed every sentence, seemed for a little while to swell the clamours of Mrs. Wilson's newly awakened conscience. But, alas! the impression was transient; the chains of systematic delusion were too firmly rivetted—the habits of self-deception too strong, to be overcome.

Jane, fearful that the violence of her aunt's passion would over destroy her reason, sought only, for the remainder of the day and the following night, to sooth and quiet her. She remained by her bedside, and silently watched, and prayed. Mrs. Wilson's sleep was disturbed, but she awoke somewhat refreshed, and quite composed. Her first action was to tear David's letter into a thousand fragments. She was never known afterwards to allude to its contents, nor to her conversation with Jane. There was a restlessness through the remainder of her life, which betrayed the secret gnawings of conscience. Still it is believed, she quelled her convictions as Cromwell is reported to have done, when, as his historian says, he asked Goodwin, one of his preachers, if the doctrine were true, that the elect should never fall, nor suffer a final reprobation!—"Nothing more certain," replied the preacher. "Then I am safe," said the protector; "for I am sure I was once in a state of grace."

Mrs. Wilson survived these events but a few years. She was finally carried off by the scrofula, a disease from which she had suffered all her life, and which had probably increased the natural asperity of her temper; as all evils, physical as well as moral, certainly make us worse, if they do not make us better. Elvira was summoned to her death-bed; but she arrived too late to receive either the reproaches or forgiveness of her mother. Jane faithfully attended her through her last illness, and most kindly ministered to the diseases of her body. Her mind no human comfort could reach; no earthly skill touch its secret springs. The disease was attended with delirium; and she had no rational communication with any one from the beginning of her illness. This Jane afterwards sincerely deplored to Mr. Lloyd, who replied, "I would not sit like the Egyptians in judgment on the dead. Thy aunt has gone with her record to Him who alone knows the secrets of the heart, and therefore is alone qualified to judge His creatures; but for our own benefit, Jane, and for the sake of those whose probation is not past, let us ever remember the wise saying of William Penn, 'a man cannot be the better for that religion for which his neighbour is the worse.' I have no doubt thy aunt has suffered some natural compunctions for her gross failure in the performance of her duties; but she felt safe in a sound faith. It is reported, that one of the

Popes said of himself, that 'as Eneas Sylvius he was a damnable heretic, but as Pius II, an orthodox Pope.'"

"Then you believe," replied Jane, "that my unhappy aunt deceived herself by her clamorous profession?"

"Undoubtedly. Ought we to wonder that she effected that imposition on herself, by the aid of self-love, (of all love the most blinding,) since we have heard, in her funeral sermons, her religious experiences detailed as the triumphs of a saint; her strict attention on religious ordinances commended, as if they were the end and not the means of a religious life; since we (who cannot remember a single gracious act of humility in her whole life) have been told, as a proof of her gracious state, that the last rational words she pronounced were, that she 'was of sinners the chief?' There seems to be a curious spiritual alchymy in the utterance of these words; for we cannot say, that those who use them mean to 'palter in a double sense,' but they are too often spoken and received as the evidence of a hopeful state. Professions and declarations have crept in among the protestants, to take the place of the mortifications and penances of the ancient church; so prone are men to find some easier way to heaven than the toilsome path of obedience."

CHAPTER XVI

God, the best maker of all marriages,
Combine your hearts in one.
Henry V

We have anticipated our story, tempted by a natural desire to conclude the history of Mrs. Wilson, that its deep shade might not interfere with the bright lights that are falling on the destiny of our heroine. After the dissolution of her engagement with Erskine, Jane continued her humble vocation of school-mistress for some months. Rebecca Lloyd had from the beginning been one of her pupils, and a favourite among them; and so devotedly did the child love her instructress, that Mr. Lloyd often thought impulse was as sure a guide for her affections as reason for his. Jane's care of his child furnished him occasion, and excuse when he needed it, for frequent intercourse with her; and, in this intercourse, there were none of those mysterious embarrassments (mysterious, because inexplicable to all but the parties) that so often check the progress of affection. Jane, released from the thraldom in which she had been bound to Erskine, was as happy as a redeemed captive. Her tastes and her views were similar to Mr. Lloyd's, and she found in his society a delightful exchange and a rich compensation for the solitude to which her mind and affections had been condemned.

We are ignorant, perhaps Jane was, of the precise moment when gratitude melted into love, and friendship resigned the reigns to his more absolute dominion. But it was not long after this, nor quite 'a year and a day' (the period of mourning usually allotted to a faithful husband) after her separation from Erskine, that, as she was sitting with Mrs. Harvey in her little parlour, Mr. Lloyd entered with his child. After the customary greetings, Mrs. Harvey suddenly recollected that some domestic duties demanded her presence, and saying with an arch smile to Mr. Lloyd that she 'hoped he would overlook her absence,' she left the room. Little

Rebecca was sitting on her father's knee; she took from his bosom a miniature of her mother, which he always wore there, and seemed intently studying the face which the artist had delineated with masterly power. "Do the angels look like my mother?" she asked.

"Why, my child?"

"I thought, father, they might look like her, she looks so bright and so good." She kissed the picture, and after a moment's pause, added, "Jane looks like mother, all but the cap; dost not thee think, father, Jane would look pretty in a quaker cap?" Mr. Lloyd kissed his little girl, and said nothing. Rebecca's eyes followed the direction of her father's: "Oh, Jane!" she exclaimed, "thou dost not look like mother now, thy cheeks are as red as my new doll's."

The child's observation of her treacherous cheek had certainly no tendency to lessen poor Jane's colour. She would have been glad to hide her face any where, but it was broad daylight, and there was now no escape from the declaration which had been hovering on Mr. Lloyd's lips for some weeks, and which was now made in spite of Rebecca's presence. It cannot be denied, in deference to the opinion of some very fastidious ladies, that Jane was prepared for it; for though the marks of love are not quite as obvious, as the lively Rosalind describes them, yet we believe that except in the case of very wary lovers—cautious veterans— they are first observed by the objects of the passion.

We are warned from attempting to describe the scene to which our little pioneer had led the way, by the fine remark of a sentimentalist, who compares the language of lovers to the most delicate fruits of a warm climate—very delicious where they grow, but not capable of transportation. Much is expressed and understood in a few sentences, which would be quite unintelligible to those whose faculties are not quickened by *la grande passion*, and who therefore cannot be expected to comprehend the mystics of love.

The result of the interview was perfectly satisfactory to both parties; and as this was one of the occasions when all the sands of time are 'diamond sparks,' it is impossible to say when it would have come to a conclusion, had it not been for little Rebecca, who seemed to preside over the destinies of that day.

Her father had interpreted his conversation with Jane to his child, and had succeeded in rendering the object and the result of it level to her comprehension, and she had lavished her joy in loud exclamations and tender caresses; till finding she was no longer noticed, she had withdrawn to a window, and was amusing herself with gazing at the passengers in the street, when she suddenly turned to Jane, and raising the window at the same moment, she said, "Oh, there goes Mary to lecture, may I call her and tell her?"

At this moment the sweet child might have asked any thing without the chance of a refusal, and a ready assent was no sooner granted, than she screamed and beckoned to Mary, who immediately obeyed her summons.

Mary entered, and Rebecca closing the door after her, said, "I guess thee will not want to go to lecture to-day, Mary, for I have a most beautiful secret to tell thee, hold down thy ear, and promise never to tell as long as thy name is Mary Hull;" and then, unable any longer to subdue her voice to a whisper, she jumped up and clapped her hands, and shouted, "Joy, joy, joy! Mary, Jane Elton is coming to live with us all the days of her life, and is going to be my own mother."

Mary looked to Mr. Lloyd, and then to Jane, and read in their faces the confirmation of the happy tidings; and to Rebecca's utter amazement, the tears streamed from her eyes. "Oh, Mary!" said she, turning disappointed away, "now I am ashamed of thee, I thought thee would be as glad as I am."

But Mr. Lloyd and Jane knew how to understand this expression of her feelings; they advanced to her and gave her their hands; she joined them: "the Lord hath heard my prayer," she said, and she wept aloud.

"I thank thee, Mary," replied Mr. Lloyd; "God grant I may deserve thy confidence."

"If she has prayed for it, what then does she cry for?" said Rebecca, who stood beside her father, watching Mary's inexplicable emotion, and vainly trying to get some clue to it.

"Come with me, my child, and I will tell thee," replied her father, and he very discreetly led out the child, and left Jane with her faithful friend.

The moment he had closed the door, Mary said smiling through her tears of joy, "It has taken me by surprise at last, but for all that I am not quite so blind as you may think. Do you remember, Jane, telling me one day when you laid your book down to listen to Mr. Lloyd, who was talking to Rebecca, that since your mother's voice had been silent, you had never heard one so sweet as Mr. Lloyd's? I thought to myself then you seemed to feel just as I do when I hear the sound of James' voice; not that I mean to compare myself to you, or James to Mr. Lloyd, but it is the *nature of the feeling*— it is the same in the high and the low, the rich and the poor."

"Was that all the ground of your suspicion?" asked Jane, smiling at her friend's boasted sagacity.

"No, not quite all; James has been very impatient for our marriage; and from time to time I have told Mr. Lloyd I wished he would look out for some one to take charge of his house, and I advised him not to get a very young person, for, says I, they are apt to be flighty. I never saw one that was not, but Jane Elton. He smiled and blushed, and asked me what made me think that you was so much above the rest of your sex, and so I told him, and he never seemed to weary with talking about you."

"I am rejoiced," replied Jane, "that your partiality to me reconciles you to the disparity in our ages."

"Oh, that is nothing; that is, in your case it is nothing. Let us see, eleven years. In most cases it would be too much, to be sure; there is just four years between James and I, that is just right, I think; but then, dear Jane, you are so different from other people, you need not go by common rules."

The overflowing of Mary's heart was checked by the entrance of some company. As she parted with Jane, she whispered, "I shall not think of leaving Mr. Lloyd till you are married, be it sooner or later; when I see you in your own home, it will be time enough to think of my affairs."

There still remained a delicate point to adjust: Mr. Lloyd had been brought up a Quaker, and he had seen no reason to depart from the faith or mode of worship which had come down to him from his ancestors, and for which he felt on that account (as who does not?) an attachment and veneration. He rarely, if ever, entered into discussions upon religious subjects, and probably did not feel much zeal for some of the peculiarities of his sect. He was not disposed to question their utility in their ordinary operation upon common character. He knew how salutary were the restraints of discipline upon the mass of men, and he considered the discipline of habits and opinions infinitely more salutary than the direct and coarse interference of power. He perceived, or thought he perceived, that as a body of men, the 'Friends' were upon the whole more happy and prosperous than any other. No contentions ever came among them. This circumstance Mr. Lloyd ascribed in a considerable degree to the uniformity of their opinions, habits, and lives, and to their custom of restricting their family alliances within the limits of their own sect. Mr. Lloyd regarded with complacency most of the characteristics of his own religious society; and those which he could not wholly approve, he was yet disposed to regard in the most favourable light; but he was no sectarian: his understanding was too much elevated, and his affections were too diffusive to be confined within the bounds of sect. Such ties could not bind such a spirit. If any sectarian peculiarities had interfered to restrain him in the exercise of his duty, or while acting under the strong impulses of his generous nature, he would have shaken them off 'like dew-drops from a lion's mane.' Exclusion from the society would have been painful to him for many reasons, but the fear of it could not occasion a moment's hesitation in his offering his hand to a woman whom he loved and valued, and whose whole life he saw animated by the essential spirit of Christianity. He determined now to inform his society of his choice, and to submit to the censure and exclusion from membership that must follow. But Mr. Lloyd was saved the painful necessity of breaking ties which were so strong that they might be called natural bonds.

Jane had been early led to inquire into the particular modification of religion professed by her benefactor, and respect for him had probably lent additional weight to every argument in its favour; this was natural; and it was natural too, that after her matured judgment sanctioned her early preference, she should from motives of delicacy have hesitated to declare it. If it cannot be denied that this proselyte was won by the virtues of Mr. Lloyd, it is to be presumed that no Christian will deny the rightful power of such an argument.

If the reader is not disposed to allow that Jane's choice of the religion of her friend was the result of the purity and simplicity of her character, the preference she always gave to the spirit over the letter, to the practice over the profession, she must call to her aid the decision of the poet, who says that

"Minds are for sects of various kinds *decreed*,
As different soils are formed for different seed."

Not a word had passed between Mr. Lloyd and Jane on the subject of the mental deliberations and resolves of each, when a few days after their engagement, Jane said to him, "I have a mind to improve the fatal hint of my little mischievous friend, and see how becoming I can make a "quaker cap."

"What dost thou mean, Jane?" inquired Mr. Lloyd, who seemed a little puzzled by the gravity of her face, which was not quite in keeping with the playfulness of her words.

"Seriously," she replied, with your consent and approbation, "I mean to be a 'member by request' of your society of friends."

"Shall my people be thy people?" exclaimed Mr. Lloyd with great animation. This, indeed, converts to pure gold the only circumstance that alloyed my happiness; but do not imagine, dear Jane, that I think it of the least consequence, by what name the different members of the christian family are called."

"But you think it right and *orderly*," she replied, smiling, "that the wife should take the name of the husband?"

"I think it most happy, certainly."

There remained now no reason for deferring the marriage longer than was rendered necessary by the delays attending the admission of a new member into the friends' society.

It was a beautiful morning in the beginning of May—the mist had rolled away from the valley, and wreathed with silvery clouds the sides and summits of the mountains—the air was sweet with the 'herald blossoms' of spring—and nature, rising from her wintry bed, was throwing on her woods and fields her drapery of tender green—when a carriage, containing Mr. Lloyd, Mary Hull, and little Rebecca, stopped at Mrs. Harvey's door; Jane, arrayed for a journey, stood awaiting it on the piazza; old John, the basket-maker, was beside her, leaning on his cane, and good Mrs. Harvey was giving Jane's baggage to James, who carried it to the carriage. "Farewell, dear Jane," said Mrs. Harvey, affectionately kissing her;—"now go, but do not forget there are other 'friends' in the world, beside quakers. Return to us soon; we are all impatient to see you the happy mistress of the house in which you was born."

John followed her to the carriage, and respectfully taking her hand and Mr. Lloyd's—"You've been my best friends," said he; "take an old man's blessing, whose sun, thanks to the Lord who brought Jemmy back! is setting without a cloud. God grant you both," he added, joining their hands, "a long and a happy day. Truly says the good book, 'light is sown for the righteous, and joy for the upright in heart.'"

James was the only person that did not seem to have his portion of the common gladness. He had, with a poor grace, consented to defer his nuptials till Mary's return from Philadelphia. He did not mind the time, he said, "five or six weeks would not break his heart, though he had waited almost as long as Jacob now; and he was not of a distrustful make; but it was a long way to Philadelphia, and the Lord only knew what might happen." But nothing did happen; at least, nothing to justify our constant lover's forebodings.

Jane was received with cordiality into the friends' society, and their hands were joined, whose hearts were 'knit together.'

The travellers returned, in a few weeks, to ——, happy in each other, and devoting themselves to the good and happiness of the human family. Their good works shone before men; and "they, seeing them, glorified their Father in heaven." We dare not presume upon the good nature of our readers so far, as to give the detail of Mary's wedding; at which, our little friend Rebecca, was the happy mistress of ceremonies.

There yet remains something to be told of one of the persons of our humble history, whom our readers may have forgotten, but to whom Mr. Lloyd extended his kind regards—the poor lunatic, crazy Bet. He believed that her reason might be restored by skillful management—by confinement to one place, and one set of objects, and by the sedative influence of gentle manners, and regular habits in her attendants. He induced Mary, in whose judiciousness and zeal he placed implicit confidence, to undertake the execution of his plan; but after a faithful experiment of a few months, they were obliged to relinquish all hope of restoring the mind to its right balance. Mary said, when the weather was dull, she was as quiet as any body; but if the sun shone out suddenly, it seemed as if its bright beams touched her brain. A thunder-storm, or a clear moon-light, would throw her back into her wild ways. "The poor thing," Mary added, "had such a tender heart, that there seemed to be no way to harden it. If she sees a lamb die, or hears a mournful note from a bird, when she has her *low* feelings, she'll weep more than some mothers at the loss of a child."

No cure could be effected; but Mary's house continued to be the favourite resort of the interesting vagrant. Her visits there became more frequent and longer protracted. Mary observed, that the excitement of her mind was exhausting her life, without Bet's seeming conscious of decay of strength, or any species of suffering.

The last time Mary saw her, was a brilliant night during the full harvest moon; she came to her house late in the evening; the wildness of her eye was tempered with an affecting softness; her cheek was brightened with the hectic flush that looks like 'mockery of the tomb'—Mary observed her to tremble, and perceived that there was an alarming fluttering in her pulse. "You are not well," said she.

"No, I am not well," Bet replied, in a low plaintive tone; "but I shall be soon—here," said she, placing Mary's hand on her heart—"do not you feel it struggling to be free."

Mary was startled—the beating was so irregular, it seemed that every pulsation must be the last. "Oh!" she exclaimed, "poor creature, let me put you to bed; you are not fit to be sitting here."

"Oh, no!" Bet replied, in the same feeble, mournful tone; "I cannot stay here. The spirits of heaven are keeping a festival by the light of the blessed moon. Hark! do you not hear them, Mary?"—and she sung so low that her voice sounded like distant music:

"Sister spirit, come away!"

"And do you not see their white robes?" she added, pointing through the window to the vapour that curled along the margin of the river, and floated on the bosom of the meadow.

Mary called to her husband, and whispered, "The poor thing is near death; let us get her on the bed."

Bet overheard her. "No, do not touch me," she exclaimed; "the spirit cannot soar here." She suddenly sprang on her feet, as if she had caught a new inspiration, and darted towards the door. Mary's infant, sleeping in the cradle, arrested her eye; she knelt for a moment beside it and folded her hands on her breast. Then rising, she said to Mary, "The prayer of the dying sanctifies." The door was open, and she passed through it so suddenly that they hardly suspected her intention before she was gone. The next morning she was discovered in the church-yard, her head resting on the grassy mound that covered the remains of her lover. Her spirit had passed to its eternal rest!

NOTE TO PAGE 85

"For the news had come that Shays' men would cover their front with the captives."

The exhaustion occasioned in Massachusetts by her struggles to support the revolutionary contest, in which her efforts were, at least, equal to those of any other state, and the taxes, which, at the close of the war, were necessarily imposed upon the citizens by the state government, were the principal causes of the disturbances in 1786–7, which are now talked of by some of the older inhabitants, and particularly in the western part of the commonwealth, as the *"Shays war."* It was so called from Daniel Shays, one of the principal insurgents, and now (1822) a peaceable citizen and revolutionary pensioner in the western part of the state of New-York.

This rebellion is certainly a stain upon the character of Massachusetts— almost the only one. It may, nevertheless, serve to exhibit in a favourable light the humane and orderly character of her inhabitants. If there were no wrongs to be redressed, there were heavy sufferings and privations to be borne. The stimulus of the revolutionary war had not wholly subsided, and the vague and fanciful anticipations of all the blessings to be conferred by "glorious liberty," had passed away. The people found that they had liberty indeed, but it was not what they had painted to their fancies. They enjoyed a republican government, but with it came increased taxation, poverty, and toil. Their means were rather straightened than enlarged. From the embarrassment and confusion of the times, debts had multiplied and accumulated; courts were established, and the laws were enforced.

The organization of courts and the collection of debts, formed one of the principal grounds of discontent. The court-houses were attacked, and their session sometimes prevented. The party in favour of the state government, and, of course, of the support of the laws, was commonly called the *court party*. An Englishman might smile at such an application of the term.

The insurrectionary spirit was very general throughout the commonwealth; and it might be said that the western counties were in the possession of the rebels against republicanism. It endured, however, but for a few months, and was chiefly put down by the voluntary and spirited exertions of the peaceable inhabitants. While it lasted, there was, of course, a considerable degree of license, and occasional pilfering, for it could hardly be called plunder; but there was little destruction of property, and no cruelty. Sometimes a few individuals of the court party, and sometimes a few *Shaysites* were made prisoners; and in such cases they were shut up in rooms during the stay of the conquering party, and occasionally marched off with them on their retreat.

It is probable that about fifteen or twenty individuals perished in battle during the Shays war. Not one suffered by the sentence of a civil magistrate.

The most severe engagement which occurred during the contest, took place in Sheffield, on the 27th of February, 1787. The government party was composed of militia from Sheffield and Barrington; in number about eighty men, and commanded by Colonel John Ashley, of Sheffield. This party, hearing that the rebels had appeared in force, in Stockbridge, where they had committed some depredations, and taken several prisoners, pursued them for some time without success, and did not fall in with them until their return to Sheffield, to which place the rebels had marched by a different route. The insurgents were more numerous, but possessed less confidence than the government party. This circumstance was every where observable during the contest. Upon this occasion, as the most effectual protection, they placed their prisoners in front of their line, and between themselves and their assailants. They probably expected a parley, and that the parties would separate without bloodshed. This had sometimes happened before, from the great reluctance which all felt to proceed to extremities against their neighbours and acquaintances. But Colonel Ashley was a man of determined spirit, and fully convinced that energetic measures had become necessary, he ordered his men to fire. They knew their friends and remonstrated. The Colonel exclaimed, "God have *marcy* on their souls, but pour in your fire!" They did so, and after an engagement of about six minutes, the rebels fled. Their loss was two men killed, and about thirty, including their captain, wounded. The loss of the government party was two men killed, and one wounded. Of the former number, one was a prisoner who had been forced into the front of the rebel line.

If the remembrance of this commotion had not been preserved by the classical pen of Minot, its traditions would, probably, expire in one or two generations.

This is the only civil war which has ever been waged in our country, unless the war of the revolution can be so called.